BOUGHT WITH BLOOD

BOUGHT WITH BLOOD

Ann Quinton

Severn House Large Print
London & New York

This first large print edition published in Great Britain 2002 by
SEVERN HOUSE LARGE PRINT BOOKS LTD of
9-15, High Street, Sutton, Surrey, SM1 1DF.
First world regular print edition published 2001 by
Severn House Publishers, London and New York.
This first large print edition published in the USA 2002 by
SEVERN HOUSE PUBLISHERS INC., of
595 Madison Avenue, New York, NY 10022

British Library Cataloguing in Publication Data

Quinton, Ann
    Bought with blood. - Large print ed. - (A Holroyd and
    Morland mystery)
    1. Police - Englar
    2. Detective and n
    3. Large type book
    I. Title
    823.9'14 [F]

    ISBN 0-7278-7167-6

GLOUCESTERSHIRE COUNTY LIBRARY	
992202123	
Cypher	25.10.03
	£18.99

Except where actual h
described for the story
publication are fictitio
is purely coincidental.

Printed and bound in Great Britain by
MPG Books Ltd, Bodmin, Cornwall.

For Neill, who pointed me in the right direction, and Kathryn, who helped me along the way.

I should like to thank the many people who helped me with the research for this book, in particular Ann Colvill, Simon Grew, Helen Kingsland and Jeremy Trowell.

O, think upon the conquest of my father,
My tender years, and let us not forgo
That for a trifle that was bought with blood.

Henry VI, Part 1, act 4, scene 2

One

The two women approached the gap in the hedge. Through it they could see the outline of a dilapidated farmhouse, partially obscured by the overgrown trees and shrubs surrounding it.

'Are you sure this is the right place?' asked the younger woman.

'Of course I'm sure,' replied her companion. 'I spent all my holidays here as a child. I know it was a long time ago but I'm not completely gaga. This is definitely Holmewood Farm but I agree it looks very run-down.'

'Perhaps the owner has died. It's certainly not a working farm now.'

'According to the agent the owner is a Matthew Gorham. He's known as a recluse. Collects antiques and pictures but has little to do with the local community.'

'There you are. If he's still living here, he's not going to take kindly to us poking our noses into his affairs.'

'Don't be so negative, Reid. We're not doing any harm. I have very happy memories of my holidays here and I just want to look over the place again and relive some of my childhood.'

Reid Frobisher looked at her great-aunt with a mixture of affection and exasperation. 'So, what do you suggest we do? The main gate is locked and looks as if it hasn't been opened in years. I should say callers are clearly not welcome.'

'There should be another gate round the side. The path from it led to the back of the house. The scullery door was the one that was always used in the old days. The front door and the front parlour were only opened for funerals and weddings.'

'Come on, I can see you are determined to get inside.' Reid put her arm through Edith Culham's and they walked back down the unmade road and turned down the lane that led round the side of the garden. 'There is probably a Rottweiler or a Doberman on guard.'

So overgrown was the hedgerow that they didn't see the side gate until they were right upon it. It sagged from its hinges, the paint was so blistered and worn that it was impossible to tell what the original colour had been and the latch was broken but secured by strands of wire and copious lengths of rope.

'What do you suggest we do now? Unravel this lot?'

'It's ridiculous,' said Edith Culham. 'If there is someone in residence, he must get in and out somehow. I think this Matthew Gorham must be dead and the place has been shut up and left. In which case, I don't see why we shouldn't have a little nose around.'

'And how do we get in?' asked Reid patiently.

'Through the gap in the hedge, of course. Do use your initiative. I am sure we can push through. What a pity I didn't bring my walking stick.'

The elder woman retraced her steps and her great-niece shrugged in resignation and followed her.

'Hold that branch back and flatten those brambles, and then I think I can squeeze through,' commanded Edith.

'Better let me go first, I'm bigger than you.'

Reid Frobisher pushed her way through the jungle of uncut hedge and undergrowth, gathering scratches and stings as she did so.

'Are you sure you want to go through with this? From the look of the house your memories are going to take a sad knock.'

'Of course I do! I haven't come all this way to be disappointed at this stage.' Edith Culham burst through the opening in the hedge like a cork from a bottle and looked about her.

'Criminal neglect. That's what it is. Look at the state of that roof – it must let water in!'

The house was divided into two distinct parts. One section was thatched and the thatch appeared to have slipped so the edge hung in grey, wispy swags over the cracked guttering. The other half was tiled, and the tiles lay haphazardly over the rafters, revealing holes in the roof. At some stage the walls had been whitewashed but they were now a dirty beige colour and from where they were standing none of the windows on view appeared to have curtains. Some were boarded up and others were half covered with rickety shutters. Fruit trees, unpruned for years, advanced on the building, their gnarled and twisted branches shedding dead leaves over the unmown grass and barely discernible paths.

As the two women stared in distress at the picture of neglect and decay, there was the sound of furious barking and a man's voice coming from round the other side of the house.

'What did I tell you? We'll probably end up in A & E having anti-rabies jabs.'

'We've just come to pay a visit, a perfectly legitimate excuse.'

Reid forbore to say that to the owner it

might look more like breaking and entering and turned towards where the commotion was coming from. A large, black dog of indeterminate breed, accompanied by a man, appeared round the corner and headed towards them. The man was limping and looking as angry as his dog, which was snarling ferociously. He was a man in his seventies with grey, spiky hair crammed under a flat tweed cap and with a bushy grey beard. He was dressed in what appeared to be a dressing gown tied round the middle with a piece of string, worn over a collarless shirt and dark trousers. He was carrying a shotgun.

'What are you doing trespassing on my land? I'll set the dog on you!' he bawled, and the dog danced nearer, regarding them balefully and baring its teeth.

'Are you the owner of this place?' demanded Edith Culham.

'Course I am, and nobody steps foot in here!'

'Then you want to mend the hole in your hedge,' she retorted, and Reid hurriedly intervened.

'Mr Gorham – it is Mr Gorham, isn't it? – we're sorry to intrude in this way but we couldn't get the gate open. My aunt used to stay here at one time and she just wants to visit and have a look round.'

'What do you think this is – an effing

stately home? This is my property and I won't have anyone near it. Now clear off or you'll be sorry!'

He was handling the shotgun suggestively, and the elderly woman looked at it askance.

'Is that thing loaded?'

'You don't think it's a toy, do you? If you're not out of here in two minutes you'll get a load of shot up your backsides!'

'Come on, Edith. You can't argue with a madman.'

'The police shall get to know about this.'

'Police!' he snorted in disgust. 'You're the ones who are in the wrong, come to steal my property! How about giving them a nip, Paddy?'

The dog growled and snaked towards them, and the two women beat a hasty retreat, struggling back through the hedge and adding to their collection of scratches and grazes.

'I really thought we were going to be savaged by the dog or shot. He was quite mad.'

Reid Frobisher was regaling her friend, Rachel Morland, with details of her visit to Holmewood Farm, and Rachel listened sympathetically, refilling their coffee cups as she did so. It was a late September evening, and the two women were sitting in the living room of Rachel's cottage at Melbury Magna.

14

'Did you report it to the police?'

'No. Aunt Edith has gone back to Yorkshire and as we *were* trespassing I didn't want to make too much of it, but I wondered if you could mention it to Nick. I know he's CID but he could have a word in the right quarter if he thinks some action should be taken.'

'The old chap certainly sounds unbalanced and a danger to himself and everyone around him. You can tell Nick yourself – he's supposed to be calling round later – that's if he's not called out on a case.'

'So, how are the wedding plans coming along? It's not long now, is it?'

'They're not,' said Rachel shortly, pushing away her cup and saucer and running her fingers through her short, dark curls.

'*Not*? You haven't broken up? I don't believe this! Or are you having pre-wedding nerves?'

Reid regarded her friend in dismay. They had only known each other since Rachel had moved down to Dorset to take up her position as senior physiotherapist at Casterford General Hospital, but they had clicked straight away after meeting at a local history society gathering of which she, an English teacher at the local high school, was secretary. She knew that Rachel was a widow; her husband had been a vicar and Rachel herself was closely involved with the Church.

Perhaps she was having a crisis of conscience about marrying a divorced man.

'Nick is not free to marry me.' Rachel spoke flatly, shunting the milk jug and sugar bowl round the tray. 'He's not divorced.'

'Not divorced! But I thought—?'

'So did I. So did he. Oh, it's quite ridiculous really. Unbelievable. The sort of thing that happens on stage in a farce.'

'Whatever do you mean?'

'His wife left him in the early '90s. Two years later she sued for divorce – I think it was termed a no fault divorce. The case went through the court and he received his decree nisi in early '93. Six weeks later he received what he thought was his decree absolute through the post. He was so upset and angry about the whole business that he just rammed the envelope into a drawer without opening it.'

'How like a man. When my divorce came through I was so relieved and elated I wanted to frame the document and hang it on the wall. But I can just see your Nick doing that. He's very impetuous, isn't he?'

'That's just the point. He's not my Nick, not any more. He has to produce his decree absolute for the registrar before *our* marriage can take place. When he found the envelope and opened it, he discovered it wasn't the decree at all. It was a letter from his wife's solicitor stating that she had changed her

16

mind and didn't want to go through with the divorce after all.'

'My God! But I don't understand – surely she must have contacted him again when he didn't reply to it?'

'He was out of the country. He was so fed up with the state his life was in that he took the opportunity to go and work in some African state for a few months, helping to monitor an election, on secondment from the police force. When he returned, he got a transfer to a different part of the country. As far as he was concerned his life with Maureen was over, finished. He had put it behind him and moved on.'

'So what happens now?'

'He's applying through the court now for a decree absolute. He says it is only a formality and there will be no trouble about it being granted, but somehow I don't feel the same. He's still a married man. That probably sounds crazy to you.'

'On account of me having a live-in partner who I have no intention of marrying?'

'No, I don't mean that. How you live your life is your affair, and I wouldn't dream of interfering or condemnation, but *you* are not *me*.'

'We're talking religious scruples here, aren't we?'

'I'm not sure...Yes, I suppose so. I *am* a lay reader and I still hope to be priested one day, although that's a long way in the future. The whole affair with Nick has been a struggle with my religious principles.'

'But you're not *having* an affair with him, are you?'

'No, we've been saving ourselves for marriage.' Rachel gave a wry little grin at her friend.

'I must say I'm surprised your church was happy about you marrying a divorcee.'

'The Church of England is much more tolerant about these things nowadays.'

'But you're not marrying in church?'

'No. I'm sure we could get a dispensation from the Bishop but it wouldn't feel right. Why should I, a lay official, be allowed to marry in church when this is denied other divorced couples? No, we'll have ... would have had a civic ceremony and a church blessing afterwards. Peter Stevenson, my vicar, is very happy to do it.'

'I don't see what the problem is. After all, you and Nick both thought he was divorced and it is only a temporary hiccup, a short delay while it's sorted out. Don't let your scruples get in the way of your happiness. In other words, don't risk losing him. Nick is quite something. If I wasn't taken I could fall for him myself.'

'I feel so fed up about the whole thing. I just don't want to think about it any more at the moment.'

Rachel got up and rummaged in the drawer of the dresser and produced a bar of chocolate.

'Let's indulge ourselves. One of the old dears I'm treating insists on bringing me these little gifts. I think she feels that I need fattening up.'

'Lucky you. I've only to look at something like this and I put on weight, but what the hell...'

Rachel peeled back the wrapper, snapped the bar in two and pushed half across the table to her friend.

'Let's change the subject. There's something I've been meaning to tell you, something I thought would interest you.'

'I'm all agog. Do tell.'

'Peter Stevenson has been sorting out the effects of one of our ex-parishioners. He was the verger at St James's before he retired, and he died recently leaving no living relatives. He'd never married and he was as poor as the proverbial church mouse, but he left the little cottage in which he had lived all his life – and its contents – to the parish. The cottage is desperately in need of modernisation but should realise a reasonable sum for the church when it is sold. The furniture and contents are pretty worthless. However, Peter was going through the clutter in the attic when he came across this cache of letters. He thinks they were written by

Thomas Hardy, so I thought it would be right up your street.'

'You mean *the* Thomas Hardy?'

'Yes. He lived locally, didn't he?'

'He most certainly did! He's one of Dorset's claims to fame. This is fascinating.'

'I suppose they could be of value to autograph hunters or anyone interested in Hardy. They were signed TH and written to someone he just addressed by the initials AC. They were about the new book he had written and I think Peter said the first one was dated around 1908. You're not listening to me, are you?'

'Oh, but I am. Just run that past me again.'

'Some letters written by Thomas Hardy to a friend,' said Rachel patiently, 'talking about the new novel he was working on. Are you alright, Reid?'

'Thomas Hardy wrote his last novel in the 1890s.' Reid spoke slowly and carefully as if to a child. *'Jude the Obscure* was published in 1895 and caused such a furore amongst the critics and his reading public, dealing as it did with adultery and other unmentionable subjects in Victorian society, that he vowed never to write another novel again but to concentrate on his poetry – which he did. He never produced another novel.'

'He never published another novel,' corrected Rachel.

Reid stared at her friend. 'You're right. He

never published another novel but if these letters are genuine he *did* write one. This is dynamite! Wait till I tell Tony!'

Tony Pomfret was Reid's lover. He was an ex-actor who, disillusioned by the uncertain life of treading the boards, had switched careers to bookselling. He and a partner ran an antiquarian bookshop in Casterford.

'I suppose he would know the value of the letters and would know how to go about selling them.'

'Can I see the letters? Can I show them to him?'

'I'll ask Peter, but I don't see why not. He'll be surprised at them causing so much interest.'

'But, Rachel my innocent, don't you see? It's not just the existence of the letters. If he wrote another novel, what happened to it? Where is the manuscript?'

Nick Holroyd reread the communication from the county court for the sixth time and threw it down on his desk in disgust. Judge Jefferson, or Judge Jeffries as he was known in the firm, was just being bloody-minded. The old sod! He had crossed swords with him on several occasions in court and the old devil was getting his own back. What was Rachel going to say about this further hiatus? He would soon find out.

He shuffled the reports he was working on into some sort of order, grabbed his fleece, shouldered himself into it and slammed the door behind him. With a murder enquiry brought to a successful close and now in the hands of the CPS, as well as a breakthrough in a recent spate of larceny cases, he was owed some leave. Leave which he had planned to use for honeymoon and house-moving. And now this...

He called out goodnight to the duty sergeant as he passed the front desk, and then strode across the tarmac to his car, which was parked in a far corner of the car park. A long, hot summer had given way to a cold, miserable autumn which seemed to be metamorphosing into winter before they had even reached October. He shivered and pulled on his gloves before gunning the engine and driving off.

Melbury Magna was six miles from police HQ and as he left the outskirts of Casterford and reached open countryside it started to rain. Brown, sodden leaves slashed against the windscreen and danced in the headlights like discoloured confetti as the strengthening wind bowed the trees. When he reached Rachel's cottage and saw the car parked outside he groaned. Her friend Reid was visiting; this was all he needed. Not that he'd got anything against her, quite the opposite. She was an attractive woman with a well-developed sense of humour and he liked her. The boyfriend was another matter. He and Tony Pomfret had nothing in common. He found the bookseller shallow and immature and knew that he was regarded as Mr Plod by Pomfret. Hopefully he wouldn't also be there.

Reid Frobisher took one look at his face when he followed Rachel into the sitting room and rose to go.

'I'm just off. No, really. I have a pile of essays to correct and I'm sure you two have a lot to discuss.'

'Tell Nick about your encounter at Holmewood Farm before you go,' said Rachel.

'Cold Comfort Farm, more like – and definitely something nasty in the woodshed.'

She explained what had happened to her and her great-aunt and Nick frowned.

'I'll certainly pass it on and get them to check if he has a certificate for the shotgun. If he has, it sounds as if it ought to be revoked and the gun confiscated. Was it loaded?'

'I don't honestly know. I'm not into guns, but he certainly threatened to loose it off at us. Actually, I think the dog frightened me more. It was a vicious thing and I'm not sure he could control it.'

'His name rings a bell. I seem to remember something about him having a run-in with some young thugs from Casterford about six months ago. They were after some valuables he was supposed to have stored in an out-house.'

'By the look of him and his property you wouldn't think he had two pence to rub together but Aunt Edith had heard that he has a valuable collection of antiques.'

'If that is so, he needs a visit from our security adviser to get a proper alarm system installed instead of acting as a one-man vigilante. Were you actually on his land?'

'It would have been difficult to pay a visit without treading his acres, but don't worry, I wouldn't dream of returning; I value my skin too much.'

'I'll see that he gets a warning. Neighbour-hood Watch is all very well; it's when people lose confidence in the police and take the law into their own hands that trouble starts.'

'I shouldn't think he's even heard of Neighbourhood Watch. He doesn't trust anyone, full stop.'

Reid gathered up her handbag and extracted her car keys. 'Is it still raining?'

'It's a filthy night. Take care, the roads are really slippery.'

'I'll see you on Friday,' she said to Rachel. 'Tony has got a rehearsal but he may join us later.'

'How is Tony?' asked Nick, more out of politeness than a desire to know.

'He's very busy at the moment getting *West*

Side Story off the ground. It's an ambitious project, especially working with amateurs. He had the brilliant idea of involving my sixth-formers and local youth club members as well as the operatic society. The show is about teenagers after all – a modern *Romeo and Juliet* – and they are very enthusiastic, if inexperienced.'

'If it helps to keep them off the streets I'm all for it.'

Rachel saw Reid out and when she returned to the sitting room Nick had taken off his coat and was mooching around with his hands in his pockets.

'Don't I get a kiss?' she asked.

'You may not want to when you hear my news.'

'Something is wrong. I knew it the moment I saw you.'

'I've had a letter from the county court about my divorce...'

'And...?'

'Judge Jeffries, in his wisdom, will not process it until Maureen is notified and brought into the equation.'

'But why? I thought you said...'

'Quite. There is no reason why he shouldn't have granted it. There were no children involved, no property settlements to be sorted out. He is just being awkward.'

'So what happens now?'

'Maureen has to be contacted, and the

25

onus is on me to find her.'

'Have you any idea where she is?'

'Not a clue. It's been eight years, for Christ's sake— Sorry, Rachel. She could have emigrated, be living on the other side of the world. All I know is that the last time we were in communication she was still living in the Midlands. She may have re-married – no, she couldn't have.'

'How are you going to find her?'

'Well, I suppose I'm in the right profession for tracing missing persons, but I can't do it. I've still got contacts in the Northampton-shire police force. One of my ex-colleagues is now working as a private investigator. I'll put him on to it. It could take time, though. We'll have to postpone our arrangements.'

'Yes. It's a good thing we weren't planning an elaborate ceremony with a large guest list.'

'Don't speak of it in the past tense. We *will* get married, sooner rather than later, I hope. Oh, Rachel, I couldn't bear to lose you. How could I have been so bloody stupid! Don't hold it against me.'

He pulled her to him and buried his face in her hair. She returned his embrace, cling-ing to him for a few moments before dis-engaging herself.

'Suppose when she is found she won't agree to the divorce?'

'There is nothing she can do to stop it.

26

We've been separated over ten years. It is just a formality but it has to be done.'

'I've never asked you – did you get married in church?'

'No, it was at a registry office on a cold February morning. But I don't want to talk about Maureen. That's over and done with. We married far too young and were totally unsuited. I was upset when she walked out on me but it was my pride that took a battering. I wasn't heartbroken.'

'Nick, you can still move in.'

'Rachel...'

'I mean it. We're committed to each other, we don't have to wait for a piece of paper.'

'Stop it, stop it,' he groaned. 'I want you more than I've ever wanted anything, but it wouldn't be fair on you. We'd enjoy it. I promise we'd enjoy it, but afterwards... your conscience would trouble you – you wouldn't be able to square it with your religious principles.'

'But...'

'Sssh. Don't make it any harder for me. We said we'd wait and we're going to. I've still got the lease on my flat. I'll renew it for a further period.'

At that moment Nick's mobile phone rang. He swore and fished it out of his pocket. Rachel listened as he answered the caller in monosyllables and raised his eyebrows at her in resignation.

'You've got to go,' she said when he rang off.

'I'm afraid so. It's this damn name-and-shame campaign. Somehow the press are getting names and addresses of people on the Sex Offenders Register and publishing them. We've had a tip-off that there's a gang moving in on a house on the Marsden estate tonight and we're expecting trouble.'

'It's horrible. I've no sympathy with these people, but presumably they've served their sentences and paid for their crime and they have to live somewhere. Someone starts rabble-rousing and the general public get carried away and start a witch-hunt. Those pictures on television last week were quite frightening. Women and children waving banners and chanting slogans, and the children far too young to understand what it was all about. What sort of example is that to impressionable youngsters? Talk about mass hysteria!

'Mob violence is frightening and it can escalate so quickly. And it's not just the women and children. You've got gangs of right-wing neo-Nazis climbing on the bandwagon, stirring things up. Climbing on *their* backs is our criminal fraternity, ready to take the opportunity to do a little looting.'

'You can't believe it's happening here in a rural county like Dorset.'

'Don't forget there are a lot of affluent

28

people living in this area and the more you have to defend the more paranoic you become about security. I must go. I'll give you a ring tomorrow.'

He gave her a quick hug and a kiss and was gone. As she heard the car drive off she gave a wry smile and sank back into her chair. Saved by the bell. Another night spent in her virginal bed whilst her emotions ran riot. Her intention to become a priest had been put on hold, her marriage plans were also on hold – what was she saving herself for?

She gathered up her prayer book and bible and went upstairs to her bedroom to make her evening devotions.

Two

'I should like to know where the leak is coming from. I intend to find out.' Superintendent Tom Powell frowned at the serried ranks of police personnel facing him and tapped the sheet of paper he held in his hand.

'Somehow the press are getting hold of the names and addresses of people on the Sex Offenders Register living in this area.'

'Sir, it doesn't have to come from us. It

could be social services,' an earnest young police constable piped up. 'They're in the know and have more direct contact with these people than us.'

'Point taken, Vulliamy, and I should imagine there is another internal enquiry taking place at this very moment amongst the social services departments. However, I have every intention of making sure that no more disclosures are laid at our door; so, if there is some misguided person in this force who thinks he is doing a public duty – take heed. I won't tolerate it. And I won't tolerate it for two reasons: one, whatever we personally feel about these perverted creatures and their vile inclinations, they have been punished and are entitled to our protection; and two, we're hard pressed enough without having to waste resources controlling incited herds screaming that their children are going to be defiled and murdered in their beds! And what is more, they were mistaken in their target last night. He was not a paedophile as the public see it. OK, he *was* on the register, but not for molesting young children. If someone had bothered to read the case history, they would know that he was charged with having intercourse with a fifteen-year-old girl who, for the record, lied about her age and seduced *him*. He has paid the price and tried to put it behind him, and now this.'

'Where is he now?'

'Social services have put him and his family up in a safe house until they can resettle them at a new address.'

'That's one way of beating the housing list,' quipped a member of his audience and the superintendent glared at him.

'This is no laughing matter. Have you thought of the effect on his innocent family? How do you think his wife feels? She'd forgiven him and they were making a new start. And what about his young family, trapped in their house with a maddened crowd baying outside?'

'He's going a bit over the top, isn't he?' muttered a sergeant at the back. 'Fucking hell, it's that crowd he should be addressing, not us!'

'It's his pet hobby horse at the moment, controlling crowd hysteria,' said his near neighbour sotto voce. 'We'd be getting the same lecture if it was a football mob run amok.'

'Have you got something to contribute to the discussion, Palmerston?' The superintendent singled him out. 'Or are you confessing to being the mole?'

'Who, me, sir? No, of course not, sir.'

'Then perhaps you will allow me to continue,' said Tom Powell sarcastically. 'Whilst we were dispersing the crowd and evacuating the family at number 23 Leydon Grove, number 32, 36 and 44 were being done over. A large number of televisions, videos and assorted goods walked off into the night.'

After Morning Service that Sunday Rachel Morland went back to the vicarage for lunch with Peter and Jenny Stevenson and their family. After the meal they discussed parish affairs and then Rachel mentioned Reid Frobisher's reactions and enthusiasm when told about the Thomas Hardy letters.

'Do you mean they could be *really* valuable?' asked Jenny, twisting back a lock of hair that had escaped from her topknot. She was a tall, elegant woman, slim and naturally blonde, who had held down a high-powered job as PA to the managing director of a software company before her marriage to Peter. As far as Rachel could tell, she had made the switch from technology and power politics to parish priest's wife without too much trauma. Peter was one of the modern breed of Church of England priests, trendy and outgoing, more concerned with reaching out to the people than abiding by archaic canon law, and Jenny supported him wholeheartedly. Instead of power dressing, she now wore denim skirts, brightly-coloured scarves and charity-shop gear. If she ever had regrets about her changed lifestyle, she kept them to herself.

'More than we first thought. If they are genuine, they relate to work that no one knew existed.'

'You mean the book he was working on. Did he finish it?'

'You've studied them more closely than I,' said Rachel to Peter. 'Did he mention a finished novel?'

'Let's go and have another look at them. I brought them back from the cottage, as I thought they would be safer here.'

'I must reread my Hardy,' said Jenny. 'I went through a period when I thought he was very romantic, especially his poetry. I remember a poem about a young girl dying from a botched abortion. Very moving and tragic.'

'I shouldn't have thought that went down any better with his Victorian readership than *Jude the Obscure*,' said Rachel, getting up to follow her hosts out of the room. 'What about the washing-up?'

'The children can do it,' said Jenny firmly, to a chorus of groans from her son and daughter. 'So far they have contributed nothing to the running of the household this weekend. And, Debby, stop jiggling your brace about. It's quite revolting, apart from defeating its purpose.'

Debby clicked her brace up and down with her tongue a few more times, then snapped it into place and grinned at her mother through a mouthful of wire.

'It's my turn to do the washing-up.'

'No, it's not,' said her brother. 'I did the wiping-up last time.'

The three adults left the children arguing amicably between themselves and went into Peter's study, Jenny remarking as they went, 'According to them, we are the only family in the entire school not to have a dishwasher – apart from the two-legged ones, that is.'

Peter opened the drawer of his desk and took from it a folder from which he extracted some sheets of paper.

'Here we are. There are six in all. I suppose the handwriting should be easy to verify. Have a read.'

Rachel skimmed through the letters. They were written on good quality paper which was discoloured with age, the ink faded and the writing difficult to read where they had been folded.

'There's a gap between them,' she said, looking up. 'These four are all about the book he is working on, then there's an interval of eighteen months, and then these two telling his friend that he has finished the novel and is not sure what to do with it.'

'I think he must have kept up a regular correspondence with this AC but later someone – maybe AC himself – only kept the ones referring to the book.'

'And we've no idea who AC was?'

'They were in Bill Curtis's possession. Maybe it was an ancestor of his. As far as I know, he and his family have always lived in the area.'

'This is fascinating. He's even given it a title, but I can't make it out, can you?'

Peter Stevenson helped her to flatten out the sheet of paper, but the writing in the fold was almost illegible.

'*The*— can't read the next bit,' he said, 'then *Blood...*'

'May I borrow these and pass them on to Reid to show to Tony?'

'I don't see why not. He's the obvious person to advise us as to value and what to do with them. I ought to photocopy them first, but the blessed machine has broken down again.'

'I'll take good care of them. I wonder what happened to it – the book, I mean. He must have decided not to try and get it published, but he wouldn't have destroyed it, surely?'

'If your Reid is right, it certainly didn't become part of his known oeuvre. We'll probably never know.'

Rachel put the letters back in the folder and placed it in the large envelope Jenny produced for the purpose.

'How is *cherchez la femme* going on?' she asked Rachel.

'No luck so far. Nick has got a private investigator working on it. It all seems so sordid, somehow.'

'It is astonishing how easy it is in this day and age, with all the computer and government records, to disappear. What will happen if she can't be found?'

'I haven't dared think about that. It is surprising that *she* hasn't wanted to remarry. I presume she was quite an attractive woman.'

'Yes, Nick certainly knows how to pick them,' said Peter, grinning at her. 'I can't imagine him falling for an old hag.'

'I'll ignore that remark, and now I must be off. Thanks for the lunch.'

'Any time, Rachel, you know we love to have you,' said Jenny, handing her her coat. 'At least whilst you are here the children remember their manners and don't behave like ravening beasts at the table.'

'They're good kids, don't knock them. About these letters; do you want Tony Pomfret to put out feelers to possible interested buyers?'

'Before any decision is made to dispose of them it will have to have the backing of the PCC, but see how he feels about it. I should imagine getting the London dealers interested and auctioning them would realise the best sum, but he would be entitled to a commission if he did the groundwork,' said Peter.

'Tony will claim his cut, don't worry.'

'That's not a very charitable remark.'

'No, it isn't, but you don't know Tony like I do. He looks after number one.'

'Your friend Reid doesn't seem to have these reservations.'

'She worships him. He can do no wrong in her eyes, but I'm not so sure that he is so committed. I think he uses her.'

'Well, they say there is one who gives and one who takes in every relationship. If they are happy—'

'Who am I to interfere? You're right. It is none of my business, but I hope he doesn't hurt her.'

And am I the giver or the taker? mused Rachel as she drove away from the vicarage.

'Another set of Dickens, mangled, moth-eaten and mildewed. Why do people think that just because books are old and have leather bindings they are valuable?' Gordon Barnes was sorting through a box of books and talking over his shoulder to his colleague, who was brewing coffee in the little cubbyhole they called the office.

'The collection wasn't worth buying?' Tony Pomfret slopped milk over the table top and mopped it up with his handkerchief.

'We're not going to get rich on it, certainly, but there are one or two interesting items.'

Barnes picked up a pile of the books and carried them over to a table near the window where the light was better. He was a man in his early fifties, of medium height, with no distinguishing features. He had a pale buttoned-up face and neatly trimmed, greying hair; the sort of person once seen, easily forgotten, leaving no lasting impression on the beholder. He glanced through the window and straightened up.

'Your woman is coming.'

'Reid? Aha, perhaps she's got the letters. Our luck may have turned.' Tony Pomfret bounced into the main body of the shop carrying two mugs. If Gordon Barnes was a colourless, nondescript man, his partner was the complete opposite, being flamboyant in looks and personality. His hair was a very dark red, almost mahogany in colour, and it swept back from his forehead in luxuriant waves, curling in at the nape of his neck. Long, thick eyelashes fringed his green eyes, and he had a tall, rangy figure that was just beginning to show signs of overindulgence in food and drink. He was not fat and had not yet got a corporation, but the signs were there: a certain flabbiness and an incipient thickening of the waistline. He wore green corduroy trousers, a purple silk shirt and multicoloured deck shoes, and certainly looked more the thespian than an antiquarian bookseller.

'Dear heart, did you get them?' He swept Reid into an embrace on the doorstep and drew her into the shop.

'Get what?' Reid knew perfectly well what he meant but felt that her presence rather than a handful of letters should take precedence. 'Hello, Gordon, how are tricks?'

'The better for your appearance, my dear. Are you shirking classes?'

'I have two free periods on Monday afternoons. I met up with Rachel Morland in the lunch hour and she passed this correspondence on to me, so I thought I would bring it round so that you can both look at it.'

'Thoughtful of you,' said Gordon Barnes whilst Tony Pomfret looked annoyed. 'Would you like a coffee?'

Reid decided that she would and Gordon went off to make her one.

'I thought you'd bring them home this evening and we could examine them together,' said Tony peevishly.

'I've already seen them and I thought this was a joint effort between you and Gordon. You were going to involve him, weren't you? You can't keep something like this to yourself and, after all, Gordon has far more experience than you in the world of books.'

'Just because he has been in the business longer doesn't make him any more expert than myself. Still, I'm jumping the gun; we've got to verify them first before we start getting excited.'

'Tony, these belong to the church. You do understand that?'

'Sure, but I'm being consulted professionally, aren't I?'

'Well, I'm not so sure about that. When Rachel mentioned them I realised their significance and suggested that you should have a look at them. Anyway, here they are. See what you think.'

Reid accepted her mug of coffee from Gordon, and the two men cleared the books off the table and spread out the letters.

'I looked in a biography of Thomas Hardy and there were photographs of some of his manuscripts,' she said. 'The writing in those looks identical.'

'It certainly looks genuine,' said Barnes. 'If it's not, it's a very good forgery. I think they are the real thing. The paper looks authentic for the period. What do you think, Tony?'

'You know the provenance, don't you, Reid? If, as you say, they have been kept amongst family papers for God knows how long, I don't see how or why they should be forgeries.'

Reid left them poring over the letters and wandered round the bookshop. Business was slack on a Monday afternoon and there were no other customers. It was difficult to see how they made a living out of it. Tony always pleaded penury but perhaps Gordon had money behind him. She knew little about him; he looked as if he had been born middle-aged and he appeared to have no relatives or close ties. She had always thought he was a closet homosexual but Tony had insisted that he was not.

'He has no inclinations towards either sex,' he had said when she had brought up the subject. 'Gordon was missing when they gave out sexual instincts. I don't think he has ever had a carnal urge or felt desire in his entire life towards man or woman. Poor Gordon, he doesn't know what he's missing.' And Tony had lunged for her and they had ended up between the sheets.

She smiled to herself. Tony certainly had no hang-ups about sex but she wondered how long she would hold his fidelity. She was only too aware that she was in her mid-thirties and when he was taking rehearsals he was mixing with nubile young women half her age. Still, she had earned Brownie points over these letters; perhaps this evening would be a good time to bring up the other subject which was exercising her at the moment. Tony was not going to be pleased.

She strolled back to the two men, who were in deep discussion and looking very intense. She hadn't seen Gordon so animated for a long while.

'Well?'

'We think they are the real McCoy.' Tony

grinned at her.

'The vicar will be pleased to know that. Apparently he thinks you should approach some of the big boys in London with a view to auctioning them. What do you think? Can you put a rough value on them?'

'Oh, I think they would arouse consider-able interest in two different camps. You've got the autograph hunters on one side and the Hardy scholars on the other, but I think we should hold fire for a while and not rush into anything rashly.'

'What do you mean?'

'Reid, dear, it's the *contents* of the letters that matters,' said Barnes, squinting at her through his glasses.

'Don't be dim, Reid,' interposed Tony. 'You mentioned it yourself when you told me about the letters. What happened to this novel he described to his friend? Before we go public I think we ought to have a go at trying to *find* the lost manuscript.'

The coach trundled into the bus station and drew to a halt. The doors opened, disgorging passengers on to the tarmac. One of the last to descend was a youth in his late teens carrying a rucksack and a large grip. He moved away from the coach, dumped his bags on the ground and looked about him. It was one o'clock and the streets converging on the bus station were busy with lunchtime traffic and pedestrians. Beyond the bays, with their destination boards, was a café. He picked up his luggage and walked over to it.

Inside, the air reeked of smoke and chips. Formica-topped tables in red and cream ran the length of the room, and he deposited his gear at one of them and went over to the counter. He chose a ham roll and a dough-nut from the glass display cabinet, added a Coke to his tray, paid for them and carried them back to his table. As he chewed his roll he felt panic spreading through him. What was he doing here? He shouldn't be here, he was doing it all wrong... He stared round the building as if seeking inspiration from the crowds, and his eyes alighted on a group of youths sitting in the corner. His casual glance turned to one of amazement as he thought he recognised one of them. It couldn't be— Why was *he* in Dorset?

As if aware of the eyes boring into him from the other side of the room, the youth looked up and their eyes locked.

'I don't believe it! What the hell are you doing here?' He got up and left his group of friends.

'Kevin?'

'You're the last person I expected to see in Casterford. Why are you here?'

'I'm having a year out before university.'

'University, eh? I thought guys having a year out backpacked to places like India and

Australia, not sunny Dorset.'

'Later. I've got some business to sort out first. I can't believe it's you; do you really live here?'

'People do, you know. It's not a bad area.'

'But a long way from Yorkshire.'

'Yeah.' Kevin Compton sat down at the table. He was a small, compact youth with straw-coloured hair and a round, open face. 'After St Kilda's I was sent to a home in Ripon, but it wasn't much better. Nobody was interested in you. I acted up, cut school, got in with bad company. I really screwed up, nearly ended up in a Young Offenders Centre. Then I met this guy. He was a holy Joe, ran this youth club. He found out that I was interested in electronics and arranged for me to be taken on as an electronics apprentice at Mathies here in Casterford. I didn't want to leave Yorkshire but I reckoned it was my last chance. And it's worked out. I've been here three years and I wouldn't go back up north for anything. What about you?'

'I guess I was lucky. When St Kilda's closed down I was fostered. Passed around a bit but ended up with this family who really cared. Accepted me as one of their own and made sure I stuck to my schooling. Didn't have their brains but they encouraged my interest in wildlife and natural history, so I decided to try and make a career out of it.'

'So you've come to these parts to study wildlife? Paint?'

'Not exactly. Well, I may do some...'

'OK, tell me to get lost.'

'No, really Kevin, it's great to see you. I often think about St Kilda's, don't you?'

'Nightmares, more like. Where are you staying?'

'Don't know, I've only just arrived. A B&B somewhere for a few weeks.'

'They cost. How about coming back to my place?'

'You've got your own pad?'

'There's a group of us who share a house.'

'You mean a squat?'

'No, it's all legal and above board. There's this big house that's divided into bedsits, and I rent one of them.'

'A hostel?'

'Not the sort you're thinking of. It's a Housing Association project. We've got our own rooms but there's a communal kitchen and lounge. How about it?'

'I don't know. I'm only going to be here a short time. I just want somewhere to doss down, not take on a tenancy.'

'No problem. You can have Dan's room. He's off hiking round South America. He won't mind.'

'If you're sure...'

'Come and meet some of the others. It will be great to have someone from my neck of the woods, speaking the same dialect. Help me to keep my end up. Though the Yankee accent is coming along.'

'Yankee?'

'Sure thing. Some of us are involved in this musical that's going to be put on locally. *West Side Story* – you know, the Jets and Sharks. Great stuff. They'll probably grab you – there's a shortage of men. Is this all your stuff?'

Kevin Compton hefted the grip and his newly-discovered friend swung the rucksack over his shoulder and followed him out of the café looking dazed.

Martin Boyd, head of English at Casterford High School, flung himself into a chair in the staffroom, took off his glasses and rubbed his eyes. School was over but he was loath to go home. He had a load of sixth-form essays to correct but he was half-minded to do it here on the school premises where he was not likely to be disturbed. His office was cramped, with only two hard, upright chairs, but here in the staffroom he could relax in an easy chair, which was more than he could do at home. His house was in chaos from building work and Fiona was sure to want him to do some task that would certainly take priority in her eyes over his school work. He sighed and stared at the pile of folders he had dropped on the table, then went over to the worktop in the corner and switched on the kettle.

He was sipping his mug of tea when he heard footsteps in the corridor. Damn, he'd forgotten about the cleaners. There was no peace or quiet anywhere. He looked up resignedly as the door opened and was surprised to see Reid Frobisher.

'Hello, I didn't expect to find anyone still here,' she said, striding into the room and loosening her scarf.

'I could say the same. I thought you were one of the cleaners.'

'I came back to collect that OFSTED report. You look as if you're settled for the evening.'

'I thought I'd get some of this lot out of the way.' He gestured to the folders. 'Saves carting them home with me, and we're in such an upheaval at the moment – the builders, you know.'

'I thought your new kitchen was finished and up and running.'

'It is. We're having a conservatory built on to the back of the house now and they're having to break through walls.'

'Heavens. I don't know how you can afford it on your salary, even though you earn oodles more than me.'

'Neither do I, but Fiona gets these ideas and likes things to look nice.'

I bet she does, thought Reid savagely. In

her opinion Martin's wife was a spoilt individual who still thought she was daddy's darling, whose every whim had to be satisfied. She hadn't come to terms with living on a teacher's salary, and poor Martin strove so hard to please her, not realising that she would never be content.

'Anyway,' said Boyd, polishing his glasses furiously, 'you've been holding out on me.'

'What do you mean?'

'These letters purported to be by Thomas Hardy.'

'How do you know about them?'

'Tony mentioned them to me last night after rehearsal. He was surprised you hadn't already told me of their existence.'

'He had no right to do that. I'm sorry, Martin, but he was consulted confidentially. The way this news is spreading, some reporter is going to get hold of it and then it will be a free-for-all.'

'Who do they belong to?'

'They are the property of St James's Church in Barminster.'

'And where are they?'

'They are on their way back there now,' said Reid shortly.

'You've got them. They're in your brief-case,' he said, successfully interpreting the way in which she had tightened her hold on the case she was clutching. 'Let me have a look at them, please? My interest is only academic. You know Thomas Hardy is one of my pet subjects.'

'Alright, but don't let on I've shown them to you, and *don't* mention this to anyone else.'

Once more the letters were spread out for perusal and Martin Boyd pored over them, emitting little sighs of excitement.

'Fascinating.' He straightened up. 'Tony thinks an attempt should be made to find the lost manuscript.'

'The decision is not his to make, and where would you start looking?'

'Hardy was still married to Emma Gifford then, and living at Max Gate.'

'It wouldn't still be there.'

'Hardly likely. Max Gate is in private ownership and I have no idea how many times it has changed hands since his death, but it is opened to the public several times a week.'

Reid giggled and Boyd looked surprised.

'I've just got this vision of Tony joining a party of sightseers and going round the place tapping on the walls and trying to find a secret hideaway. No, I think the manuscript was suppressed by Hardy himself. He probably destroyed it when he realised he was never going to be able to publish it during his lifetime.'

'No, I don't believe he would have destroyed it. Think, Reid, could *you* scrap something you'd created and worked on for months? You might decide it wasn't good enough for other eyes, or the subject matter was too risky, but I bet you couldn't bring yourself to actually destroy it, I know I couldn't. When I was younger I wrote poetry. Utter crap, I realise now, but I've kept it, stowed away in the back of a cupboard somewhere, forgotten but preserved.'

'I didn't know you were a poet, Martin.'

'I'm not, that's just what I'm telling you.'

'So, if he kept it,' mused Reid, 'it should have been found amongst his effects after he died. His second wife was much younger than him and outlived him. Surely if she had discovered it she would have realised its significance?'

'Maybe *he* didn't keep it but passed it on to someone else for safekeeping. Although he mourned Emma excessively and was stricken with remorse after she died, they became increasingly estranged in the years before her death. She would probably have been horrified at the idea of him writing another novel that might set society by the ears again. He was earning a good living from his poetry and articles and public engagements, and she was meeting and rubbing shoulders with all the famous people of the day and moving in elite circles. She wouldn't have wanted him to rock the boat.'

'Martin, what a horrible collection of clichés! What an example to our pupils!'

'Still, you get my meaning. My bet is that he wrote it secretly and nobody knew about it except this friend to whom he was writing. Take it a step further – he finished the novel and was in a turmoil about what to do with it, so what did he do?'

'Passed it on to this friend for safekeeping,' said Reid slowly.

'Got it in one! Probably asked him to hang on to it until the climate was more favourable for publication, or may even have asked him to submit it to his publishers posthumously.'

'This is sheer supposition.'

'Of course, but you've got to start somewhere. And, don't forget, the manuscript has never turned up. If it wasn't destroyed, it must be somewhere.'

'Thrown out with the rubbish years ago when some house clearer got to work, more. like.'

'Yes, I expect so, but it is exciting to speculate.'

Reid rummaged in her locker and found the report she needed and put that and the folder of letters into her case.

'How did the rehearsal go last night from your point of view?'

'They're actually enthusiastic – the boys, I mean. Anyone knows the girls will jump at any excuse to plaster themselves with make-up and strut their stuff on stage, but the lads are getting really keen. Of course, it's the fight scenes that have grabbed them. Tony's making a good job of choreographing those. The rumble is quite tricky and could be really dangerous. Timing is everything, but at the moment they are willing to do exactly what they are told. It's when someone decides to do their own thing that we could get trouble. I don't want half my A-level students down with broken legs or stab wounds or worse.'

'I was amazed at how well they were singing when I went down last week. They really sounded quite professional.'

'Don't forget many of the cast are members of the operatic society, and presumably being able to sing is the entrée to becoming a member, but I agree with you. Bernstein was a genius, and the music is so dynamic it carries you along. And, of course, the lyrics appeal to them – apart from the lovey-dovey stuff.'

'It must help to make Shakespeare more interesting when they see his ideas are still relevant today.'

'It's just a case of balancing the merits of Shakespeare brought up to date and playing down the fact that Juliet was only fourteen.'

'Tony says you still want some more boys and young men to complete the cast.'

'Yes, another two or three are needed.'

'He's trying to persuade Gordon Barnes to take a small part.'

'Oh yes, Glad Hand, the MC in the dance-hall scene. It's a non-singing part and he's only on stage for a short while, but I don't think he's had any success so far.'

'I can't imagine Gordon taking part in any sort of acting role. To expose himself on stage would be his idea of hell, I should imagine, and I think young people are an alien species to him.'

'It's such a small role that none of the operatic society men will demean themselves taking it on.'

'I'm sure Tony will be able to twist someone's arm. Well, I must be on my way. Have fun!'

Reid Frobisher swung her handbag over her shoulder, picked up her briefcase and went off down the corridor. After she had gone Martin Boyd stared into space for some time, deep in thought, before sighing and applying himself to the pile of essays.

The phone call came just as Nick Holroyd was about to leave the house. He listened in growing astonishment and disquiet to what his caller was saying and after he put down the phone he sat in shock for a long time unable to take in what he had been told. How would Rachel cope with this? How could *he* cope with it? He needed a drink, a stiff drink, but not at this hour of the morning. He glanced at his watch. He should be at work but he couldn't face his colleagues and the bustle of the station at the moment. Nor could he face Rachel.

He got in his car and drove out of Casterford, aimlessly following narrow country roads, oblivious of where he was going. For once the weather was fine. A gentle sun shone out of a cerulean sky over fields of golden stubble and newly-ploughed acres. A tractor was labouring up the slope alongside the lane he was traversing, the ploughshare behind it turning the furrows and attracting hoards of screaming seagulls. They wheeled across his line of vision, dazzling white against the blue sky, and the smell of newly dug soil assailed his nostrils. The hedgerows were turning and scarlet hips and darker crimson hawthorn berries gleamed amongst the greens and browns.

He rounded a corner and found himself facing a country churchyard, in the middle of which a small crooked church sat surrounded by dusty yews and crooked tombstones. A church. This was Rachel's domain, where she would seek comfort and strength. He was not a believer, he couldn't pray, but he found himself parking the car on the grass verge and walking towards the porch. Inside the church it was surprisingly light.

54

The walls had been whitewashed and many of the windows contained plain glass instead of the usual heavy stained glass. He sat down in a pew near the back and looked about him. Buckets of flowers and foliage stood around on the floor with baskets of fruit and vegetables and a sheaf of corn. Harvest festival. Soon these offerings would be descended on by a bevy of well-meaning women determined to beautify their place of worship for the annual ritual of harvest thanksgiving.

He wondered how long he would be in sole possession of the church and leant back, letting the peaceful atmosphere wash over him. Dust motes danced in the sunbeams and the sweet smell of apples mingled with the pungent scent of chrysanthemums and root vegetables. There was the sound of someone moving about in the vestry and Nick resigned himself to company. However, it wasn't a female flower arranger who emerged through the door, but Peter Stevenson. Belatedly, Nick remembered that although Stevenson was vicar of St James's in Barminster he was also priest-in-charge of a cluster of neighbouring village churches of which this must be one.

The priest did not notice him at first and Nick studied him as he walked amongst the harvest offerings humming softly beneath his breath. His appearance reminded him of the Holman Hunt painting *The Light of the World*, which hung in St Paul's Cathedral. The same long, flowing hair and beard and benign expression, except that the Pre-Raphaelite subject didn't sport a gold earring in one ear. Peter *was* wearing a dog collar but it was partly obscured by a shapeless sweatshirt, and his jeans and trainers had seen better days. Surely this style of dress didn't go down very well with his elderly congregation? Yet Rachel said, and he had noticed it himself, that he was attracting increasing numbers of teenagers and young people with families to his services. But not in a little moribund village like this?

Peter noticed him and came over.

'You're not here on official business, I hope?'

Nick assured him that he was not, and had just called in for a few minutes peace and quiet.

'You've chosen the wrong day, I'm afraid. The good ladies will soon be amongst us.'

'Yes, I realise that. Well, I'll be on my way.'

'Is anything wrong, Nick?' Peter straddled a pew end and looked at him searchingly.

'Why? Do you do confessions too?'

'I'm not a Roman Catholic priest, we don't go in for the confessional box, but I'm here to listen if anyone wants to talk something through.' Peter spoke lightly and started to move away. He knew better than to force himself on Rachel's fiancé. Nick was not in the fold; he vehemently resisted the whole idea of religion, but the cleric knew that he was already hooked, although he would never admit it, by a slender thread of interest and unwilling longing, and would one day be reeled in. But it needed a very light, delicate hand on the rod, to continue the fishy analogies, thought Peter, and he was adept at that.

'You know about the trouble Rachel and I have been having?' asked the policeman abruptly.

'About your divorce, which is not yet legal? Yes.'

'It's more complicated than that.' Nick stared wide-eyed at the priest and opened his hands.

'I think I may be a father. I think I may have a son.'

Three

Rachel Morland was in the Physiotherapy Department dealing with her last appointment of the morning. It was an elderly man suffering from back trouble and she finished up with a session of ultrasound.

'There we are, Mr Biggs, how does it feel now?'

'More comfortable. It's always better when you treat me but it plays up when I try to do anything.'

'Try not to do anything that exacerbates it. You're retired now, aren't you, so you must take it easy. No digging in that garden or heavy lifting. Remember to bend your knees rather than your back and sit up straight, don't slouch.'

Whilst he dressed she consulted her work chart, pencilled him in a vacant slot and wrote out an appointment card.

'Is the same time next week alright?' she asked him when he reappeared from the cubicle.

'Yes. I can catch a bus which brings me right to the door.'

'Good. I've written it down for you in case you forget. Take care, and remember, no lifting or twisting movements.'

After he had gone she sorted out some equipment and checked her afternoon appointments. With one of her staff ill and another on holiday the department was stretched and it was a struggle to cope with the workload. She looked up as a figure loomed behind the frosted glass door, and frowned. Not another patient, surely? Had she forgotten someone? The door opened and Nick Holroyd walked in. His hair was ruffled as if he had been running his fingers through it, and there was a taut expression on his face.

'Nick?'

'We've got to talk,' he said abruptly. 'This is your lunch hour isn't it?'

'I can only take about thirty minutes. I was going to pop down to the staff canteen.'

'Is it private there?'

'Perhaps the hospital restaurant would be a better idea. What's the matter? What has happened?'

'I'll tell you in a minute. Let's go and get some food first.'

'I don't think I'm hungry now. You've got me worried.'

'Soup,' said Nick, steering her out of the door. 'Soup is what we need, the great comfort food.'

Why do we need comfort food? thought Rachel, but he refused to say anything more until they were seated at a table in the corner of the restaurant, bowls of Scotch broth and a basket of rolls in front of them.

'This has something to do with Maureen, hasn't it?' Rachel took a sip of her soup, gasped as the hot liquid hit her throat and put down her spoon.

'Yes. I heard from my contact today. He discovered that after we split up she went to live in a village called Geddington near Kettering. Eight months after she left me she had a baby. A son.'

Rachel stared at him. 'A son. Are you saying it was *your* child?'

'I don't know.'

'I see.' She fumbled with her roll and the knife slipped from her hand and clattered on to the table.

'No, you don't see, Rachel.' He spoke urgently. 'You've got it all wrong.'

'Wrong? No, I don't think so. If you think it may be your child, you must have still been sleeping with her. I understood that you had been estranged a long while before you actually separated.'

'We were, Rachel. This was a one-off thing. Please try and understand. She was having this affair with a married man. It had been going on for ages, was an on-off relationship. I don't think he had any intention of leaving his wife for her, but she thought differently. Anyway, he told her it was finished and we talked it over and decided to have one last try at saving our marriage. We went away for the weekend, but it was hopeless – there was nothing left between us and she was still infatuated with this chap. We both knew then that it was the end, and she moved out a few weeks later—'

'So, this baby could be yours or the other man's?'

'Yes.'

'But surely if she had thought it was yours she would have contacted you?'

'I told you, I went abroad immediately after she left. When I came back there were a couple of letters from her waiting for me but I tore them up without reading them. Hell, Rachel, I don't come out of this very well, do I?'

'It was a very natural reaction at the time.' She placed her hand over his and he clutched it. 'Did she make no more attempts to keep in touch with you?'

'I transferred to Norfolk as soon as I got back from Africa. I deliberately cut myself off from all my old ties and I never went back.'

'Still, if she had thought you were the father, she would have sought some sort of maintenance arrangement, surely? Especially now the Child Support Act is in place.'

'You'd think so. Perhaps she couldn't find me.'

'As a serving policeman you wouldn't be difficult to trace.'

'True, so the fact that I haven't had the Child Support Agency breathing down my neck must mean that her lover was the father.'

'But you're not sure.'

'No, and I've got to be. You do understand, don't you, Rachel? Somewhere out there is an eight-year-old boy who may or may not be my son. I've got to know the truth.'

'How will you discover that?'

'Dave came up with some more information. She didn't stay long in Geddington. About eighteen months later she moved again and really went to ground.'

'He doesn't know where she went?'

'Not at the moment, but he's working on it. From the enquiries he's made he thinks she went up north. He'll find her. Dave is one of the best.'

Nick remembered his soup and started to eat it. Rachel stared round the restaurant. There was a good cross-section of the community represented: patients idling away time until their appointments, families snatching a snack between visiting sick relatives and people with desperation sketched on their faces who had been persuaded away from a death bed by concerned medical staff but were unable to eat or drink and were awaiting the final summons. At a nearby table a young boy sat with his parents drinking a Coke. He had fair, floppy hair and blue eyes and was absorbed in the gurgling noises he was making through his straw. He could be Nick's son, she reflected. He was about the right age and he certainly had Nick's colouring. She pulled herself together.

'Does this make a difference – to us, I mean?'

'Of course not. I still feel the same about you, and I hope it hasn't altered your feelings for me. But you do see that I have to find out?'

'Yes, you must. When your man catches up with her you'll be able to ask her, always supposing she knows which one of you is the father.'

'I hadn't thought of that. She may never have been sure, but it could be sorted by DNA testing.'

He pushed aside his bowl and said slowly, 'If I have a son, I'm prepared – I *want* to share some responsibility in his upbringing, but first I need to be damn sure he *is* my child before I offer any sort of support, emotional or financial.'

'She may not welcome the idea of you suddenly turning up claiming a share in her son. Don't get me wrong, I agree with your sentiments, they do you credit, but she's managed without you for eight years when she *could* have got in touch if she had really wanted to – have you thought that she might be bigamously married to someone else and have other children?'

'That hadn't crossed my mind. Ye Gods! That would put the cat among the pigeons! Still, I have to find her, child or no child, to get my degree absolute granted. That is the most important thing; so that *we* can get married and have children.'

The boy at the next table was getting bored. He drummed his heels on his chair and flicked breadcrumbs from plate to plate. He saw her looking at him and grinned widely. She found herself grinning back. Yes, the biological clock was alive and ticking away, but was it potent enough to take on board the idea of a stepson?

The noise was getting louder. At first it had sounded like the humming of bees. A gentle background noise that had puzzled the man waiting in the house. He had not been able to identify it initially, but as it got closer and the pitch rose he recognised the clamour of human voices and felt sick with fear. There was a mob out there intent on retribution and he was the target. This was what he had been afraid would happen ever since the local newspaper had started its campaign.

64

Had they named him? Were the crowd chanting his name as they converged on his part of the town?

He switched off the light and crept upstairs in darkness. He edged cautiously across the front bedroom floor and peered out from behind a curtain. There was a flickering glow at the end of the street but it wasn't coming from the street lights. Torch beams mingled with flaming brands held aloft by the mob who were starting to pour down the road, and in the red luminance he could see banners also being held aloft and waved. He couldn't read what was on them from this distance but he knew what it would be: 'Perverts out!', 'Protect our Children!', 'Hang the Paedophiles!', ' Merv the Perv!'

He could hear them now, though he couldn't distinguish what they were shouting. They were howling like animals and there were children too, adding their treble chants to the tumult. Innocent children, children he identified with— They were like a lynch mob from the deep South, baying for blood – and it was *his* blood they were after.

He was too petrified to move, frozen with terror as they surged up the street towards his hideout. He had been so afraid of this happening, had tried to make contingency plans and had plotted his escape, but now it was actually taking place he felt helpless and unable to act. They were almost at the gate and the shouting was now a roar. 'Come out, Mervyn!'

'Merv the Perv!'

'Mervyn the Monster – we know you're there!'

He cringed further back behind the curtain and watched transfixed as two men kicked open the gate and smashed the flowerpots lining the path. In her excitement a fat, monstrous woman in a pink anorak tipped over the tripper she was pushing and her two toddlers toppled out, their screams adding to the tumult.

He *must* do something. He had packed a case and it stood ready under the stairs. His whole life's belongings reduced to one piece of baggage. He had wanted to include his collection of photos but common sense had prevailed. In the end he had burnt them in the grate, and charred black fragments still spilled over the hearth and a faint smell of burning hung in the air. Through the internet he had made contact with others of his ilk. He had resisted at first, not wanting to be drawn back into that network of corruption and vice which could lead to only one thing – him reoffending. But *they* had left him no choice. *They* wouldn't leave him alone to live his life in peace. He had tried so hard to put his past behind him and behave normally. But he wasn't normal and that screaming mob outside was driving him back to his old world and the proclivities that excited and fuelled him.

There was the crash of breaking glass as a window down stairs was smashed and a flaming brand was thrown through the jagged hole. They were torching the place – he *must* move! He half ran, half fell down the stairs and snatched up his suitcase, hesitating momentarily as fire snaked up the hall curtains and reached flaming fingers towards the bannister. He scrambled through the kitchen and opened the back door with shaking fingers. It was dark and silent in the overgrown garden; the mob had not yet found its way to the back entrance. Sobbing under his breath he plunged through the undergrowth towards the door in the high fence. It had not been opened for some time and he wrestled fruitlessly with the latch before giving up and heaving himself over the fence. He stumbled and twisted his ankle as he hit the pavement.

From behind him came shouts of frustration and anger. They had broken into the house and found him gone. He lurched to his feet and staggered through the maze of back streets and alleys, seeking out the address he had memorised.

Reid Frobisher left her car in the school car

park and walked the short distance to the little supermarket on the nearby Buckton estate. As she walked she felt the strange pricking sensation between her shoulder blades; she was being followed. She turned round sharply but there was no one to be seen except a group of boys fooling around on the pavement behind her. They grinned sheepishly when they saw her watching them and moved off round the corner.

This was ridiculous. She was becoming paranoid, conjuring up things that were not there. But she was sure she was not imagining the sensation that someone was stalking her, dogging her footsteps. Several times she had almost glimpsed him. Him? A shadow or movement seen out of the corner of her eye, a sense of being watched and monitored, but when she turned round there was no one there. There had also been the phone calls. Only three, and each time when she had picked up the receiver there had been silence. No heavy breathing but she had been sure that there was someone on the other end listening intently. Was this connected with the phone calls, and was the anonymous caller upping the ante and now stalking her?

The strange thing was, it had only happened when Tony was not there; as if someone was watching and knew when he went out and she was there alone. Not a happy thought. And Tony had been quite derisory, dismissing the calls as wrong numbers when she had told him. Come to think of it, this feeling of being stalked had only started since the business of the Thomas Hardy letters had come up, but how could there possibly be a connection? The question of the missing manuscript was exercising a lot of people. Tony and Gordon were trying to trace all Hardy's known local friends; a mammoth task and to her mind quite hopeless. They were in contact with the Thomas Hardy Society and were searching local archives. Meanwhile, at school Martin Boyd pestered her about how the search was going and hinted that he was doing some research. Well, let them get on with it. She had more important things to think about.

She bought some groceries and added a bottle of wine and a bunch of flowers to her purchases in the supermarket and took them back to the car. She stowed them in the back and checked her watch. Rachel should be back from work. It was time she brought her friend up to date on her exciting, scary news. She manoeuvred out of the school gates and took the road to Melbury Magna. Tony would be expecting her to cook their evening meal. Hard luck!

Rachel was sorting out the agenda for a meeting that evening and wondering if she had time or could be bothered to prepare a meal, when Reid arrived.

'I had to see you,' she said when Rachel opened the door. 'I'm not interrupting anything, am I?'

'No. I've got a meeting later this evening and I was just thinking of rustling up a meal.'

'You don't have to bother, I've got it all here.' Reid indicated her basket. 'A quiche – just needs heating up – salad ingredients, yoghurts and fruit – and these.' She handed the flowers and bottle of wine over. 'Don't look so suspicious! I'm not trying to sweeten you up. I'm just hoping *you* will be pleased at my news.'

'What news? What is this all about?'

'All will be revealed in good time. Now, you put the oven on and I shall make the salad.'

They made small talk over the meal and when they had finished Reid picked up the bottle of wine.

'Let's finish this up.'

'Not for me. I don't think it would go down very well if I breathed alcoholic fumes all over the PCC. You shouldn't either if you're going to drive.'

Reid put down the bottle regretfully and Rachel went into the kitchen to make coffee. When she returned with the tray her friend was looking pensive.

'Come on, tell me what is worrying you.'

'I'm not worried. Just a little anxious *and* elated and all mixed up.'

Rachel raised her eyebrows and her friend smiled and leaned forward.

'You're younger than me but do you ever feel the ticking of the biological clock?'

'What an extraordinary question!'

'Extraordinary? Why?'

'Because I *was* thinking about it only the other day. Don't tell me *you're* getting broody?'

'Yes, but not in the way you think. Anyway, you've got plenty of time to start producing; you're surely not worrying that you're too old?'

'No, I hope not, but Nick has made a discovery...'

She told Reid about what he had learnt from the investigator tracing his ex-wife and Reid listened intently.

'That's quite startling news. How does Nick feel about it? Will it make any difference to the divorce?'

'I think he has mixed feelings, as I have. / to the divorce – I really don't know. Every-thing seems to be one big muddle at the moment.'

'How strange, all these children suddenly turning up and turning our lives upside down.'

'What do you mean?'

71

'I also have a child.'

'Reid!'

Reid got up and stalked about the room. 'This will probably shock you. You're such a principled person.'

'You mean, I'm an old-fashioned prude.'

'No, of course I don't, but I'm a very different person. You know I married at a very young age and it didn't work out. Well, I was sexually active much earlier than that. I had an affair with a married man whilst I was still at school and I got pregnant. You can imagine how mother reacted.'

Rachel could. She had only met Reid's mother once, but had recognised the elderly widow as a patronising, bigoted snob.

'You had the child?'

'Yes. By the time mother found out it was too late for an abortion.'

'What about the father?'

'He never knew. Even besotted as I was, I realised that he would never leave his wife and family. He never knew he had another child, and a few years later he was killed in a car crash.'

'Poor Reid, it must have been difficult for you.'

'It was. I wanted to keep the child but she insisted on adoption. We're talking about the early 1980s, not the '50s. We were into the permissive society. It wasn't such a disaster, single mothers were becoming more common, but mother wouldn't hear of it. She bullied and nagged me and went on about my career and how my brilliant future would be ruined. I *was* bright at school and I was set to get good A-level results and a place at university and – and eventually I gave in. The baby was due in the summer holidays and she sent me away to this ghastly place for the birth. All my friends thought I was travelling, having a super time seeing the world, when actually— Anyway, he was born – it was a boy – and taken from me immediately. I only had one glimpse of him before he was snatched away.'

'How awful!'

'It was an easy birth and I quickly recovered. I went back to school in the autumn and continued my studies, eventually going on to university. Nobody knew, except mother and I, but I never forgot him. I used to wonder where he was, what he was doing, whether he knew he was an adopted child— I expected, in the fullness of time, to have other children, but it never happened. My marriage was a disaster from start to finish and afterwards I had several unsatisfactory affairs. Then I met Tony. Tony is not father material. He has no desire to perpetuate his line and I'm too old to argue and plead and go through all the business of nappies and broken nights and restricted freedom. I have come to terms with the fact that I shall never have another child, but last year I found myself continually thinking of the son I *did* have. In the end I decided to try and do something to trace him.'

'And you've found him? How wonderful!'

'No, you're jumping the gun. It wasn't as simple as that. I applied to go on the Adoption Contact Register. I had to fill in this application form giving details of myself and the original birth registration etc. and I was put on the register. But then things ground to a halt. You see, although the Registrar General established my relationship with my adopted son, nothing could be done unless *he* wanted to trace me, his real mother, and had also registered.'

'You mean, you can only have contact with him if he wants to find you?'

'Yes. All I could do was wait and hope he would be curious to find out his blood ties. The months went by and I tried to put it at the back of my mind and not dwell on it, and then a few weeks ago I got this letter telling me a register link had occurred. My son had applied to go on the register – he wanted to find *me* – and my name and address had been sent to him.'

'That's marvellous! So what happens now?'

'I have to wait for him to make contact. The ball is in his court – it is up to him to decide if he really wants to meet up with me.

But just think, Rachel, any minute now I could hear from him, a letter asking for us to meet – I'm not sure how I shall cope with it exactly—'

'Don't forget he already has another mother and father, his adoptive parents. They've brought him up and he is bound to them by loyalty and affection.'

'Oh, I know. I can never take their place. I'm the bad mother who gave him up for adoption, but he wants to find me – there is some tie – you know, blood thicker than water.'

'How does Tony feel about all this?'

Reid's face fell. 'He can't understand it. He thinks we're okay as we are and he can't understand my compulsion to find my long-lost baby. He's not bothered by the fact that I had an illegitimate baby, I think he's more concerned with how it's going to affect the status quo. He doesn't want a teenager suddenly descending on us and moving in.'

'One can sympathise with that point of view but it wouldn't be a case of him coming to live with you, would it? He already has a family. How old is he?'

'Ben is nineteen. I called him Ben but I don't know if he kept that name. He may have changed it, or the people who adopted him may have chosen another name.'

'Well, I think it's wonderful news and I hope he soon makes contact with you. Now,

I really have to get ready for this meeting.'

'Don't worry, I'm on my way. I hope Tony has managed to feed himself. He's got another rehearsal tonight. I'm becoming a real grass widow. Still, I've got plenty of school work to do.'

Reid gathered up her belongings and made for the door.

'Every time the phone rings I wonder if it's Ben, and I look out for the post each morning wondering if there will be a letter from him.'

'I hope everything works out well. Good luck.'

'Mervyn Dooley. Fifty-six years old. Several convictions for sexual offences. Now out on licence.' Superintendent Tom Powell was holding a briefing. 'This time they targeted a real nasty. Fancies little boys *and* little girls. Came out six months ago and has been closely monitored ever since. His probation officer reckons he's a high risk and could reoffend.'

'Then why is he out on licence?'

'That's the way it works. He's done a couple of treatment programmes and he reckons he's cured of his perverted tastes. As long as we knew where he was and he knew that we were keeping an eye on him and temptation wasn't put in his way he was probably safe. Now he's been driven underground he could be a real danger. If only the misguided public would realise that by acting as it does it is more likely to bring about what it fears. He's disappeared; neither us nor social services can keep tabs on him any longer. He's gone to ground and is now probably swelling the ranks of a paedophile ring. Someone is slipping names to the press and I hope to God they now realise how deluded and reckless they have been.

'Megan's Law is not working in the States and a similar law is not viable here. If the names of people on the Sex Offenders Register are available to everyone, it will drive the pervs underground for fear of reprisals, just as happened last night. The ringleaders of that mob are going to be brought to justice. It was sheer luck the fire brigade got there in time and the entire house didn't burn down. Next time someone's going to get killed, and not necessarily the pervert they're hunting.'

'Do you think Dooley has left our patch?'

'We can only hope,' said Tom Powell heavily. 'We know something else from his record. He was involved with a children's home up north that was closed down in the early '90s. There were rumours of sexual abuse but by the time the authorities were alerted the children in care and those in charge of them were scattered and there was not enough evidence to bring a case. So, as I say, a dangerous man – and one who, however he behaves now, could be facing further prosecution if the past catches up with him.'

Tony Pomfret had already left for rehearsal when Reid Frobisher returned home, and the house was in darkness. She left the car in the drive and the security light switched on as she walked up the path and approached the front door. The curtains were drawn in the downstairs rooms but he hadn't left a light on inside as she was always urging him to do. She fumbled in her bag for her key and unlocked the front door, stepping into the hall and snapping on the light.

A smell of curry and garlic wafted from the kitchen and she grinned to herself. Good, he'd had a take-away, the sink wouldn't be full of pots and pans left for her to wash. On the infrequent occasions when Tony was persuaded to try out his culinary skills he usually produced a passable meal but the kitchen was a disaster area. Every crock and utensil was called into use and abandoned, dirty, at the culmination of his efforts. She hung up her coat, kicked off her shoes and padded through into the dining room, where the sight of piles of exercise books on the table made her groan. She supposed she had better get on with the essay marking. She had the whole evening to herself, though she could think of far better ways of spending it, but first she must get her slippers from the bedroom.

As she mounted the stairs in her stockinged feet she stubbed her toe on a pair of shoes Tony had left on a step and she swore under her breath. She bent down and massaged her foot and it was then that she heard it. Not so much a noise as the sensation that someone was crossing the floor above her head. She froze and listened intently, her heart thudding in her chest. There it was again, very soft but definitely a footfall. Someone was in the back bedroom.

Panic surged through her. The stalker was here, in her house, and she was alone and vulnerable. He was lying in wait for her and she was helpless. The phone was near the front door, separated from her by the length of the hall and the stairs she had almost climbed. If she tried to get back to it he would hear and get her before she could reach it, and the extension was in the front bedroom. She felt hysteria flooding through her and clamped her hand over her mouth to cut off the cry that was rising in her throat. He was lurking, waiting to pounce, but she knew he was there. She was not the unsuspecting victim he was expecting, and she must take advantage of this. If she moved extremely carefully she might be able to get to the front bedroom and the other phone before he realised she was upstairs with him. She crept up the few remaining stairs and paused, her eyes alighting on the bronze statue that stood on a pedestal near the top of the staircase. It would make a good weapon, and her fingers closed round it and lifted it off the stand. It was cold and smooth beneath her touch, and she grasped it firmly and moved stealthily across the landing to the front bedroom.

The door was ajar, and very, very slowly she eased it open and crossed the threshold. The curtains were undrawn and light from the streetlamp outside filtered into the room, providing some illumination. She focussed on the phone standing on the bedside cabinet on the far side of the bed and moved cautiously towards it. There was a muffled sound from near the window and she swung round. Silhouetted against the diffused light was a figure, tall, black and immobile.

He was here in the same room as her, not in the back bedroom as she had thought. She squeaked in fright and stumbled back towards the door, her shaking fingers seeking the light switch. She found it and pressed it down and the features of the room sprang into prominence. The figure didn't move, he seemed as transfixed as her. They stared at each other across the room. She saw a young man with dark, untidy hair, dressed in jeans and a denim jacket. He was holding no weapon and made no attempt to attack her. She took a tentative step forward.

'Who are you? What are you doing here?'

He didn't answer and she stepped nearer to him, somehow no longer afraid. He was regarding her intently out of dark-fringed hazel eyes set in a pale, freckled face. She felt a frisson go through her. It was like looking at a mirror image. She suddenly knew who he was. The knowledge exploded inside her and she thought she was going to faint.

'You're Ben – my son!' she croaked.

'The son you gave away!' came back the reply.

Four

The rehearsal had gone well. Tony Pomfret had started with the first act and then when Emma Spendlove, the choreographer, arrived they concentrated on the dance-hall scene. The clumsy, adolescent boys roped in to swell the numbers were gradually being licked into shape. Emma was an exacting teacher, driving them mercilessly and making them repeat movements over and over again until she was satisfied that they had got it right. After an hour and a half working out, they were exhausted – still reasonably keen but starting to grumble. Tony decided it was time to intervene.

'Okay, folks, we'll call it a day. You've all worked hard and it is coming along, but we need some more males. If you look at your libretti you will see that the boys should outnumber the girls. I don't want to reduce the number of our girls – you're doing fine, ladies – so we must do some more recruiting.'

'I've met up with an old friend who's come to stay in the area,' said Kevin Compton, who was Baby John in the show. 'I might be able to persuade him to take part.'

'Good. Bring him along to the next rehearsal. When he sees the female line-up I'm sure we won't be able to keep him away.'

There were sniggers from some of the boys but several of the young women looked annoyed. Tony just grinned and patted the shoulders of those nearest to him.

'Right, off you go. Next rehearsal on Tuesday and I want the girls at seven. We're going to do the Miss America number so be ready and willing. Eight thirty for everyone else.'

'You really are an MCP,' said Emma Spendlove as the cast trooped off. 'If you're not careful you'll have a mutiny on your hands.'

'Nonsense. They lap it up. You have to keep it light otherwise some of those chicks get too intense.'

'You mean they develop crushes on you? A middle-aged, conceited has-been? When there are all those virile young men bursting with testosterone and hormones.'

'I always knew you fancied me. It's the attraction of the older man as far as they are concerned, but don't worry, I can deal with it.'

'It's not you I'm thinking of.'

'Emma, do me a favour. Do I look like a man who's into teenage groupies? Frankly, they leave me cold. I must be getting old.'

'Poor Tony, I feel real sorry for you.' Emma draped a sweater over her leotard and pulled on her boots. 'I thought you said your colleague was coming this evening to suss out the part of Glad Hand?'

'He hasn't shown up. Probably got cold feet. I know the part is supposed to be for a younger man, but when you see Gordon you'll know what I mean about him being right for the part. Oh, thanks, Barry' – this to the rehearsal pianist, who had shut the lid of the piano and was sorting out his music. 'You did a grand job.'

'I should get danger money. It's a *fiendish* score. I shall probably want a finger transplant by the time it's over.'

'Well, at least you must admit it is more

interesting than Rodgers and Hammer-
stein.'

'More challenging, certainly. Goodnight.'

Barry Thomas tucked his music case
under his arm and made for the door. He
almost collided with the man who hovered
in the doorway casting tentative glances
round the hall.

'Can I help you?'

'Yes— er, no. It's Tony I want – I can see
him over there, thanks.' He advanced
cautiously across the floor to where Tony
was talking to Emma Spendlove. Tony broke
off when he saw him.

'Gordon, you old sod, I thought you were
coming to rehearsal?'

'I have come,' said Gordon reluctantly.

'It's nearly a quarter to ten.' Tony checked
his watch.

'I didn't think you'd finish as early as this.'

'We've worked them hard and let them go
early this evening. Have you met Emma, our
choreographer?'

'How do you do?' he mumbled, not meeting her eyes.

'Emma, this is our Glad Hand.'

'I haven't agreed yet,' said Gordon hastily.
'You know I haven't.'

'Have you studied the libretto I gave you?'

'Yes. It's not a very *sympathetic* part, is it?
They all make fun of him.'

'He's a do-gooder. It is only a cameo part

but a very important part of that scene. Now you're here, let's go and share a jar at the Cock and Pie. You coming, Emma?'

'No, I want an early night. I'm off to town tomorrow on the seven thirty train.'

'Right, see you next week.'

They parted company in the car park and Tony and Gordon walked the short distance to the local pub. It stood on the corner of the High Street and looked much the same as it had when it was first licensed in the early seventeenth century. Somehow it had escaped any modernisation attempts by the local brewery. It had no canned music, fake antiques or themed decor. Those in search of more sophisticated drinking favoured the King's Head or the Newt and Cucumber further along the street, but to those in the know, the drab-looking Cock and Pie was a little gem that offered real ale to its clientele.

Gordon found an unoccupied table in the corner of the lounge whilst Tony made his way to the bar. He returned with two foaming pints and set them down carefully.

'It was a shame you missed the rehearsal this evening,' he said, taking a swig out of his glass. 'I wanted you to see how the scene played out.'

'What would I have to wear?'

'An ordinary sober suit like the one you're wearing now. You're not one of the Jets and Sharks; just a perfectly respectable middle-aged man trying to instil some decorum into these feuding teenagers.'

Privately, Tony thought Gordon was a perfect fit for the part. He wouldn't need to act, just be himself, but he had to be tactful in his persuasion.

'I wouldn't be expected to hang around all evening when the show is running?'

'No, just do your little bit then you can go home. Nearer the time we can work out a timetable for when you are needed. It will be fun, Gordon, and do you good to mix with some young people, as well as helping me out of a hole.'

'I'm not making any promises but I'll come to your next rehearsal.' Gordon lit a cigarette and squinted through the smoke at his companion. 'The reason I was late tonight was because I was working on the provenance of those letters.'

'Did you get anywhere?' Tony leaned forward eagerly.

'I think I may have. Reid said those letters were in the possession of a Bill Curtis. As they were written to someone with the initials AC, I think we can safely assume that the C stands for Curtis and AC was an ancestor of Bill Curtis.'

'Yes, we've already discussed this,' said Tony impatiently. 'It is pure supposition, though I think we must work on that assumption.'

'Now, this Bill Curtis was eighty when he died, which means he was born in 1920. Hardy didn't die until 1928, so he could have actually known him as a child.'

'You're not saying the letters were written to a child.'

'No, but they could have been written to his father or grandfather. Most likely his grandfather, as one would suppose he was writing to a contemporary.'

'So, you're saying Bill Curtis's grandfather was A. Curtis. It should be easy to check.'

'I have and he wasn't.'

Gordon ground out his cigarette and tapped the ashtray with a finger. 'Bill Curtis's father was George Curtis and his grandfather was William Curtis.'

'So, your supposition was wrong.'

'No, William Curtis had a brother, Arthur – Bill's great-uncle.'

'Aha, that sounds more promising. You *have* been busy.'

'It's easy to research ancestry now. So many people are into tracing their family tree. There are societies and even evening classes geared to doing just that.'

'What is the next step?'

'Try and find out where this Arthur Curtis lived. People didn't move far in those days. It was a tight-knit community and people stayed in the same area all their lives.'

'We don't actually know where Bill Curtis lived, do we? Only that it was in one of the villages that come under the umbrella of the Reverend Stevenson at Barminster.'

'You're not thinking it could be hidden in *that* cottage surely?'

'No,' said Tony regretfully, 'it's been cleared out and the only thing of any importance was the cache of letters.'

'It's strange that they should have survived; someone must have realised their significance somewhere along the line. Was this Bill Curtis an educated chap?'

'No, a real old country codger from what Reid gathered from Rachel Morland. A pillar of the local church, but certainly not into literature. His reading was probably confined to his weekly pools coupon and the tabloid newspapers.'

'Is the vicar doing any research into this?'

'No, he's waiting for us to pronounce a verdict and point him in the direction of the most lucrative sale.'

'Well, I think we should stall on that for the time being; I'm just getting my teeth into it.'

'Don't forget, any money realised belongs to the church.'

'But think of the commission.'

'Quite. There are commissions and commissions, aren't there? And think of the publicity. Our little business could become

88

famous. A nice slap in the eye for the big boys at Hay-on-Wye!'

Reid Frobisher sank on to the nearest bedroom chair and clutched the arm for support. She had always thought the expression about one's legs turning to jelly to be a figure of speech; now she knew better. Her legs had given way. She looked up at the motionless youth radiating disapproval and blurted out, 'How did you get in?'

'There was a man here.'

'Tony, my partner. Did he let you in?'

'He went out into the garden. I slipped in the back door when he wasn't looking.'

So much for security. 'You've been here all evening waiting for me?'

He ignored the question. 'Is he your husband?'

'No. As I said, he's my partner. We live together.'

'You're not married?'

'I was once, a long while ago.'

'Was he my father?'

'No. Your father – was a married man who already had a family. He died not long after you were born.'

'He didn't want me either.'

'He never knew about you.'

'I was an accident you wanted to forget, to be rid of.'

'Don't judge me, Ben.' Suddenly she was

galvanised into action. She *had* to make him understand her version of what had happened. 'I suppose to be truthful, I did give you away. But I did *not* want to. God knows I didn't want to— Please try and understand. I was only a schoolgirl, on my own, with no hope of support from your father, under pressure from my family to give you up. In the end I did what I thought was best for you. An adoptive family could give you all the things I couldn't provide – *two* parents, a stable home life, material possessions – so I agreed.'

'Yes, well, that didn't happen, did it?'

'What do you mean?'

He remained silent and she moved towards him. She put out a hand to touch him but sensed his recoil and dropped her arm to her side. She was suddenly aware of how cold it was and shivered.

'What are we doing up here in the cold, talking in whispers in the dark? Come downstairs and I'll put the kettle on.'

She blundered to the door and snapped on the landing light. He suddenly looked less menacing and disproving; more like a highly-strung, spooked colt. He shrugged but followed her down the stairs into the kitchen.

'Will you have something to eat? Are you hungry?'

'No, thanks.'

'Coffee? Tea? Or what about a beer? I know there is some in the fridge—' She knew she was gabbling and tried to get a grip on herself. He agreed to a beer and she handed him a can and a glass and started to pour herself a glass of milk, but changed her mind and got the bottle of brandy out of a cupboard. She poured herself a generous shot and added a little water. She took a sip of it, choked and blew her nose violently. Ben perched himself gingerly on the edge of a kitchen stool and as he drank his beer she studied him. In her mind's eye she had always thought of him as a young boy, but of course he wasn't. He was a man, a grown man, even though he was still in his teens. Youths his age were married, held down responsible jobs, were mature adults, but he still had a pubescent vulnerability about him that smote her and awakened a latent protective feeling.

'What did you mean about your adoptive family? You *were* adopted. I signed the papers. They were chosen with care.'

Ben put down his glass and studied his fingernails.

'They brought me up until I was six. They'd told me I was adopted, how they had chosen me, but I just looked on them as my mum and dad. Then they were killed in a car crash. There was no one else, no aunts or uncles or other relations willing to take me on, so I was taken into care. I went to live in a children's home.'

'Ben! How awful! I didn't know. If only I had known... Every time I thought about you my one comfort was knowing that you were being looked after as part of a loving family—'

Her son looked sceptical. 'I don't believe you thought of me at all. You'd passed me on, got rid of the responsibility. I don't suppose you gave me another thought.'

'Oh, I most certainly did! I swear to you, I did. I never forgot you, not for one minute. I can assure you that never a day passed without me thinking of you, wondering what you were doing, what you looked like—'

'So, why didn't you try and find out?'

'Because there was nothing I could do. You know that,' she said sharply. 'You know how the system works. *You* had to be the one to find *me*, and you had to be eighteen before you could do it. All I could do was make sure I was put on the register of birth mothers seeking their offspring; which I did as soon as your eighteenth birthday arrived. I've been hoping ever since that you would want to find me and would also register and make contact – but I didn't expect it to be like this; you turning up out of the blue and – and *stalking* me.'

'I've done this all wrong, haven't I?' Ben got up and mooched round the room, his hands rammed into his pockets. 'I should have written to you or phoned or made contact through a counsellor.'

'It was you – those phone calls.'

'Yes.'

'But *why*? Why didn't you speak, identify yourself?'

'I just wanted to hear your voice and to see what you looked like.'

'You mean you wanted to look me over and decide whether you really wanted to get to know me?'

'Yes, I guess so.' He looked sheepish. 'I got cold feet when your name and address were given to me and I learned that you wanted to make contact. It was my decision and I wondered just what I had started. So, I decided to come to Dorset and ... and—'

'Spy on me?'

Ben shrugged. 'I'm sorry if I frightened you. You weren't supposed to be aware of me. I'm obviously not as good at surveillance as I thought I was. You didn't go to the police?'

'No.' She looked at him in sudden anxiety. 'You're not on the run, are you?'

'Christ, no!' He chuckled. 'I'm not in trouble. That's not why I've come here—'

'I *do* have a name, you know, Ben. Don't look so horrified. I don't expect you to call me mother; why not settle for Reid?'

'What sort of name is that?'

'The one my mother – *your* grandmother – gave me. She came from a well-to-do old Scottish family and she wanted to carry on the family name, so I was saddled with it as a first name.'

'I like it, it suits you.'

Now, what did he mean by that? she thought, taking another sip of her brandy and pushing the glass to one side.

'Do I take it you liked what you saw?'

'What?'

'I didn't horrify you or put you off. You decided you could bear to become acquainted and you came here tonight with the purpose of making yourself known to me?'

'Not exactly. I mean, I wanted – I want – to get to know you, but tonight was just an impulse. I was waiting outside the house and I saw the opportunity to get inside and I took it. I think I surprised myself as much as I surprised you.'

'Well, that's honest. So where do we go from here? Pretend we've met through the official channels and start again? I want to know all about you. Tell me what happened, the children's home, everything.'

Ben fiddled with his empty beer can and she silently opened the fridge and handed him another. He put it down on the table and stared at it unseeingly.

'I lived at the home for four years.'

'And was it … *bad*?'

'I survived,' he said simply. 'When I was ten it was closed down and I was fostered out. I was moved around from one family to another – I guess I was a difficult sod. I never seemed to fit in— Anyway, when I was thirteen I went to live with this family in York and that was different. They were great – they still are – they took me into their family and really cared for me, and I felt I belonged for the first time.'

There was animation and approval in his voice and she felt a pang of jealousy shoot through her.

'They were strict,' he continued, 'and made me work hard at school. Clive is a tutor at the university and he wants me to go on to higher education. I've always been interested in wildlife – birds and animals and plants – and he suggested I make a career in nature conservation. I got the A-levels I needed and I've got a place at Bishop Burton College in East Yorkshire to read for a BSc in conservation management starting next autumn. I'm having a year out at the moment.'

'That's marvellous. I should think it is a very interesting and rewarding field of work to get into. Your foster parents have done well by you. Do they know you've been trying to trace your real mother?'

'Yes, they encouraged me, but they don't know that I'm here now. They think I'm hitch-hiking in Cornwall.'

'Where are you staying? You're not sleeping rough, are you?'

He laughed ruefully. 'You don't have to put me up, Reid, I've got accommodation.'

'Don't get me wrong. I so much want to get to know you. We've got so much catching up to do, but I wouldn't presume that at this stage you'd even want to move in.'

'I met up with an old friend as soon as I arrived in the area. He used to be at St Kilda's – the home – with me. He's living in a housing association let and I've got a temporary room there.'

'Who is he?'

'His name is Kevin Compton. He works for an electrical company.'

'And he's our Baby John, unless I'm mistaken.'

'You know him?'

'Small, blonde, baby-faced? If it's the same Kevin Compton who's taking part in the local production of *West Side Story*, then yes, I have met him.'

'What a coincidence. Yes, he's very involved with the musical. He wants me to take part in it as well.'

'If you do, you'll be Tony's friend for life.' Ben looked a question.

'Tony is my partner, the man you saw here earlier this evening. He is the producer of *West Side Story* and is very keen to recruit a few more males.'

'Does he know about me?'

'Yes, I've told him. We don't have any secrets from each other.'

'And does he mind?'

'That I had an illegitimate baby?' she said starkly, and he flinched. 'No. Tony believes that what I did before I met him is my business and nothing to do with him. He's just not so sure that I'm doing the right thing by delving into the past, afraid that I might be opening up a can of worms.' She saw the expression on his face and laughed.

'Don't look so worried, you're a very attractive can of worms and I certainly don't want to put the lid back on again.' She shook her head. 'I don't even know your surname.'

'Latimer. That was the name of the people who adopted me, and I've always kept it.'

'Ben Latimer,' she said slowly. 'Well, Ben, you'll be a hit with Tony as well if you agree to be in his blasted musical. You are going to stay, aren't you?' she asked, suddenly anxious that he might disappear as suddenly as he had come. 'You're not planning to rush back up north, are you? Whatever happened in the past, I've found you at long last and I want the chance to get to know you.'

'I hadn't really thought beyond coming here and looking for you. I reckon I'll stay around for a while.'

From outside came the sound of a car

pulling into the drive. A car door slammed, feet scrunched up the gravel path and a key was inserted into the front door.

'Come and meet Tony,' said Reid, at long last daring to lay a hand on her son's arm and drawing him into the hall.

Nick Holroyd had been put in charge of the investigation into the vigilante attacks and their fallout. After a difficult session with Tom Powell he was bringing Tim Court, his sergeant, up to date with the latest developments.

'As a result of the second raid, six of them have been bailed to appear later on charges of criminal damage and affray, and two others on the same charges plus that of endangering life, but they are not the ringleaders. They are the pawns who were incited to carry out the mayhem.'

'So, who is behind it?' Detective Sergeant Tim Court was a large, phlegmatic man with a youthful face and untidy habits. He never sat if he could lounge and his clothes always looked slept in. He was older than he appeared, had been married for many years and was the father of two young children. He had known his share of tragedy; a cot death had robbed him of his eldest son and resulted in his wife having a nervous breakdown – but that was in the past. He never referred to it, and his calm, imperturbable manner was a good foil to his colleague's more volatile and impetuous character.

'You pays your money and takes your pick. The Super thinks we've been infiltrated by a far-right group, and they could be the motivators. Possibly an arm of the National Democrats, who are linked to the old National Front. According to a spokesman from the anti-Nazi magazine, *Searchlight*, they often get involved in campaigns to out paedophiles, as it gives them a veneer of respectability; don't ask me why. The yobs we arrested say letters were put through their doors giving them Mervyn Dooley's name and address. Of course, they were anonymous and none of them were kept.' Nick leaned back against his desk and hunched his shoulders. 'On the other hand, it could be a larceny scam.'

'Not exactly a well-heeled area; not many pickings around there, I should have thought.'

'The corner supermarket in the next street was done over.'

'It's owned by a Pakistani couple. That could point to it being a racial attack and tie it in with a right-wing group.'

'Yes, but what about the Mercedes – top of the range model – that was nicked in nearby Goat Street?'

'I didn't know about that. What was a

Merc doing in Goat Street?'

'Parked near a knocking shop. It's owner has only just reported it missing, financial considerations finally getting the better of fear of his sexual shenanigans coming to light.'

'Probably just an opportunist snatch. With all the kerfuffle going on in those streets it's amazing it wasn't torched.'

'I think we'll go and visit the Patels. See if they can shed any light on their burglary.'

The district where Mervyn Dooley had lived and the Patels had their shop was not a part of Casterford that tourists ever got to see. The picturesque town centre and the surrounding rolling countryside were a mecca for visitors and holidaymakers, who would be unaware and surprised that such an area existed. What had been genteel Victorian respectability in the last century had sunk into poverty and disrepute in this. Most of the solid terraced villas had been turned into bedsits and flats and the gardens carved up for blocks of lock-up garages and storage units. A proliferation of small shops had sprung up in the last twenty years but they were cheap, downmarket stores that came and went with depressing regularity.

As they drove towards the Patel's super-market the hazy sunshine accentuated the shabby appearance of the buildings and streets. They passed a run-down-looking garage that dealt in second-hand cars, and Court remarked that he wouldn't buy a Dinky car from such a dealer. The main window of the Patel's shop was still boarded up, but it was open for business as usual. Ram Patel was a small, plump man with a very dark complexion and full of restless energy. His wife was timid, with a poor command of the English language. She surveyed the world through heavy, horn-rimmed spectacles that looked at odds with the orange, gauzy sari she was wearing. Both Patels were highly nervous and looked with trepidation at the two tall officers as they entered the shop, but once they had been shown warrant cards Mr Patel became highly voluble.

'I don't like this, Inspector, not at all. I am losing my stock and I am afraid for my family.'

'How did they get in? Through the smashed window, or did they force the door?'

'No, sir, the door was not touched. They threw a brick through the window and it fell right over here near the counter, and there was glass everywhere about.'

'So they came in through here—' Nick indicated the boarded-up window, 'and looted the place?'

'No, no, I am telling you, nobody came in here. Nothing was taken – but the mess, the terrible mess—'

'But you reported burglary and the loss of most of your liquor and cigarette stocks.'

'They were taken from my storeroom at the back. They came through my back yard.'

Nick and Court exchanged glances.

'Now, let me get this clear. Whilst the mob was advancing down this street and hefting bricks through your shop window, your storeroom at the back of the building was being ransacked by someone else?'

'That is what I am telling you, Inspector. They took the panels off of my fence and got into the yard.'

'And where were you when all this was going on?'

It turned out that the Patels and their two young children had been huddled together in the dark in their living quarters over the shop, too terrified to move.

'Why didn't you phone the police?'

'The phone is down here, behind the counter.'

Why not get a mobile phone and an alarm system? thought Nick with resignation. An inspection of the premises showed where the intruders had removed three fence panels from the rotting, sagging fence and broken the flimsy lock and bolts on the door of the store. Crates of beer, boxes of wine and cartons of cigarettes had been removed quickly and efficiently under cover of the rampaging crowd.

'That was no haphazard looting,' said Court later, when they got back in the car. 'That was organised crime.'

'I agree. Somebody knew where the valuable stuff was kept and how laughable their security measures were and either cashed in on it—'

'Or started the riot in the first place for just that purpose,' finished Court, snapping on his seat belt. 'Where now?'

'I think we'll have a nose round Dooley's old pad. We might get a clue as to where he has scarpered to.'

'If he's left our patch – and if he's got any sense he'll be miles away – it's someone else's problem.'

'Wherever he's gone they need to be warned. He's not going to turn up at the local station and say, "Please, sir, I'm here."'

The house where Mervyn Dooley had lived was still cordoned off and the front door and windows boarded up, but Nick had borrowed the key to the back door from forensics. An alleyway ran along the back of the row of gardens, with doorways leading off into each fenced property. It took some physical shouldering to get the gate into Dooley's place open, and when they got through they found themselves in an overgrown wilderness.

'Well, he certainly wasn't a gardener,' said Court, pushing through the long grass and

103

leaving a bruised trail.

'He hadn't been here long and it wasn't his property. Would you bother to cultivate land that didn't belong to you?'

'Not if I could help it. The wife is into home-grown vegetables,' said Court gloomily.

The smell of charred timbers was very strong when they let themselves into the house. Scorched wood and fabric and the very pungent aroma that always followed the combination of fire and water when a conflagration had been doused by the fire brigade. There were dirty pots and pans in the sink, and a crumb-strewn plate and a mug containing congealing dregs on the kitchen table, but a quick look round revealed that Dooley had got by with the minimum of utensils. The gas oven was old and filthy and looked hazardous, and the fridge contained only a couple of eggs, a tub of margarine and a half-empty bottle of very sour milk.

The rest of the house was little better equipped; basic furniture, no pictures or ornaments, and the only touch of luxury a television set in the living room. There were no electrical appliances, no telephone and no computer equipment.

'Well, he didn't occupy himself downloading porn from the internet,' said Nick, looking with distaste round the room.

'Presumably he left in an almighty hurry and won't have taken much with him but there's not much left behind either. What an existence!'

'There's something in the fireplace,' said Court, bending down and scrutinising the charred scraps scattered in the grate and over the hearth. 'Looks like he'd been burning photos. Can't make out what they were but I think we can use our imaginations, eh?'

'He's left no paperwork behind.' Nick was opening and shutting drawers in frustration. 'No letters, no bills or receipts, no address book, no bank books, no diary. Zilch.'

The two bedrooms revealed nothing of interest. The bed had been hastily made in the main bedroom where Dooley had slept, and one dirty sock lay underneath in a mat of dust balls. A pair of cotton trousers and a short-sleeved shirt hung in the wardrobe cupboard, and some dirty underwear had been stuffed in a drawer of the chest of drawers, but no other personal belongings were to be found apart from two disposable razors and a scrap of soap in the bathroom.

'We're wasting our time,' said Nick as they clattered downstairs again. 'I wonder where the little rat is holed up now.'

Five

The call came through on Rachel's mobile as she was tramping the endless corridors of Casterford General Hospital, having been on a visit to the Geriatric Department to assess some patients. She pulled it out of her pocket and tuned in and Reid's voice came wailing into her ear.

'Rachel, you must help me. I don't know what to do.'

'What's happened? What is wrong?'

'I think I may have lost him again and I've only just found him! It's all Tony's fault!'

'Reid, what *are* you talking about?'

'Ben. My son. Sorry, I'm not making much sense. He turned up out of the blue and I think Tony's frightened him off!'

'Look, I can't talk now.' Rachel dodged out of the way of a trolley being trundled along by a porter, its occupant comatose and attached to a number of drips.

'Oh God, I'm sorry. Are you in the middle of treating someone?'

'No, I'm negotiating the wastelands of corridor country. Can I ring you back later?'

'Can you get away in your lunch hour – can we meet up for a coffee or something?'

'Well—'

'Please, Rachel, it's important. I *must* discuss it with you.'

'I can only spare thirty minutes, we're short staffed at the moment.'

'That's fine. How about the Green Café at one o'clock? It's not far from the hospital and it won't take me long in the car.'

'Don't you have to do playground duty?'

'Someone else can look after the sodding little buggers today, this is important. Oh God! I hope I haven't blown it. I'll see you there.'

She really is rattled, thought Rachel, tucking her phone back in her tunic pocket. Reid usually tried to restrain her colourful language in front of her friend, much to Rachel's secret amusement, but today she had been far too upset to bother. She had set so much store by this meeting with her unknown son; what could have gone wrong? Well, she would soon find out. She broke out of her reverie to point a bemused old lady in the right direction for the eye clinic.

Reid was waiting for her when she reached the Green Café just after one o'clock. She was sitting at a window seat anxiously scanning the street outside. She beckoned to Rachel and pounced eagerly on her as she wended her way through the tightly-packed tables.

'I've ordered coffee and toasted sandwiches. Is that alright?'

'Yes, fine.' Rachel undid her coat, slipped it off and sat down opposite her friend. Reid looked strung up. Her hazel eyes were as bright and alert as usual, too bright perhaps, and there were dark smudges under them. The hair round her ears was in tight corkscrews as if she had been winding a pencil through it.

'Now, what is this all about? Your son has made contact with you?'

'Yes, he arrived on the doorstep yesterday evening – or, rather, I found him in the house.'

'Inside the house? You mean he appeared out of nowhere and Tony let him in?'

'No, Tony wasn't there. He'd been stalking me, you see.'

'*Stalking* you? *Tony*?'

'No, don't be daft. *Ben.*'

'How about starting at the beginning. I know you said there was a link-up between you through the Adoption Contact Register, and you were hoping he would get in touch with you. You expected a letter or a phone call—'

'Well, I got the phone calls but not in the manner you mean. He decided to check me out first before he made contact.'

The waitress brought their order to the table, interrupting Reid's flow, but after the food had been set in front of them and the coffee poured she continued, 'I never told you because it would have sounded as if I had flipped or was becoming paranoid, but over the last couple of weeks I felt that I was being watched – followed. Phone calls with no one on the other end when I answered – that sort of thing. Yesterday evening I got home mid-evening – knowing that Tony would already have gone to rehearsal and expecting to have the house to myself – and realised that there was someone upstairs. It was Ben. He'd managed to slip inside when Tony wasn't looking.'

'How frightening! You must have been petrified.'

'I was scared stiff until I realised who he was.'

'Did he have any proof?' ventured Rachel cautiously.

'I recognised him. As soon as I set eyes on him I knew who he was. Oh, Rachel, I can't tell you how I felt – it was miraculous – all those years when I'd wondered about him – how he was, where he was – and then these last few months when I'd begun to hope that at long last we would meet – and suddenly he was there in front of me, and I thought I was going to *burst* with happiness—'

'How did he react?'

Reid grimaced. 'He certainly didn't throw himself on me shouting "Mother"! In fact, he accused me of giving him away.'

'That's about par for the course.'

'Yes, I suppose so. The atmosphere was very chilly at first, until I explained the circumstances of his birth and adoption, and then he brought me up to date with his life— And that was what was so terrible.' Reid fixed rueful eyes on Rachel as she told her about the events that had taken place in Ben's upbringing. 'If I had only known...'

'Well, he seems to have fallen on his feet now.'

'Yes, he's hoping to work in nature conservation. He's got his life all planned – I just don't know where I come into it...'

'So, what happened next?' Rachel glanced surreptitiously at her watch.

'We talked and talked and then Tony came home.'

'And?'

'You know Tony. He was perfectly civil but he behaved as if Ben was a complete outsider.'

Which, of course, he was as far as Tony was concerned, thought Rachel. Ben had rattled his cage and he wouldn't be enthusiastic about anyone who looked like usurping part of Reid's attention and affections.

'It was alright to start with,' continued Reid. 'Tony was showing an interest and asking about his ambitions and plans, but then he made it perfectly clear that he thought that was the end of the matter. Ben and I had met up and satisfied each other's curiosity, and now we'd part again and go our separate ways. Can you *believe* it?'

Rachel could but forbore to say so.

'I could have wrung Tony's neck!' Reid stirred her coffee cup savagely. 'He was being so possessive of me— And then Ben suddenly said he had to go, and he got up and literally *ran* out of the house. I was so gobsmacked I just sat there for a few seconds, then I went after him. I caught up with him in the front garden. He was almost through the gate. I blurted out, when was I going to see him again and he just shrugged and didn't answer and then he was gone...'

Reid relived the scene, remembering how she had nearly tripped over a crack in the paving as she had plunged after him. The early-evening mist had turned into fog and it had distorted the shapes of the trees. They had hung like amorphous pyramids on the edge of her vision, limbs wreathed in grey shrouds, dripping moisture where they dipped over the path. The gate had clattered as Ben had pulled it open. She saw again his hand, a white, disembodied prosthesis, clutching the top rail, his body a dark mass out of which his pale face gleamed like a monk's from a cowl. She had called after

111

him and he hadn't replied, and from behind her had come Tony's voice yelling from inside, 'For Christ's sake shut the door, it's like Siberia in here!' She stared at her friend tragically.

'Do you know where he's staying?' asked Rachel practically.

'No— Yes. He's staying with a Kevin Compton. Apparently they know each other from way back in Yorkshire. Kevin has got a part in Tony's musical.'

'Then Tony will know his address, won't he?'

'Ye ... s.'

'You could phone him and suggest another meeting. I should leave it for a few days. Don't rush him. This has been as traumatic for him as it has been for you. Take it step by step and don't look so worried. I'm sure it will work itself out.'

'I had thought that perhaps Ben could be persuaded to take part in *West Side Story*. Tony's anxious to recruit at least one more male.'

'Well, there you are. Get Tony to ask this – what was his name? Kevin? – to ask Kevin to bring him along to a rehearsal. If Ben agrees to take part it will please Tony and give them both a chance to get to know each other.'

'That's brilliant, but I think it would sound better coming from you.'

'From me? But I'm nothing to do with

West Side Story.'

'Well, actually, that's another thing I meant to discuss with you. I promised Tony I would ask you.'

'Ask me just what? What have you been conniving at behind my back?'

'He wondered if you would help out as prompt.'

'Oh, no. Don't you think I've got enough on my plate at the moment? What with working full-time, being a part-time lay priest and my marriage plans—'

'But they're on hold at the moment, aren't they? It will help to take your mind off it. *Please* Rachel, it would only be from time to time. I've agreed to be the official prompt, you'd just be spelling me, helping out when you'd got a spare evening. It's not difficult; you just have to sit in a corner and give them a nudge when they forget their lines.'

'I imagine you have to be very alert and keep your wits about you. It is quite a responsibility. I really can't take on anything else.'

'Please, Rachel, don't dismiss it out of hand. Think it over first.'

'Okay, I'll give it some thought. Now I really must be going.'

'Don't forget you promised to persuade Tony to involve Ben in the show.'

'I did nothing of the sort,' protested Rachel, looking at her friend with exasperation.

'I thought we could all get together for a meal or something. Tony and me and you and Nick.'

'Why Nick?'

'Well, Nick's having to come to terms with a problematic child, isn't he? He and Tony have got that in common.'

'I don't think we're talking the same thing here,' pointed out Rachel.

'You'll earn my undying gratitude. Is Nick terribly tied up at the moment?'

'So-so. He's hopefully coming round for a meal tomorrow evening.'

'Then you can both come round here instead.'

'No, it would be better if you and Tony came to us. Nick won't find that so obvious.'

'Thanks, Rachel, I'm really grateful. Let me help with the food.'

'No. It won't be haute cuisine but I'll rustle up something. Now, I must go or I'll be having patients queuing up for me.' Rachel put on her coat and opened her handbag. 'How much do I owe for this?'

'It's my treat, that's the least I can do. What time tomorrow night?'

'Eightish? That will give me time to shop and prepare something. I'll see you then.'

She hurried out of the café, leaving Reid still sitting at the table. Nick is not going to be very pleased about this, she thought, as she half-ran, half-walked the short distance

114

back to the hospital. He reckoned Tony was arrogant and too fond of getting his own way, and he certainly took advantage of Reid. Still, Reid seemed to be quite adept in the manipulative stakes herself. Why can't I just say no? she asked herself, and knew the answer immediately. Because she wanted to meet Ben and get to know him. He sounded an interesting young man and she wanted to see how the situation developed. Forget altruism and helping out a friend, she was just plain nosey.

Mervyn Dooley leaned back against the tree and fought for breath. He could feel his heartbeat. It thudded in his ribcage, in his ears, pulsating through his body. His throat and chest were raw and burning and his legs were trembling. He had been walking for hours but he had no idea what distance he had covered; whether it was five miles, ten miles or fifteen – but it felt like fifty. He also had no idea where he was. He had deliberately travelled cross-country, avoiding all but the minor roads, even plodding across ploughed fields, where the saturated clods had dragged at his feet like quicksand.

At one point he had struggled from an overgrown footpath on to a grass verge where a signpost pointed the way to Cerne Abbas. He knew vaguely that this was a tourist attraction but he couldn't remember

why. He had turned his back on the picturesque cluster of houses round the church,
skirted the edge of the village and toiled up
the slope behind. Pausing for breath he had
glanced back over the roofs and chimneys to
the hill opposite and there, facing him, had
been the Cerne Abbas Giant. Crude, power-
ful and flaunting its manhood, the enormous figure carved out of the hillside turf
had seemed to mock him, and he had shuddered and averted his eyes and stumbled on.

Now, miles further on, he was too exhausted to walk any further. He slid down
until he was sitting on the ground, ignoring
the damp grass, and pressed his shoulders
against the trunk of a tree. Instead of
clearing his head, the long tramp had made
him even more muddled. He was no nearer
sorting out his future or planning his next
moves than when he had taken to his heels
to escape the mob in Casterford. He knew
he should get as far away from the area as
possible but, insanely, he wanted to stay in
Dorset. The industrial north was his roots.
He was a townie born and bred, and the
temptations and hazards of living in an
urban community had fed his inclinations
and dark desires. If anyone had told him
only a short while ago that he would take
to a rural environment he would have said
they were off their trolley. But unlike most
townies the countryside didn't scare him.

He liked the open spaces and the wind and the rain, that seemed so much more elemental sweeping across fields and woods than across the concrete jungle. The lack of street lights he found exciting. To be able to merge into the night, to become as one with the shadows, unseen, unnoticed, appealed to his nature. The strange noises that pervaded the night scene – the rustles, grunts, hoots and occasional bark – didn't frighten him either. He found them strangely comforting, indication of the presence of unidentified animals and birds going about their business and ignoring him as he ignored them.

But it was madness to stay around here. To start with, if the police picked him up he would be back in the slammer before he could blink. He was out on licence and he was committing an offence by not notifying the fuzz of his whereabouts. With his photograph flaunted all over the local papers, they would be on the lookout for him. He was trying to alter his appearance, growing a beard and letting his hair grow to match, and he wore dark glasses when he couldn't avoid human contact, but that was probably unwise. Anyone wearing shades in this dull, autumn weather was more likely to draw attention to themselves.

The other reason why he should take himself as far away as possible – and what had triggered off his panic today – was the encounter he had had outside the bus station. One minute he had been slinking through the crowds, straining to read the destination boards, the next he had found himself confronted by a face from the past. The very remembrance of it sent a fresh stab of panic through him. Had he been recognised? Surely not – and yet... There had been no indication of recognition, but the chance meeting had probably startled him equally. Later, when he had thought about it, he might decide to act. If he fingers me, I shall be really done for, groaned Dooley, holding his head in his hands and trying not to think of his corrupt past, which was threatening to catch up with him.

Should he go back to his bolt-hole and sit it out until they made arrangements to send him on? The foul little room he had been holed up in like a rat in a sewer was known as a halfway house. The way out was a new life on the Continent. Holland – Amsterdam. Where one of the best-organised rings in the world would draw him into its orbit. The delights and temptations beckoned him, and he shivered in anticipation. There he would have access to everything he had ever desired, but there would be no backing out. Once he was sucked back into that web of perversion and intrigue he would be lost forever, and he knew he had to make one last effort to escape. He could go straight, he knew he could. The treatment programmes he had undergone whilst inside had shown him there was another way of life. He wouldn't reoffend, if only they would give him a chance.

It started to rain and he huddled against the tree seeking what shelter he could from the practically leafless canopy overhead. If only it was summer, he could camp out; isolate himself and live off the land until the furore died down and people forgot about him. But this time of the year? When it was already cold and wet and could only get worse? No one could live outside in the winter, but perhaps he could doss down in a barn or find a deserted cottage in which to squat.

He dragged himself upright, pulled his collar up about his ears and plodded along the path out of the wood, his feet squelching through the soggy leaves and mud.

'I really don't know why you had to ask them round for a meal; we don't very often have an evening to ourselves.'

'Oh, Nick, don't be difficult. I've explained it all to you.' Rachel paused in the act of whipping a bowl of cream and glanced at her fiancé, who was clumsily chopping up tomatoes and peppers on the kitchen table.

'Reid is in a state, and it's the least I can do. It's not every day your long-lost son turns up, and she needs to play this right. Tony must be made to see him as a blessing rather than a threat.'

'I can understand Tony not welcoming a teenage lad suddenly descending on them and creating a *ménage à trois*.'

'He's not a lad, he's nineteen and there is no question of him moving in with them. He's already got a foster family behind him and further education planned in another part of the country. This is a diversion for him. When he was old enough he decided he wanted to trace his real mother, and now he and Reid have met up and we've got to help them establish some sort of relationship, so that they keep in touch and don't lose each other again.'

'I don't like this "we". It really isn't anything to do with us. You've got to let people sort out their own lives.'

'You mean I'm interfering? Doing a Pollyanna?'

'Who the hell is Pollyanna?'

'Oh, forget it. Have you finished that salad yet?'

'What else goes in it?'

'There is a bag of mixed leaves in the fridge and a bunch of chives. Snip them up finely – the chives I mean – and then you can make the dressing.'

Rachel opened the fridge door and pulled out the bag of lettuce leaves. She struggled to open it and Nick gently took it from her and slit it open with his knife.

'There you are. There's no need to get worked up, too. Two women in a distraught mood is not a good recipe for a dinner party. I promise to behave, and I'll do what I can to ease things along. Have you met him yet?'

'Ben? No. That's one of the reasons why I agreed to help out as prompt. Reid really needs me along for moral support. She thought that if we can get Ben involved in *West Side Story*, it would provide an opportunity to get to know him better without any emotional pressure.'

'I thought you were far too busy to take on anything else.'

'I've got to do something to fill the time now our marriage plans are on hold.'

She wished the words unsaid as soon as they were uttered. Nick went very still and stared at her with an inscrutable expression on his face.

'I'm sorry. I shouldn't have said that.'

'No, you had every right to,' he said slowly, putting the knife down carefully on the table.

'It's just that I'm so mixed up, so – unsettled. Have you heard anything?'

'Not yet, but I expect Dave to get in touch any day now. It's going to be alright, Rachel.' He put his arms round her and held her close. 'We're going to get married, nothing can stop us. This is just a formality, a little hitch.'

'Not quite. You may have a son. He's real, Nick, not just a statistic you can push to one side.'

'Maureen had a child. Yes, that's a fact, but I don't think he's *my* child, or I would have known years ago. I need to be sure, I want to know the real truth, but—' he raised his hands in a gesture of resignation. 'I guess men feel differently about these things. It's a cerebral exercise; I don't feel any emotional involvement, and it has nothing to do with *us*.'

Rachel buried her face into the curve of his shoulder and relaxed against him.

'We nearly had a row, didn't we? Kiss me, Nick.'

He brought his lips down on hers and they clung together in a passionate embrace. He ran his fingers through her curls and groaned as he fought for control.

'I don't want to break this up but what time are you expecting them?'

'About eight.' She glanced at the clock. 'Help! I didn't realise it was as late as this. They will soon be here. Can you lay the table whilst I see to the salmon?'

Tony was in an expansive mood when he and Reid arrived a little later. He gave Rachel a smacking kiss and told her she was his second favourite woman, then thrust a bottle of wine into Nick's hands with a stage wink. He was wearing a plum-coloured velvet jacket over a multicoloured brocade waistcoat and an indigo shirt.

'Have you been raiding the stage wardrobe?' demanded Nick, pretending to be dazzled by the sartorial display.

'Why should the women have it all their own way? I like giving them a run for their money.'

'Well, you won't have any competition from me,' said Rachel, looking down ruefully at her sensible dark skirt and cream blouse. 'Go on in and Nick will fix your drinks.'

Reid declined to join the men in the living room and followed Rachel into the kitchen. Once inside, she slammed the door shut and pounced on her friend, a big grin on her face.

'You're never going to believe this. He's already done it – what I wanted – Tony, I mean.'

'For an English teacher you show a remarkable disrespect for the English language.'

Reid ignored this. 'He rang up Kevin Compton – completely off his own bat without me even mentioning it – and Kevin put Ben on the line. After a little persuasion he agreed to come to a rehearsal and give it a go. He's coming along on Thursday with Kevin. Is that alright with you?'

'I have a meeting but I can probably postpone it.'

'Tony thinks he's eager for us to meet again and has agreed that *West Side Story* would be handy as a means of our getting together without compromising his independence.'

'Which is just what we wanted, isn't it – and just what I have been telling Nick. I'm looking forward to meeting him, and I promise I won't bombard him with questions or pressurise him.'

'You'll like him, Rachel. He really is a charming young man, quite diffident and—' Reid paused and screwed up her face. 'If I say "immature" it sounds derogatory, but there is something very young and innocent about him. He's not nearly so – so adult as many of my sixth-formers. They smoke and drink and I'm sure most of them know more about sex than I – and I'm talking participation here, not theory – and I wouldn't mind betting half of them have dabbled in drugs.'

'Not the hard stuff!'

'I hope to God not. No, I mean pot and ecstasy. But where there is a market for *those*, the dealers move in and one thing leads to another. We try to combat it, to get across the message that drugs are a fool's pastime. We arrange talks from the drugs squad, show films, that sort of thing – but there is always some young fool who thinks it's hip to experiment. I can assure you, Rachel, that teaching nowadays is not just a case of cramming academic facts into un-willing skulls.'

'No. I often wonder just what the role of the Church of England is in combatting drug abuse.'

'Don't get me started on religion.'

'We are getting profound. You'd better go through and join the men, they'll be wondering what has happened to us.'

'Can't I do something to help?'

'It's all under control – but you can take the soup bowls through with you.'

The meal progressed agreeably. Rachel was relieved that Nick was behaving himself and not deliberately needling Tony. As for Tony, he was being very avuncular, talking as if the business of Reid tracing Ben had been his idea in the first place. He was knocking back the wine and, although not drunk, it was making him even more loqua-cious than usual.

'If it makes Reid happy, who am I to inter-fere?' He speared a grape on his cheese knife and held it up for inspection.

'It was rather a shock at first, I must admit. I suppose it's not every day a fully-grown stepson – I suppose I can call him my stepson – arrives on the doorstep.'

Nick and Rachel exchanged glances, but Tony was in full flow and didn't notice.

'But we got on like a house on fire, didn't we, Reid?'

He wasn't expecting an answer, and his partner raised her eyebrows and shrugged at Rachel.

'He's got a career all lined up. Wants to be a naturalist, work in conservation. Save the planet and all that. Very fashionable at the moment, but you know the study of natural history is not just a modern phenomenon. Pliny the Elder published thirty-seven volumes on the subject back in Roman times.'

'Fancy you knowing a fact like that,' said Rachel, passing round the cheeseboard.

'I *am* a bookseller.'

'I usually think of you as a – retired actor.'

Tony frowned, obviously not liking the euphemism 'retired', and Reid chipped in, 'Once an actor, always an actor. Listen to you now; you're declaiming, not conversing.'

'I'll tell you something else,' said her partner, ignoring the interruption. 'Did you know that Pliny was so interested in natural phenomena that when Vesuvius erupted he hurried to Pompeii to investigate and was killed by the fumes?'

'Fascinating,' drawled Nick. 'Who *was* this Pliny?'

'If you are sure you've all had enough, let's

126

go through to the other room and I'll make coffee,' said Rachel hurriedly.

'Lovely meal,' said Reid, crumpling up her napkin and rising from the table. 'Was there any input from you, Nick?'

'The salad was my lowly effort, and I shall make the coffee.'

Later, when the coffee had been poured and drunk, Tony leaned back in his seat and regarded Nick maliciously.

'So, how are tricks, Nick? Still busy?'

'Policing is an ongoing thing,' said Nick shortly.

'I hate that expression "ongoing",' said Reid. 'It's almost as bad as "at this moment in time".'

'What's happening to this paedophile business? Have you caught the little jerk yet?'

'I presume you are talking about the man who was almost a victim of mob violence, and not the thug behind it.'

'Yes, Merv the Perv. Christ! You sound as if you're on his side!'

'Driving a known paedophile underground is not the best way of protecting the community.'

'Pity they didn't kill him. Those sort of people shouldn't be allowed to live.'

'Surely we've progressed beyond the law of the jungle?' protested Rachel.

'You know what it says in your Bible: *An eye for an eye and a tooth for a tooth*.'

127

'It's not *my* Bible, and that quote comes from the Old Testament.'

'Does that make a difference?'

'Actually, Tony, quite a lot. But I'm not going into that now.'

'I didn't think you belonged to the flog 'em, hang 'em brigade,' Nick challenged Tony. 'I thought you were more left-wing.'

'I've no time for perverts, preying on young girls. It's virile young men who should be getting into their knickers, not dirty old men.'

'Well, that puts you out of the equation, doesn't it?'

At that moment the phone rang and Rachel went out thankfully into the hall to answer it. She came back a few minutes later looking worried.

'That was Peter Stevenson. The vicarage has been broken into.'

'Has he reported it?' asked Nick.

'Not yet. As far as they can tell nothing has been taken except the letters. The Thomas Hardy letters.'

'Holy shit! I hope someone has photocopied them!' exclaimed Tony.

'How many people know of their existence?' demanded Nick of Rachel.

'Too many. Tony and his partner were consulted about their value. Did you mention them to anyone else, Tony?'

'No, of course not.'

'That's not true,' put in Reid. 'You told Martin Boyd, our head of English. Probably most of the staff have got to hear about it by now.'

'And all the members of St James's PCC know.'

'They weren't all *that* valuable, were they?' Nick put down his coffee cup and looked at his watch.

'It's not so much the value of the letters as the significance of the contents,' said Tony. 'Though how possessing the letters is going to help anyone to actually find the missing manuscript is beyond me.'

'I'll go over to St James's now.' Nick stood up and moved towards the door. 'It will have to be officially reported, but I'll check out what has happened.'

'Before you go, Nick, there is just something I want you to sort out for me,' said Tony portentously. 'In the last scene of *West Side Story* we have a gun on stage where Tony gets shot. Can you fix up a firearms licence for us, or whatever we have to have?'

'Are you serious, man? You're not talking about firing a real gun? You want a blank firer. Try a sports or a joke shop!'

With that rejoinder Nick made his exit, whispering into Rachel's ear as they hugged briefly in the hall, 'Get rid of the bloody guests before I return!'

Six

In the event Nick did not get back to Rachel that evening. When he arrived at St James's vicarage he found that Peter and Jenny Stevenson had revised their original belief that only the letters had been stolen.

'It's good of you to come, Nick,' said Peter as he welcomed him into the house. 'We've discovered that it wasn't just the letters; some money is missing from the house-keeping kitty and several Children's Society collecting boxes, waiting to be opened and counted.'

'How did they get in?'

'Broke the fanlight in the kitchen window, reached down and undid the casement and climbed in through that.'

'You were out?'

'Yes, we both had meetings.'

'And the children?'

'Christopher was at a Scout meeting and Debbie is staying the night with a friend. Someone must have seen us all go out and decided to try their luck, though what sort of haul they were expecting from a vicarage I can't imagine.'

'You're assuming it was a random raid. Suppose someone was after the letters.'

'You mean they took the other stuff to make us think it was just a casual break-in?'

'It is possible. Where were they kept – the letters – under lock and key?'

'You'd better come and see.' The cleric looked somewhat sheepish. 'The collecting boxes were standing here on the hall table.'

'How much would have been in them?'

'It's difficult to say, but we're not talking great sums. The housekeeping money was in a pot on the dresser in the kitchen.' Jenny saw Nick's face. 'Don't say it. I know we were negligent, but there is very little spare cash or valuables in a ministry home, as Peter has said, and he likes to believe the best of people and not be distrustful.'

Was there a slight waspish tone to her voice? wondered Nick. It would be understandable. Peter held the high ideals, but it was Jenny who had to make ends meet on what he suspected was a meagre salary.

'So, how much was in the pot?'

'About fifteen pounds,' said Peter.

'Fourteen pounds and seventy-five pence,' said Jenny crisply.

'Where were the letters kept?'

'In my study.'

Peter Stevenson led the way into his study

and pointed to the cupboard on the wall beside the desk.

'It was locked, but the key was in the top drawer of the desk and he found it.'

'The obvious place to look.' Nick sighed and looked round the room. 'Is it always as untidy as this, or did your intruder make this mess?'

'We found it like this when we got back. He'd pulled all the papers about and had gone through all the drawers.'

'And you're sure nothing else was taken?'

'My sermon notes and the Parish accounts are hardly lucrative loot,' said Peter dryly.

'These letters – were they just lying on the shelf in full view?'

'They were in a folder, an unmarked folder. It looks as if he's been through all the other folders and envelopes.'

Peter indicated the scattered piles on the shelves, surprised that the police officer was not examining them more closely. He discovered why when Nick spoke.

'We'll get forensics in and they can go over the place, but I doubt if they'll find any fingerprints. I think our man was definitely after the letters and he'll have worn gloves and taken great care not to leave any evidence behind. Have you got copies of the letters?'

'No. I was going to photocopy them but the machine is on the blink.'

'So, with the letters missing, you've got no proof of their existence?'

'The PCC are not going to like this. We had hoped to realise some money from them. Poor old Bill's other effects hardly covered the cost of his funeral. I suppose if they turn up in an auctioneer's catalogue, you may be able to trace the thief or thieves.'

'I don't think they are likely to come up on the open market. I think whoever stole them did it for what clues they might give of the whereabouts of the book Hardy mentions.'

'You really think the manuscript exists?'

'Somebody obviously does. I think perhaps we had better let the experts go over Bill Curtis's cottage in case you've missed something. Did you get the house clearers in?'

'No. The best furniture and bits and pieces we gave to a charity that helps destitute people. A lot of the stuff was so decrepit that we burnt it. He had kept stacks of old newspapers and things like that – a real hazard in that old cottage with an open fire. We had a huge bonfire in the garden and shifted it. The kids thought Guy Fawkes night had come early.'

'Hmm. Well, there's nothing to be done tonight. I'll send the team in tomorrow, and in the meantime, don't touch anything.'

Nick checked his watch as he got back into his car, and decided it was too late to go back to Rachel's place. He left a message on her answerphone sending his love and promising to be in touch tomorrow, and drove back to Casterford

The rehearsals for *West Side Story* were held in a renovated warehouse down near the waterfront. The building had been derelict for years before the council had taken it over and made it into a community centre. There was a large, barn-like hall where the rehearsals took place, a smaller hall, a coffee bar and reading room, and various other studios and offices, which were used by many local societies. Tony reckoned it was an excellent venue for his purpose. There was plenty of floor space in which to move his cast around, and the bare, echoing walls and rafters were a good substitute for the slums of New York.

Rachel and Reid met up in the coffee bar and made their way into the rehearsal hall, where Tony was putting some of the girls through their paces in the 'America' number.

'Come on, darlings, give it all you've got. You're taking the piss out of Rosalia, and we've got to hear what you're actually saying; the words are all important. Anita, I want you more centre stage, you have to dominate the scene. Now, let's go back to you, Rosalia, and your line, "That's a very pretty name, etcetera," and run through it again.'

'He's got them eating out of his hand, hasn't he?' said Rachel, grudgingly admiring the way Tony was directing his Puerto Rican chorus.

'Yes, he knows what he's doing and how to get the best out of them.'

'Is that Gordon Barnes over there? Near the backstage door?'

'Oh good, he's turned up. Apparently he's got another meeting tonight, but he said he would come here first. Tony wants to talk him through the dance-hall scene, so that he knows what it's all about. The boys are not coming along until the second half of the evening, unfortunately, but Tony's going to get the girls to walk it when they've finished this number, so that he gets some idea of what Tony's let him in for.'

Tony noticed Gordon at that moment and went over to him.

'Glad you've made it. Here is a copy of the libretto. I think your part starts on page eighteen. Have a look at it while we run through this number for the last time.'

Gordon perched gingerly on a chair and flicked through the libretto whilst Tony urged the girls through a final rendering of 'America'.

'Good, everyone, it's coming along nicely. Now, before you break for coffee, I just want you to pace through the dance-hall scene. Gordon here is hopefully going to be our Glad Hand, and I want him to get a feel for the part. It's a pity the boys are not here yet but we'll have to pretend you've all got partners.'

Tony turned to Gordon. 'The best thing would be for me to read through the part whilst you watch.'

Gordon acquiesced and Tony organised his reduced chorus and ran through the scene, emphasising Glad Hand's part.

'You see what he's trying to do? He's trying to get the Jets and the Sharks – that's the two rival gangs – to mix up and dance with each other, but they are foiling his attempts. What do you think?'

'He's not very popular with either side, is he?' said Gordon gloomily. 'They're all taking the mickey.'

'That's how it's meant to be. As I said, a small part, but important, and we need someone like you to give it gravitas.'

Tony dismissed his girls and swept Gordon over to Reid and Rachel who had been watching the scene with interest.

'You know Rachel Morland, don't you?'

'Yes, good evening, Rachel. Has he pressurised you into taking part as well?'

'I'm helping out as prompt. My days of tripping the boards ended when I left college. Has he persuaded you?'

'They used to call it a Paul Jones,' said Gordon, apparently going off at a tangent.

'What?'

'This dance that Glad Hand is trying to MC. This was in the days when people actually danced together, instead of all this modern stuff when they don't appear to make contact at all.'

'There you are, everything comes round full-circle. Have you really got to go so soon?'

'Yes, I'm late already. I'll bid you ladies good night,' he said primly to Rachel and Reid as he buttoned up his coat.

'Got your libretto?' asked Tony. 'You can hang on to that and bring it along to the next rehearsal.'

'Oh, I think I left it over there by the piano. I'll pick it up on my way out.'

Gordon made his way across the hall and was almost swept aside by the surge of men and youths flooding through the door.

'Poor Gordon, he's like a fish out of water,' said Reid, 'but he's just right for the part if you can get him to do an American accent.'

'I'll put him through his paces every day at the bookshop,' said Tony, and turned back to address the newcomers.

'We're running a little late. I'm breaking for coffee now and I want you all back here in twenty minutes. We've got a lot to get through this evening, so I hope you're all

137

raring to go.'

There was a stampede for the coffee bar, and Reid looked round the hall anxiously.

'Ben and Kevin haven't come yet. What time did you tell them?'

'Eight thirty. They should be here at any moment. Are you two coming through for a coffee?'

'I think it would be a much better idea if you went and got them and brought them back here so we can drink in peace away from the mob.'

'As you wish.' Tony shrugged and went off, and Reid fidgeted with her handbag and sighed.

'I do hope he comes. I don't know what I shall do if he chickens out.'

'Could that be him over there now?' said Rachel, nodding towards the man who was hovering in the doorway.

'Oh my, yes.' Rachel leapt to her feet, paused, and then when she saw the man looking over at them, raised an arm and waved.

The man hesitated and then came towards them. Rachel studied him closely. He was tall and slim and good-looking, she noted, and he had Rachel's colouring. I wouldn't mind claiming him for my son, she thought, and a twinge of envy rippled through her.

'Oh, Ben, I'm so glad you're here,' enthused Reid. 'Did Kevin come with you?'

'Yes, he's left something in Brett's van and he's gone back for it. Brett gave us a lift,' he explained.

'I want you to meet my friend Rachel. Rachel, this is Ben.'

Rachel smiled at him and said hello, and Ben smiled back.

'Are you a teacher, too?'

'No. I'm a physiotherapist for my sins.'

'*And* a lay reader and pillar of the local church,' said Reid. ' Rachel is into religion in a big way, so you must watch your Ps and Qs.'

'You're a priest?' He looked startled.

'No, but I hope to be one day. Does that bother you?'

'Oh no, my foster mother is very religious. She's been making noises about training for the lay ministry. She'd be interested in meeting you.'

'Are you a churchgoer, Ben?'

'Not really. I mean, I'm not really into religion but I go along at Christmas and Easter to please her. Is your church here in Casterford?'

'No, I help out at St James's in Barminster, but several smaller parishes come under its umbrella, so I suppose you could say I'm peripatetic.'

'You've timed it right,' interrupted Reid, thinking that Rachel had had enough coverage. 'They've just broken for coffee. Do you

139

want to go and join them?'

'No, I don't think so. I'm not sure this is a good idea, Reid. I'm no good at acting and Tony said it involved dancing as well, and I certainly can't dance.'

'Neither could most of them before they started rehearsing. Do you know the show?'

'I saw it once years ago, and also the film on telly. I enjoyed it, it was exciting stuff.'

Tony returned at that moment bearing a tray of coffee.

'Ah, Ben. Good, you've arrived. We'll be starting again in about ten minutes.'

'I've just told Reid, I really don't think I'm up to this. It isn't my scene at all.'

'You don't know until you've tried. I suggest you sit here with Reid and Rachel – they're acting as prompts – and watch proceedings this evening. I imagine Kevin has talked to you about it?'

'Yes, he's very keen.'

'And an excellent Baby John, but don't tell him I said so. When we finish, you can meet the rest of the cast and get to know everybody.'

The rehearsal progressed, and Ben sat with the two women, watching intently but making no comment. Reid tried to involve him in discussion about the show when there was a pause in proceedings, but Rachel could sense his reluctance, and asked him about his chosen career. Ben spoke with enthusiasm about his involvement with his local Wildlife Trust and the conservation work he had carried out with them, and she sensed that Tony was going to be disappointed. Ben was essentially a loner, quite content to spend a day in the countryside with only the birds for company. The gregarious, almost incestuous atmosphere of a group of actors, be they amateur or professional, with its exhibitionism and rivalries, was hardly likely to appeal to him. She hoped Reid could share his interests, because she didn't think they would find much common ground in a theatrical setting.

Their services as prompts were very little called on that evening. She was impressed at how well the young actors and actresses knew their lines, though she also noticed that they deviated from the script from time to time without any obvious hitches. She found herself caught up in the excitement of the action and the quality of the singing, and was quite disappointed when Tony called a halt. He came bounding over to them.

'What do you think of it?'

He was addressing Ben, but when he didn't reply Rachel jumped into the breech.

'It's very good. I'm impressed.'

'What do you think of our Maria?'

'She's got a fantastic voice—'

'But? I can tell you're going to qualify that.'

'She's almost *too* good. She's too – too sophisticated. She's good and she knows it and she seems to be almost lording it over the others, whereas she's supposed to be the youngest – naive and innocent.'

'You've got it in one. A superb voice and an accomplished actress, but she *is* lording it over the rest of the cast. And I'll tell you why. She's older than most of them – in her early twenties – and, although she went to Casterford High too, she left several years ago and she thinks she's far superior and more mature than the other school kids in the cast.'

'You're going to have to do something about her,' said Reid. 'She's making her Tony a suppliant rather than an equal. The partnership is not balanced right.'

'I'll get her on her own and give her a talking to. If I can make her see she's selling the part short by her attitude, perhaps I can persuade her to interpret it differently.'

He turned to Ben. 'Well, Ben, are you fired with enthusiasm? Ready to join us?'

'I'm sorry, Tony, but I'd only be a liability.'

He put up his hand as Tony started to protest and continued, 'I can't sing and I can't dance. I've got two left feet, and there is no way I could learn to do what they were doing tonight.'

'I'm sure we could lick you into shape.'

'No, I'm sorry, but this really isn't for me.'

'Good, don't let him bully you,' said Reid. 'He can't get it into his head that not everyone wants to risk making a fool of themselves in front of the footlights. You'll be far more help backstage, helping with the scenery and props or the lighting. Won't he, Tony?'

Tony knew when he was beaten. 'Christ, yes, we can always do with extra hands backstage. Would you be willing to help out in that way?'

'Yes, I guess so. I don't know anything about that sort of thing but I can help to hump scenery about or make it. Do you make your scenery?'

'We sometimes hire it but this time we decided to have a go at making it ourselves to save money. You're on. I'll introduce you to our stage manager, he'll be delighted to get some extra help. Now, shall we all move on to the Cock and Pie for a drink?'

'Not me,' said Ben, getting to his feet. 'I must catch up with Kevin. He'll wonder what's happened to me.'

He pushed his chair back and zipped up his jacket. Reid spoke hurriedly.

'I want you to come round for a meal. How about one evening later in the week?'

'I'm not sure. I mean, I'd like to, but I don't know yet what I'm doing.'

'Shall I phone you tomorrow to find out when you're free?'

'No, I'll phone you. I must go now. Good night, everyone!' And he made a rather hasty exit.

'He's an elusive young fellow,' said Rachel, watching him disappear through the door, 'and his own man. You're not going to persuade him to do anything against his will.'

'He's playing hard to get,' said Tony. 'He knows that will make Reid even more smitten.'

'That's an absolutely bitchy thing to say,' she snapped. 'I respect him for being honest and not giving in to your importuning. Besides, if he's helping backstage with us I'll see more of him than if he were actually taking part.'

Tony shrugged. 'Come on. The caretaker is waiting to lock up. Are you coming with us, Rachel, or is pub-crawling forbidden to those in Holy Orders?'

'Surprisingly, Tony, I am also my own man – or rather, woman – and I make my own decisions. But no, I won't join you – I want an early night.'

'Or is our favourite bit of fuzz meeting you?'

'Some people actually have to work in the evening – we haven't all got nine-to-five jobs. Goodnight.'

And Rachel swept out before her temper got the better of her and she said something that would upset Reid.

* * *

It was strange, thought Kevin Compton, how even after rehearsal was over the cast kept strictly segregated in their two gangs. Especially when you considered that many of them were in the same form at school and had known each other all their lives – and the operatic society members had all worked together on many different shows. It was as if the emotional drama engendered by *West Side Story* was so intense that it lingered on afterwards, affecting their relationships with each other. Look at them now – the Jets, of which he was one, draping the stools near the counter, and the Sharks in a tight circle in the furthest corner of the coffee bar – regarding each other with suspicion and disdain.

It was even crazier when you remembered that the criteria in choosing who would be in which gang had rested primarily on colouring. The Jets were all fair-skinned with blond or light-brown hair, whereas the Sharks were all dark and swarthy and more hispanic looking. And we're still acting the parts, he mused – this show is really getting to us. It wouldn't take much to start up a fracas here in this hall. Tension stalked the air, and a word out of place or a careless gesture would have them at each other's throats like real rival gangs.

'Wakey, wakey, Kevin!' Lisa Catling, who

played the part of Anybody's, waved her hand in front of his face. 'You haven't heard a word we've been saying. We're thinking of going on to Katy's. Are you coming?'

'No, count me out. I must go and find Ben Latimer. He'll wonder what's happened to me.'

When the others had moved off he stowed his libretto in the pocket of his anorak, crumpled up the empty crisp packets lying around and put them in the litter bin and went back into the main hall. It was empty, and only one light remained on in the corner where the piano stood. Perhaps he has gone off with Tony and his new mother, he thought, or he may be waiting for me outside. He pushed open the door and went out into the yard. It was dark amongst the outbuildings and accumulated debris that littered the area but, beyond, the car park was bathed in moonlight, and he could see that there were still some cars there. He blundered into a dustbin, swore and swerved to avoid a pile of crates. He thought he heard a noise up ahead and called out, 'Ben? Are you there?'

The moon was very bright and directly overhead. As he stepped into the car park his reflection rippled up at him from a puddle. It was the last thing he saw. He never heard his assailant, or felt the blow that felled him, only found himself falling down, down and

146

through the silver and black water that shimmered up to meet him.

'Sir? There's a report come in of an intruder out at a farm in Lackford,' Jane Perkins, the collator, called out to Nick Holroyd as he passed her door.

'Why tell me? Is no one else working in this joint?'

'It could be our Mervyn Dooley. Whoever it was was camping out in a barn and the farmer disturbed him.'

'Good thinking, Jane. Have we got a description?'

She flashed up the information on the screen and Nick read it over her shoulder.

'Middle-aged. Slight build. Unshaven and unkempt. Looked like an elderly hippie. Dressed in jeans and a dark bomber jacket and wearing trainers. Could well be. Do we know what actually happened?'

'I haven't managed to input all the information yet.' She checked her notes. 'The farmer is a Roy Sharpely. He farms at Grange Farm on the outskirts of Lackford. He went into his barn to check some machinery, and his dog got excited by something in the hayloft. He climbed up the ladder to it, leaving the dog down below, and surprised a man who had been hiding there. As soon as he saw the farmer, the intruder crawled along the rafters and managed to

147

squeeze through a gap and drop down to the ground outside. By the time the farmer got back outside, he had disappeared into the nearby wood.'

'It's a pity the dog didn't get him. Have we got any more details?'

'The farmer reckoned he'd been sleeping there. He'd made a makeshift bed out of old sacks and straw and there were the remains of a meal and some empty beer cans.'

'Well, we should get some fingerprints, and if they match up with the ones he left in the house he was living in we'll know for sure if it was Mervyn Dooley. If he *is* still in the area, we stand a good chance of picking him up. I'll get someone down there straight away.'

Tim Court was assigned to the task and, together with a fingerprints officer, drove out to Lackford. It was a bright, crisp morning and the sun, low in the sky and glinting off waterlogged fields and ditches, nearly blinded them.

'Christ!' exclaimed the detective, as a tractor suddenly loomed round the corner on a collision course. He swerved and veered up the bank. 'We need radar. What the hell did he think he was doing driving on the wrong side of the road like that?'

'He's bigger than us,' said his passenger laconically. 'Watch that mud. It looks as if he's left half the field on the road.'

'That's an offence too. Did you get his number?'

'With all that mud splattered over him? No way.'

Grange Farm was a small, mixed farm of the kind little seen these days. It was run on old-fashioned lines and looked neither prosperous nor efficient. The farmhouse was a plain, ugly building standing starkly on one side of the yard, with no gardens surrounding it or any attempt made to soften the harsh grey walls with roses or creepers. Roy Sharpely heard them draw up and came across the yard to meet them accompanied by an ancient labrador that walked stiffly and looked as if it could keel over at any moment. Its owner looked little better, thought Court as they introduced themselves. He was an old man, well past retirement age, and if he was running the farm single-handed it was no wonder it looked so neglected and run-down.

'Tell me in your own words what happened,' the policeman invited him, and Sharpely scratched his head and looked baffled.

'I went into the barn to have a look at my old seed drill, and I thought I heard a noise up in the hayloft. I didn't take much notice at first, thought it was rats. We get a lot of rats.'

I bet you do, thought Court. 'What about the dog?'

149

'Yes, well – she started to get excited and I thought, "Now, what's got into her?" She's an old dog, is Bess – and not as sharp as she used to be – but she can still tell the difference between vermin and intruders. So I told her to stay and I climbs the ladder and there he was, dodging amongst the rafters. He was too quick for me – I'm not as young as I used to be – and he got away.'

'Didn't Bess go after him?'

'Her sight's not too good these days. She really ought to be put down but I can't bring myself to do it. Her and me go back a long way and, since my wife died five years ago, she's all I've got. Couldn't bear to lose her.'

He fondled the dog's ears and she leaned against him, panting ecstatically. When pressed, he could add nothing to his description of the intruder, so the two policemen asked to be shown the barn and followed him into the building. The ladder leading up to the hayloft was rickety, with a couple of broken rungs. Tim Court looked dubiously from that to Sharpely, and the farmer interpreted the look.

'I had to be careful climbing up there and, of course, he got plenty of warning of me coming. You take care going up. I'll wait down below – but have a good look round.'

'I didn't know farms still had things like

haylofts,' said Jeff Clarke, the fingerprints officer and a country man himself, as he heaved himself up. 'I thought nowadays it was all silos and modern granaries.'

'I don't think he'd know what a silo was,' said his companion, looking round the loft. 'Well, you can see where he kipped down and the broken boards through which he escaped. You should get some good prints. I'll leave you to it and see if I can screw any more information out of Farmer Giles below.'

Court climbed back down the ladder and found Roy Sharpely rummaging through a pile of hurdles in a corner of the barn.

'Have you any idea how long he was camping out up there before you discovered him?'

'Well...'

'A couple of days? Longer?'

'It's difficult to say.' The farmer looked sheepish. 'I don't come in here all that often, and Bess wouldn't have noticed if he'd kept quiet.'

'Did he nick anything?'

'Food. I reckon he helped himself to bread and milk and bits and pieces out of the fridge. I thought my food stocks were going down quickly.'

'Good God, man! You mean he was in and out of the house as well? No, don't tell me. You're lucky you didn't lose anything else.'

'Well, there was the bike.'

'Bike? He stole a bike?' said Court sharply. 'You didn't mention that when you reported the intruder.'

'Well, I've only just discovered it's gone, haven't I?' said Sharpely in an aggrieved tone.

'Where was it kept?'

'In the old cow shed.'

'Was it an old bike? Capable of being ridden?' A penny farthing wouldn't have surprised Court.

'It were an old bike, but I had just finished doing it up for my grandson. It were in good condition – a good strong, solid machine – better than this modern rubbish, all plastic and glitter.'

'So, when did the bike go missing? You say the intruder *ran* off into the woods?'

'He must have come back again later. It was definitely there when I saw him off, but it's gone now.'

So, the intruder had wheels, be it Mervyn Dooley or someone else, thought Court in disgust. Not a car, but a cycle capable of covering considerable distances if its rider was fit enough. He could be miles away by now.

'You know who it was, don't you?' the old man said, suddenly shrewd. 'Is he dangerous?'

'We've got a good idea who it might be,

but I don't think he is a danger to the general public. I don't think he'll return, but if you do suspect he's back in the area get in touch with us immediately.'

'I'm surprised he didn't move into the farmhouse itself. I swear the old boy would-n't have noticed,' said Jeff Clarke as they drove back to Casterford.

'I can't understand why he's hanging around the district. You'd have thought he would have done a runner and been swal-lowed up by a paedophile ring in a big city by now.'

The skip was being manouevred into place. For a few seconds it swung in space, then with a clunk it hit the ground and the chains were released. It had been a tricky operation getting it in exactly the right position so that it didn't obstruct the back entrance to the community centre, but was close enough to the building to allow easy access.

The skip-hire lorry backed away and the skip remained empty for an hour until the builders and council workers arrived. An extension was being built on to the offices at the rear of the building, and this had neces-sitated the removal of a couple of old lean-to sheds. The remains of these were thrown into the skip together with some old girders and broken slates that had been lying around for some considerable time.

The men stopped for a tea break and one of them mooched round the corner to light a cigarette out of the wind.

'What about this stuff here?' he called back to his mates. 'Looks like some old cardboard packing cases.'

'It's nothing to do with our job.'

'It's been put out for rubbish. We might as well chuck it in and get rid of it. Give me a hand.'

Two of them went to help and started to move the cardboard sheets. Although not heavy, they were large and awkward to handle, and as they shifted the first two the pile overbalanced and toppled sideways, revealing a pair of dirty trainers on the end of jean-clad legs.

'Christ! There's somebody in here!'

The men scrabbled at the tilted sheets of cardboard and pushed them to one side.

'Is he dead?'

'You don't walk around with the back of your head stove in!'

The man with the cigarette choked, and it dropped from his shaking hand on to the cardboard, where it started to smoulder. He swore, bent down to beat it out and found himself staring down at a battered corpse. He backed away and was promptly sick.

'Don't touch him! We must get the police.'

'Touch him? I ain't going near him!'

'Ring them on Ernie's mobile!'

154

When the uniformed constable arrived a short while later he found four very shaken men and a murder victim awaiting his attention.

Seven

Superintendent Tom Powell sent for Nick Holroyd as soon as the call came through. He was standing with his back to the window of his office, hands deep in pockets and shoulders hunched, when Nick knocked at the door and was bade enter.

'There's been a body found at the community centre in Pankhurst Road. Some workmen clearing the site found it.'

'Foul play?'

'It's a homicide alright. He's been hit on the back of the head, half the skull crushed in. PC Hewitt was called to the scene, and from his description it could be our Mervyn Dooley. As this follows on from your investigation, I'm putting you in charge of the murder enquiry. You've got Court. Take whoever else you need, but it should be easy to wrap this one up. We don't want to expend too much time and manpower on one of the dregs of society.'

'You think one of the vigilante groups caught up with him, sir?'

'We're not paid to *think*, Inspector. I'm expecting you to find out. There will be no lack of suspects and, as the ringleaders are all out on bail, it shouldn't be too difficult to find out who had the means and opportunity. A murder charge should bring these vigilantes into line, and at the same time we've got rid of an embarrassment and a danger to the public.'

And aren't we rather jumping the gun? thought Nick as he left the Superintendent's office. We don't know yet if the murder victim *is* Mervyn Dooley. He found Tim Court in the canteen, wolfing down a late breakfast.

'Stop feeding your face, we've got a murder on our hands. Merv the Perv has possibly met a sticky end.'

He put Court in the picture as they went out to the car park, having first arranged for the SOCOs to attend the scene.

'This intruder I was checking up on at Grange Farm yesterday,' said Court. 'If it was Dooley he must have abandoned life on the range and come back to Casterford. I wonder why?'

'How far is Grange Farm from here?'

'It's on the outskirts of Lackford. About ten miles. We know he nicked the farmer's bike, so he could have covered the distance

156

easily. Strange he's still hanging around.'

'Permanently, if it *is* him. I wonder what he was doing at the community centre?'

The community centre had been closed to all users and the back cordoned off. Nick and Court ducked underneath the tape and PC Hewitt joined them.

'When was the body found?' asked Nick.

'About nine thirty. The workmen were clearing the rubbish from the yard and loading it into that skip.' Hewitt indicated the skip piled with an assortment of junk. 'They were lifting up some large cardboard packing cases from round by the old boiler room and discovered it underneath.'

'Has the police surgeon been?'

'Yes, you've just missed him. He certified death but reckoned you'd want the pathologist in on this too.'

'Let's have a look.'

Hewitt led the way to the alley beside the boiler house. The sheets of cardboard and the cartons were in great disarray, toppled this way and that. One sheet was propped diagonally against the wall, and from under it Nick could make out a pair of legs.

'Has anything been moved?'

'No. The workmen were lifting that sheet when they found him. They let it drop back and that was how it was resting when I arrived.'

Nick crouched down, peered underneath

157

and gave a startled exclamation. 'Hold it back so that I can see properly.'

Hewitt and Court did so, and Nick bent over the body and then straightened up.

'I thought you reported a middle-aged man?'

'No, sir. He's only a youngster.'

It was true, thought Nick in dismay, this was only a teenager. How many groups and youth clubs used this centre? Then he thought of Tony Pomfret's *West Side Story* production and remembered that Rachel had attended a rehearsal of it here last night. It was beginning to look horribly as if this was one of the cast.

'Where are the SOCOs? They should be here by now.'

'They're just coming, sir.'

The SOCO team arrived and, whilst they set to work and the photographer snapped the body from every angle, Nick called Dick Wickham, the pathologist, on his mobile and asked him to attend the scene.

'Have you finished?' Nick asked the photographer.

'If we can shift that sheet of cardboard I'll get some close-ups before he's moved.'

After the photographer indicated that he was satisfied, Nick once more crouched down and visually examined the corpse. The hair that wasn't bloodsoaked and matted with fragments of bone and spilled brains was fair, straw-coloured. He was small, reckoned Nick, not more than about five foot six or seven; only a young man, possibly still a child. And weren't several of the pupils from Casterford High taking part in the musical? This was getting nastier and nastier.

He donned a pair of plastic gloves and carefully slipped a hand into the pockets of the denim jacket the corpse was wearing. There was no wallet or driving licence, just some loose change, a pen, a stick of chewing gum and an old bus ticket. In the back pocket of the jeans he struck lucky and recovered a postcard. It had been posted in Spain and showed a beach scene in Benidorm. Nick turned it over and grunted in satisfaction.

'We've got a name and an address,' he said to Tim Court. 'Kevin Compton, Ranworth House, Caister Road. Until we get an identification we can't be sure this *is* Kevin Compton, but it's a pretty safe bet.'

'I think Ranworth House is one of those old Victorian houses that has been converted into flats and bedsits for single people.'

'I'll get someone over there. The other tenants may know if he has any family and where they live, but first I'm going to try someone else.' Nick took out his mobile to make a call but was interrupted by the arrival of the pathologist.

'What have you got for me?' asked Dick Wickham briskly, slamming his car door and walking eagerly towards them as if a treat was in store for him.

'A young man, been hit over the head. Discovered about an hour ago.'

Wickham swept an expert eye over the body and then bent to take a closer look at the battered head.

'Nasty. Certainly no accident. Someone took great care he wouldn't survive.'

'Any idea what the weapon was?'

'Something heavy. Could have been a metal bar. I'll be able to tell you more when I've got him on the slab. Do you know who he was?'

'We think so. How long has he been dead?'

'The old, old question. You say he was found earlier this morning?'

'Yes, at about nine thirty.'

Wickham examined the corpse. 'Rigor mortis is fully developed in his jaw and arms and legs, so he's been dead between twelve and eighteen hours. Didn't the police surgeon record the body temperature when he attended?'

'No, he just confirmed death.'

Wickham sighed. 'Help me ease his jeans down.'

Nick complied and, while Wickham busied himself with a thermometer, he studied the postcard again, now slipped into a plastic envelope.

Wickham stood up and squinted at his thermometer. 'Hmm, I reckon you can put the death at between ten o'clock and midnight, give or take the odd half-hour. He's definitely been lying there all night.'

'We think he was killed nearby and dragged behind the cardboard packing. There are bloodstains on the ground and scuff marks along the yard. Could he have been killed by a woman?'

'He was taken unawares from behind and didn't put up a fight, so, yes, a woman could have done it easily.'

At that moment one of the team who had been searching the premises came round the corner.

'I think we've found the murder weapon. There's a broken iron girder behind one of the dustbins. It looks as if it's been tossed there recently and there are what appear to be bloodstains on one end. It hasn't been touched,' he added hastily, seeing Nick's face.

The two detectives and Wickham followed him to the area where the bins were standing. Two constables were standing guard and one of them indicated the far dustbin.

'It's behind that one.'

Nick reached behind it and extracted the girder. The three men stared at it.

'This could certainly have caused that wound,' said the pathologist, 'but I'll be able to do a better match when I do the autopsy.'

'When will that be?'

'Early this afternoon. I think I can fit it in about two o'clock. Have you finished with him here?'

'Yes, he can be taken away now. Thanks, Doc.'

Nick turned to Tim Court. 'Get this girder bagged up and over to forensics. There won't be any fingerprints, but we can always dream. I'll arrange for an MIR to be set up and we'll get a team on a house-to-house locally.'

He took a last look at the body before it was moved, and grimaced. Any violent death was horrific, but when it was a child or an adolescent it was even more dreadful. Yesterday this corpse had been a young man with all his life before him, full of promise and expectations, and then, in a couple of seconds, it had all been ended. He would never know the joys of marriage and fatherhood, never play football again or take part in amateur dramatics. At this last thought he took out his phone to make the call he had been going to make earlier, then changed his mind. Tony Pomfret would be able to tell him about the rehearsal that had taken place yesterday evening and, if Kevin Compton had been one of his cast, he could also make

162

the official identification if there was no family available. Rather than ring him he would go round to the bookshop and tackle him in person; it was only a short distance from here and he should be there by mid-morning. He finished organising things at the scene of crime, got into his car and drove over to the bookshop.

Tony Pomfret was in the window arranging a display of books when Nick arrived outside. Although he raised a hand in greeting as he got out of the car, Tony ignored him and carried on with his task. The bell was one of the old-fashioned kind that jangled tinnily when he opened the door and was, supposed Nick, appropriate for an establishment that dealt with antique tomes. The whole place had an air of slightly run-down gentility; it was a setting from a Victorian novel. A great deal of effort had gone into achieving this Dickensian appearance, but it didn't suit its larger-than-life owner. Or, at least, one of its owners, amended Nick as a man in late middle-age came out of a door behind the counter. This must be Tony's partner. He certainly went with his surroundings – a Pickwick or an elderly Bob Cratchit.

'Can I help?' he asked.
'It's alright, Gordon, I'll deal with this.' Tony Pomfret appeared from behind a

bookcase. 'This is a friend of mine – Nick Holroyd, Rachel Morland's intended and a member of our gallant constabulary. Nick, this is my partner, Gordon Barnes.'

'A policeman?' Barnes looked startled. 'Is anything wrong?'

'Of course not,' said Tony. 'I suppose Rachel has got you working on this missing manuscript as well and you've come to pick our brains.'

'This is not a social call,' said Nick. 'I'm here on police business.'

'Oh my! What have we done? How have we contravened the law, Gordon, have you any idea?'

'You had a rehearsal at the Pankhurst Road community centre last night, I believe?'

'Yes. Your Rachel was there, didn't she tell you?'

'Have you got a young man in your cast called Kevin Compton?'

'Yes, he's our Baby John – and making a good job of the part, though I've had a hell of a task eradicating his Yorkshire accent. Don't tell me he's fallen foul of the fuzz. I don't believe it, he's not one of your young tearaways.'

'A man's body has been found in the vicinity of the centre. We have reason to believe it is that of Kevin Compton.'

Tony Pomfret looked thunderstruck.

'This isn't true. You're having me on?'

'Unfortunately, I'm deadly serious.'

'*Dead?* But how did he die? Was it some kind of accident?'

'If you can call being hit over the head with a heavy object an accident.'

Tony sat down abruptly on the edge of a display table and a pile of books slid to the floor.

'You're saying he's been *murdered?* I can't believe this! When did it happen? Why?'

'That is what I am trying to find out. When did you last see him?'

'At the rehearsal. It finished about ten thirty.'

'What happened then?'

Tony looked blank. 'He went off with the rest of the kids, I suppose. They go on to the pub or the bowling alley... Did you see him afterwards, Gordon? Oh no, you went off early.'

'I went to that meeting of the local book league, so I would have missed him. Not that I would have known who he was anyway. I'm sorry, Tony, it must be difficult losing a member of the cast at this stage, and dreadful for him, of course.'

'Can you give me some background information about him?' Nick asked Tony.

'I don't know anything about him,' protested Tony hurriedly. 'He's just one of my cast.'

165

'You must know something about him. How did he get involved in your show in the first place?'

'I think one of the other members brought him along. He did an audition and he was a natural for the part.'

'We know he lived at Ranworth House in Caister Road, but we need to trace his family. Do you know where he came from before he moved down here?'

'Ah, now that I can help you with. He didn't have a family, he was an orphan. Told me once he had been brought up in a series of homes up in Yorkshire. Had a hard childhood, poor little bugger. Been down here two or three years – works for Mathies.'

'So, you're saying he had no living relations?'

'That's what he said.'

'We need an official identification.'

'Oh no, don't look at me.' Tony jumped to his feet in agitation. 'I'm not doing it. Get someone from Mathies or one of his friends.'

'Tony, you knew him, working with him on your show. You don't really expect me to ask one of the other kids in your cast to do it, do you? How old was he, anyway?'

'Nineteen. Oh, God, I can't believe this!'

'It won't take long. I'll run you round to the morgue now.'

'But you said he'd been knocked about. I

really don't think I could cope with it. We're not all as hard-boiled as you, Nick.'

'You won't see the damage, I promise you. Come on, it's the least you can do for him. Once he's formally identified I can get on with the job of nailing the bastard who did for him.'

Reluctantly, Tony was persuaded into his coat and into Nick's car. His nervousness at his coming ordeal made him even more loquacious than usual. He jabbered incessantly as Nick drove through the streets of Casterford.

'I feel quite sick. I'm a very sensitive person. I shall probably pass out, you do realise that, don't you?'

'We'll deal with that when it happens,' said Nick drily.

'Do you know I've never seen a dead body before, not even my parents.'

'In your acting days you must have had corpses on stage, been one yourself. Shakespeare's plays are littered with bodies.'

'Yes, but that wasn't for real.'

'Well, think of it as broadening your experience.'

'It's alright for you, you have to deal with this sort of thing all the time. This is a first for me.'

'If you've managed to reach the age of forty plus without encountering death at first hand, you can count yourself lucky.'

167

To take his mind off it, Nick asked him about Kevin Compton.

'Who would want to kill him? Did he have any enemies that you know of?'

'I told you, he was only nineteen. Who would have enemies at that age? He's the last person you'd expect to be involved in any violence. For all his deprived background he had a very sunny, happy nature. Always smiling and very upfront. What you saw was what you got. I can't believe he had any dark secrets.'

'Somebody wanted him out of the way.'

'Couldn't it have been an accident? Where exactly did it happen?'

Nick explained briefly.

'Well, there you are, maybe he dislodged something and it fell on him.'

He was assured that this had not been the case.

'Well, maybe he saw something he shouldn't have and he had to be silenced – or maybe he was mistaken for someone else.'

'These are both possibilities to be looked into. It is why I need to know as much about him and the sort of life he led as I can discover.'

'Oh, my God!' Tony clutched his head. 'Young Ben will have to be told. Kevin more or less took him under his wing. How ever will he react? And Reid? She'll go ballistic!'

'How did Ben come to meet up with Kevin?'

'They'd been in the same home together when they were kids and recognised each other when they met accidently here in town.'

'So, Ben probably knows as much about him as anyone? Or, at least, his childhood years.'

'You'll have to ask him, won't you?' said Tony peevishly. 'I only know – knew – Kevin as an amateur thespian. I know nothing about his friends or background. Maybe he was having girlfriend trouble, though I don't think he had anyone in tow.'

Tony was silenced by their arrival at the mortuary. Although it had been rebuilt several years ago, and the interior was now a modern, gleaming steel-and-white structure, it was still reached by the old Victorian entrance at the back of the hospital. He was sweating as they walked through the tall, arched gateway and along the tiled corridor, and swallowed nervously as they entered the mortuary itself.

Nick spoke briefly to the attendant on duty, who led them over to a table, on which there was a sheeted body. He drew back the cover and Tony gave a convulsive gasp. Face upwards, the damage to the back of the head concealed, the body on the steel table looked untouched. The features were drained of colour but it was possible to see how he had looked in life. A young man in late adolescence, small for his age, with a snub nose, a wide mouth more used to smiling than frowning, and a compact, muscular physique.

Nick felt anger and regret in equal amounts. Who had cut off his life in one frenzied blow and left a waxen effigy in his place? He looked at Tony, who clutched his throat and nodded.

'I didn't hear that.'

'It's Kevin. Kevin Compton,' quavered Tony, his orator's voice singularly absent. Then he was spectacularly sick all over the floor.

Back at the incident room Nick exchanged information with other members of the team. Besides the *West Side Story* rehearsal at the centre the evening before, there had been two other group activities taking place in the building: a meeting of flower arrangers and a yoga class. Everyone at these two gatherings had to be chased up. The flower arrangers would all be women, he reckoned – and probably most of the yoga aficionados also – and were hardly likely to be in the frame, but the injury to Kevin Compton's head was such that a woman could have done it, as the pathologist had confirmed, so it had to be followed up. Somebody might have seen something that could be relevant to their enquiry.

He had obtained the names and addresses of the cast of *West Side Story* from Tony, and these were top of the list of people who had to be interviewed. Amongst the cast list were six pupils from Casterford High, and he decided to deal with them together initially. They would be shocked and upset when they learned of Kevin Compton's death, but if he acted quickly he could break the news to them himself and gauge their reactions. So far the press had not got hold of the story, but that state of affairs would not last for long; soon it would be plastered all over the newspapers and TV screens. He made a phone call to Reid Frobisher and managed to catch her in the staffroom during a free period.

'Reid? Has Tony been in touch?'

'Yes, he's just rung me. It's awful, I can't believe it!'

'Does anyone else at the school know yet?'

'I don't think so.'

'Are all the pupils involved in the musical in the same class?'

'Yes, they are doing English A-level in the sixth form.'

'So, you teach them?'

'Sometimes. Martin Boyd is head of English and in charge of sixth-form studies.'

'Tell him what has happened and ask him

to get them all together in a classroom. I'll come over and speak to them.'

'You surely don't think any of them was involved in Kevin's death?'

'I sincerely hope not, but they could have noticed something that may be important, and they should be able to tell me exactly what happened when the rehearsal broke up last night. I shall need to question you about that as well, Reid. And Ben Latimer.'

'Actually, I tried to ring him just now after Tony phoned, but he's not there. Rachel was with us as well last night, did you know?'

'Yes, she's also on my list of people to be interviewed.'

'Is it ethical for you to give her the third degree?'

'Don't be melodramatic and don't try and cloud the issue. I'll be with you in about twenty minutes, and if by any chance the press turn up first don't let them near my witnesses.'

The sun was low in the sky as he drove over to the school, and even with the visor down it reflected off the road and pavements, dazzling him. It was a glorious autumn day for once, crisp and bright with just a hint of frost in the air. The kind of day when it felt good to be alive, and he thought dismally of Kevin Compton cut down in his prime. In the course of his career he had dealt with many violent deaths and

172

far nastier scenarios than this, but somehow this one was already getting to him, although he had never known Kevin Compton, never seen him alive.

Was it because Rachel and friends were involved, however peripherally? There seemed no obvious motive for the murder. From the little he had gathered so far he didn't think Compton had been involved in any criminal activity. Nor did it seem likely that he had been having it off with someone's wife or girlfriend and been killed by a vengeful husband or partner. Though he of all people knew you couldn't make these sweeping assumptions. Every minute piece of evidence and hearsay must be pursued and followed up and maybe they would discover that he had been into drugs or was part of the Wessex underworld. But his gut reaction told him no. Probably Tony Pomfret was right, and his Baby John had seen something so sinister that he had had to be removed permanently. But what? The community centre was hardly known as a den of iniquity. Innocent pastimes and evening classes took place within its walls, but the drugs angle would have to be checked out. He knew only too well that school kids were a prime target these days with the dealers.

Martin Boyd was waiting for him at reception when he arrived at the school, and introduced himself when the detective had shown his warrant card.

'Miss Frobisher has assembled the relevant pupils in one of the sixth-form study rooms. They haven't been told the dreadful news; they think this meeting is something to do with *West Side Story*. Do they have to be involved in the investigation?'

'They were there when it happened, Mr Boyd. They *are* involved whether you like it or not, and one of them may have been a witness to the actual killing.'

'Yes, of course. I understand that a procedure has to be followed. It's just that it's such a terrible shock.'

'Are you involved in *West Side Story* yourself?'

'Yes, I've been in on it from the start and I've attended rehearsals.'

'But not last night?'

'No.'

'How did these particular pupils come to be involved in the first place? How were they chosen?'

'We were approached by members of the committee of the operatic society. It *is* a musical about teenagers, and they thought it would be a good idea to involve some of the local young people who could add verisimilitude to the proceedings. Many of the operatic society members are getting a little long in the tooth, and this musical requires a youthful image and a deal of physical exertion. We put it to the older pupils and many were eager to volunteer. They were eventually weeded out, leaving those who could sing and dance well enough to perform after coaching. From the school's point of view we encouraged it, as *Romeo and Juliet* is one of the set plays in this year's A-level curriculum – with the proviso that they didn't neglect their studies in the process.'

Martin Boyd took off his glasses and rubbed them absent mindedly on his sleeve before replacing them on his nose. Nick summed him up as being pedantic and strict but probably an excellent teacher. He also appeared very worried and harassed, but that was probably par for the course under the circumstances. It was not normal to have half one's class involved in a murder enquiry; there would be no precedent for it in the school's rules.

'They are going to be very upset by this, very disturbed.'

'I appreciate that. We can provide counselling if you wish.'

'No, we are equipped to deal with that. Well, we'd better get it over with, Inspector.'

Reid Frobisher was presiding over the room of six fidgeting boys and girls. They had copies of *Romeo and Juliet* and *West Side Story* libretti in front of them, Nick noticed, and they looked bored and uneasy. Reid raised her eyebrows at him when they walked in, then got to her feet and joined them.

'I've told them there was an incident yesterday evening at the community centre involving the cast of *West Side Story*, and that the police want to talk to them. Was that alright? They haven't any idea what I was talking about.'

Nick nodded and Martin Boyd took over.

'This is Detective Inspector Holroyd from Casterford CID. He has something to tell you.'

Nick explained briefly what had happened and there was a stunned silence. They all looked totally shocked, and then a couple of the girls started to cry.

'I know this is a great shock to you but we need to speak to you individually about what you remember of events yesterday evening. You are all over seventeen, so you are not required by law to have a parent or guardian present, but if you so wish or want a teacher to sit in on it, it can be arranged.'

There was an immediate unanimous denial of the offer, which said much for the youth of today, thought Nick.

'Has anyone any questions?'

There was a pause and then one of the girls piped up.

'Does this mean that *West Side Story* will

be cancelled?'

'A decision on that will be made later. In the meantime all rehearsals are suspended.'

Understanding and disappointment flickered across the faces staring up at him. They were horrified by what had happened but Kevin Compton had not been one of them. Not a fellow pupil who they met every day and had known for years. He had just been another member of the cast who they had met a couple of times a week over the last few months. Unless one of them *was* involved in his death, in which case he or she was an excellent actor. He made arrangements for the interviews. Martin Boyd offered a study for the purpose and Nick made a phone call and arranged for two members of his team to take over. Then he drew Reid to one side.

'I need to see Ben Latimer. Do you have any idea where I can find him?'

'No. I honestly don't know, Nick. He came down here to find me but what he does with his time is a mystery to me. I haven't liked to ask too many questions or be too pushy – he just backs off if he thinks I'm being nosey. He'll be very upset when he learns about Kevin – having known each other from way back.'

'Yes, I want to know just how and where they became acquainted. We'll need to pick him up. In the meantime, don't try and contact him, leave it to the police. And that refers to Rachel as well.'

'You mean you haven't told her yet?'

'Reid, I'm conducting a murder enquiry. Personal issues don't enter into it; there is a protocol to follow. Rachel will be told, of course. I shall put her in the picture. As I said, I need official signed statements from all of you concerning your movements yesterday evening, but we'll bend the rules and do it informally first. I want to get you and Tony and Rachel together and we'll go over the events as you remember them.'

'You want us down at the police station?'

'No, I said this was informal. A get-together this evening.'

'Then you had better come round to our place. What time?'

'Six o'clock?'

'Shall I tell Rachel or will you?'

'I will – and don't let Tony talk to the press. If I hear he's giving interviews I'll arrest him for obstructing the police in the course of their duties.'

'My, Nick! I've never seen you in your official role before. I'm impressed. Did you know that Gordon Barnes was at the rehearsal too, just for the first part of the evening?'

'Then get him along too. By the way, I think Tony may need a little TLC. He identified the body for me.'

Before he went over to Ranworth House where Kevin Compton had lived, Nick checked the list that Tony had given him to see if any other members of the cast also lived there. He discovered that a young woman called Lisa Catling had a room there. It was quite likely that no one would be around at this time of day, but hopefully there might be a porter on duty. He summoned Tim Court on his mobile and arranged to meet him outside Ranworth House, and then drove over to Caister Road.

They were in luck. Ranworth House did have a resident porter, and he concerned himself about the young inmates under his roof way above the call of duty. Ted Foreman was a man in his early sixties, a retired soldier who took his duties at Ranworth House seriously. He was tall and wiry, upright in carriage, with startling blue eyes and a thick West Country accent.

Nick and his sergeant showed their ID cards and introduced themselves. Nick explained about the death of Kevin Compton and the porter looked thunderstruck.

'You're having me on! He can't be dead!'

'I'm afraid so, Mr Foreman.'

He looked as if he was going to collapse and Court hurriedly sat him down on a chair in his office, just inside the main door.

'He's— He was so full of life. You say he's

been *murdered*?'

'We are treating his death as suspicious. Has he lived here long?'

'Going on for three years.'

'We understand he was an orphan and had no relatives – unless you know something to the contrary?'

'That's right, but he had lots of friends, got on with everybody. I wondered why he didn't come home last night.'

'Do you check on all your residents?' asked Court in surprise.

'I keep an eye on them. They're all young, some of them living away from home for the first time, and I like to think I'm acting in loco parentis.' He said this phrase slowly and grandly as if he had recently learned it from a dictionary and had been waiting for an opportunity to use it. A father figure or an interfering old man, depending on your point of view, thought Nick. A good witness who noticed things, but a man who could well be thought of as nosey and therefore deliberately not confided in. It would be interesting to discover what the other residents thought of him.

'Do you live on the premises?'

'Yes, it's my flat next door to here.'

'We're trying to find out about his background and recent movements. When did you last see him?'

'It would have been about half-past six

yesterday evening. He was going off to a rehearsal with Lisa Catling. Oh my God! If I'd known that was going to be the last time I saw him!'

'Lisa Catling is one of the people we want to speak to. Do you know where she works?'

'Down at the tourist office in App Street. You don't think that she had anything to do with it?' He was outraged.

'As you said, they were at rehearsal together yesterday evening. He was killed shortly after the rehearsal ended. We are anxious to trace his last movements and build up a picture of what happened, so we need to speak to everyone who was there. Nobody is a suspect at the moment, we are just gathering information.'

'Who would want to kill Kevin? It doesn't make sense.' Ted Foreman spoke as much to himself as to them and shook his head slowly.

'We also want to speak to another of the tenants here. A temporary resident – Ben Latimer. Do you know where he's likely to be at this time of day?'

'Well there, that's another funny thing. He didn't come home last night either.'

Eight

Rachel leaned against the washbasin feeling sick and distressed. A brief phone call from Nick a short while ago had left her reeling. She had seen Kevin Compton for the first time yesterday evening, but that didn't make his death any the less shocking. Supposing it had been Ben? Whatever would Reid do? It would completely shatter her.

She splashed some cold water over her face, patted it dry with a paper towel and stared into the mirror over the washbasin. Worried brown eyes stared back at her out of a white face and she sighed and ran her fingers through her curls and they sprang back like a dark halo round her head. But according to Nick, Ben was also missing. Supposing he had been killed, too, and his body not yet found? Or did it mean ... could it be possible that *he* had killed Kevin? Dear God, pray not, she whispered out loud, and then realised that someone else had come into the cloakroom.

'Are you talking to me?' It was Maggie Pilgrim, one of the departmental secretaries, who yanked up her skirt and surveyed in dismay the wide ladder running up the back of her tights.

'No, I was thinking out loud.'

'We ought to get danger money or at least a clothes allowance. These office chairs are *lethal*. You'd think in this day and age we'd have metal or plastic jobs with real upholstery, not rough wooden affairs that came out of the ark.'

She kicked off her shoes and wriggled out of the damaged tights, then glanced at Rachel.

'I say, are you alright? You look awful!'

'I've just had some very upsetting news.'

'Not a family bereavement, I hope?'

'No, an ... an accident to someone I knew.'

'A bad accident? Is this person *dead*?'

'Yes,' admitted Rachel. 'It's difficult to take it in.'

'Not another traffic fatality! They reckon the number of people killed on the roads in this area already tops last year's figures!'

Rachel did not disabuse her and Maggie continued, 'You're in shock. Why don't you take the rest of the day off and go home. I'll explain what has happened.'

'With my workload that's just wishful thinking. I'll be OK.'

'Are you sure you don't want to see a doctor or a nurse? I mean, we *are* in a hospital. I ought to be able to summon some sort of medical help.'

'No, I'm fine. Don't worry about me.'

'If you're sure?' Maggie shrugged dubiously and went into a cubicle. Rachel pulled herself together and went back to her office.

For the rest of that morning she was on automatic pilot. She dealt with patients, applied treatments and sorted out appointments but none of it registered. All she could think about was Kevin Compton's murder. And she had a contribution to make in helping to solve the crime. Nick wanted her to meet up with him and the others this evening to discuss the events of yesterday evening. She had to make an official statement and she couldn't recall what had happened. She remembered watching the rehearsal in progress and getting so engrossed in it that she had completely forgotten about prompting, the prompt copy lying unused in her lap. She even remembered being impressed by Kevin's performance and surprised by the professional way in which Tony had managed his cast.

She had spent some time chatting to Ben Latimer, but when exactly? And what had happened at the end of the rehearsal? She had refused Tony's offer to accompany them to the pub and returned home, but she couldn't really remember what time that had been – about ten thirty? And had Tony and Reid gone on to the pub immediately?

184

She realised with growing horror that the murder must have happened just after she had left the rehearsal hall. She could have passed within yards of the event, even witnessed it, but she remembered nothing of her departure. Certainly nothing untoward had happened or she would have remarked it. She was going to be a lousy witness; Nick wouldn't be very pleased.

'We need to see the rooms of Compton and Latimer,' said Nick to Ted Foreman. 'Presumably you have a pass key?'

'Yes.'

'Why are you so sure that neither of them came back last night?' asked Tim Court. 'You can't sit up all night listening out for them, and young people that age stay out all hours of the night. They're not under curfew.'

'Because I've been up and checked. First thing this morning, when neither of them was around for breakfast. The communal kitchen is through there and it's bedlam early in the morning. Folks wandering in and out, all trying to use the cooker and toasters at the same time and arguing about who's pinched what out of the fridge. I sort of hover around to keep an eye on them, have a cup of coffee, spin it out – and definitely neither Kevin nor Ben showed this morning. Well, Kevin couldn't have done, could he? Poor little sod.'

'Ben Latimer could have gone out early this morning before you were about.'

'No way. Besides, I've just told you – I've looked in his room. I'm sure his bed wasn't slept in last night. I can always tell, and now that I come to think of it Ben's room looked very bare. His belongings had gone – not but what they all travel light these days. He only had a grip and a rucksack, and I'm sure they weren't there.'

'Well, we can soon find out. Which rooms were theirs?'

'I'll show you. Come up with me.'

'I think you'd better stay down here, Mr Foreman, and look after things. Just tell us where to go.'

'Kevin had a room on the first floor – number 5. It's quite a large bedsit actually – got its own washbasin and loo and a gas ring. Not that he ever did much cooking up there. Very gregarious was Kevin, liked to come down and muck in with the others. Oh, Christ! I can't believe he's gone for ever!'

'And Ben Latimer?' prompted Nick.

'Number 11 on the second floor. He shouldn't really be there at all. They're not allowed to sub-let, not that I reckon he's paid any money for it. Still, it's only a temporary arrangement and it keeps the room aired whilst the real tenant is away, so I've

186

turned a blind eye.'

He handed the keys to Nick and the two policemen went upstairs, leaving Foreman looking wistfully after them.

They examined Kevin's room first. It was neat and ordered, not your usual teenager's pad. Still, if he had spent most of his childhood years in institutions he would have been used to having little personal space and having to keep his belongings tidy and shipshape, thought Nick, looking around the bedsit. The bed was made and on the wall above it was a poster of a footballer in a Manchester United strip, the sole concession to his personal tastes. Two other pictures were on the opposite wall, dull seascapes, looking as if they had hung there since the house had been built. There was a built-in wardrobe. Court pulled open the door and the two policemen examined the contents.

'What you would expect – jeans, casual shirts, sweatshirts – nothing formal.'

There was a pair of Doc Marten type boots on the floor of the wardrobe and two pairs of trainers. The drawers in the chest of drawers contained the usual underwear – socks, pants, tee shirts and a couple of belts – but tucked under a pair of old pyjama trousers in a corner they found a bank book, some pay slips and the receipt for a stereo system. There was no sign of any more

187

private or personal papers.

'Christ! They *do* travel light, don't they?' said Court. 'When I think of my bulging filing cabinet and all the bits and pieces stacked around the house, not to speak of what's up in the loft!'

There was a bar of soap on the washbasin and a wrung-out, dry flannel neatly lapped over the side. Two towels, slightly grubby but folded precisely, hung over the back of the nearby chair and a packet of disposable razors, a bottle of cheap aftershave and a box of tissues were lined up on the window sill. Nick turned his attention to the bedside cabinet, which held a table lamp, a tube of cough sweets and a current copy of *Shoot*. The cupboard underneath was stacked with old football programmes and magazines.

'No sign of him being a user.'

'No, but we'd better check the usual places,' said Nick, going into the toilet and lifting the lid of the cistern.

A short while later they were satisfied they had discovered all they could from Kevin's bedsit and moved up the stairs to Ben Latimer's room. It was much smaller than Kevin's, and contained just a bed, a couple of chairs, a cupboard and a small chest of drawers. It was empty of personal belongings. The bed was made and covered by a green candlewick bedspread of the kind that had been fashionable in the 1960s, and the whole room had a sterile feeling, as if it had not been occupied for some time.

'He's done a runner,' said Court, stating the obvious.

'At least we're not looking for another corpse. He went of his own volition.'

'Unless his killer removed his things to make us think just that.'

'And how would they have got past old Hawkeyes down below without being seen? Besides, if they have both been killed, why remove all trace of Ben but leave Compton's belongings here and his body where it would be easily discovered? It doesn't make sense.'

'He could have decided to move on and know nothing about Compton's death.'

'No, I don't buy that. It's too much of a coincidence. The two things must be connected, and it's beginning to look bad for Ben Latimer.'

And I've got to cope with Reid Frobisher this evening, thought Nick gloomily. He really ought to ask to be taken off this case because of his connections with so many of the prospective witnesses, but he knew it was a no-no. His superiors would think he was in an excellent position to milk the situation to their benefit. He sighed.

'Come on, there's nothing more we can do here. We'll let forensics go over both rooms, but I don't think they'll find anything useful.'

189

Downstairs once more, he told Ted Foreman that both rooms would be sealed and
must not be leased out again for the time
being.

'What about Kevin's belongings?'

'They'll have to keep there until we can
trace any relatives. There's nothing of value
and someone of his age is not likely to have
made a will.'

Before they left he got the names of all the
other occupants of Ranworth House and
their places of work or where they were
likely to be at that time of day, and then he
and his DC started the task of tracking them
down.

Nick was late getting to the mortuary and
Dick Wickham had already finished the
autopsy on Kevin Compton.

'I expected at least you and a couple of
your minions to attend, if only to admire my
handicraft,' said the pathologist, who was
scrubbing up when Nick arrived.

'I got held up – trying to find the bastard
who did it.'

'Got any leads yet?'

'A few. What can you tell me?'

'It's all there on tape and a full report will
be sent to you.'

'Which I shall peruse intently. Just put me
in the picture, Doc.'

Wickham finished wiping his arms and

hands and waved Nick into his office.

'Sit down and I'll go over it. He was killed by a single blow to the back of the head. There is extensive bruising in the scalp over the back of the head and, just to the midline above the occipital protruberance, there is a gaping vertical laceration with crushing of the soft tissues on its left side. Beneath this there is a comminuted fracture of the skull some 6cm in diameter, radiating from—'

'In other words,' interrupted Nick, 'he was hit with a blunt instrument. Don't blind me with science, Doc.'

'Yes, he was struck by something very heavy that was 6cm wide, which is consistent with it being a piece of girder.'

'Any other injuries on the body?'

'No, not a mark – and the other internal organs appear healthy. The stomach contained some partly-digested food.'

'No sign of being a user?'

'You didn't tell me to look for that. But no, he certainly wasn't into the hard stuff. No puncture marks on the body and he was in far too good a condition to have been a druggie.'

'But he could have been a pusher,' said Nick gloomily.

'You're investigating that angle?'

'It's as good as any. Someone had a reason to kill him. If we can find a motive we're halfway there.'

'I wouldn't like your job.'

'That sentiment is reciprocated with interest.'

'When is the inquest?'

'Probably the beginning of next week. I'll keep you informed and make sure you get good warning of the date and time.'

Nick leaned back in his chair and looked pointedly at the kettle and coffee jar that stood on the table in the corner. Wickham intercepted his gaze.

'Do you want a coffee?'

'I thought you'd never ask.'

'Most of your colleagues wouldn't dream of imbibing inside these hallowed quarters for fear they might get contaminated.'

The pathologist got up and filled the kettle, switched it on and spooned coffee into two mugs he took out of a cupboard.

'I'd have thought a man in your position would be waited on. You know, you'd snap into your intercom, "Miss So-and so, two coffees immediately," and it would come in china cups and saucers on a tray via a dishy attendant. You're spoiling my image of you.'

'The stuff from the machine is undrinkable. I prefer to make my own. Milk? Sugar?'

'Just a little milk, no sugar.'

Nick took the mug that was handed to him and took a cautious sip of the hot liquid.

'Thanks. So there is nothing else you can tell me about our friend in there?'

'No. A fit and healthy young man who should have lived to a ripe old age. A waste of life.'

'Yes. When you get a child or young person killed in a road accident it's a terrible thing, but at least it *is* an accident.'

Nick finished his coffee and put down the mug.

'That's saved my life. I must be off now and get on with my investigation. Thanks, Doc.'

'Just don't send me any more like this one. It gets to me, too, you know.'

'I hope I don't have to,' said Nick, thinking of Ben Latimer.

Later that day, Nick held a briefing with his team to correlate the evidence collected so far. It had been discovered that both the flower-arranging and yoga classes had finished at nine o'clock and all the participants had left the building well before the end of the *West Side Story* rehearsal.

'Most of them have already been interviewed, though we've still got to catch up with a few of them, and nobody noticed anything suspicious as they left,' said Tim Court. 'No dubious characters hanging around. Quite a lot of cars parked in the car park, as you'd expect, and nobody knows if there was an unknown or unaccounted for one amongst them.'

'The trouble is, the centre is completely insecure whilst it's in use,' said Nick. 'There are people going in and out all the time. Anyone seeing someone in the vicinity that they didn't know would think it was a member of one of the other groups using the facilities. However, I think we can safely assume that the only people on the premises last night, immediately prior to the murder, were people involved with *West Side Story*.'

He pointed to a sheet of paper pinned on the wall depicting the layout of the community centre. 'When the rehearsal ended at ten thirty the large hall was the only part of the building occupied, apart from the coffee bar upstairs, where a Meryl Brown, the young woman who manages the refreshments, was on duty. The younger people in the cast – which includes the sixth-formers – gathered upstairs in the coffee bar whilst the other members of the operatic society went off home, most of them collecting cars from the car park. As with the other evening-class members, nobody noticed anything untoward. That left Tony Pomfret, the producer, the two people acting as prompts and Ben Latimer in the hall. They had a short discussion and Latimer went off. That was the last time he was seen. We don't know where he went or what happened to him, but according to one witness he was expected to return to Ranworth House in the company of

Kevin Compton – isn't that so, Thomson?'

'Yes, sir,' said DC Thomson. 'The group of people in the coffee bar decided to go on to one of their houses but Compton declined to join them saying he had to meet up with Ben Latimer.'

'He actually said that he had an arranged meeting with Latimer?'

'No.' Thomson consulted his notes. 'As they drifted off downstairs, Lisa Catling asked Compton if he was going with them and he said, as far as she can remember, that he wouldn't, as he had to find Ben, who would be wondering what had happened to him.'

'Who is Lisa Catling?'

'She's the girl who plays the part of Anybody's in the show.'

A snicker ran through the room.

'And is she anybody's?' asked some joker.

'Cut it out, Coates.'

'She's probably under age anyway,' piped up someone else.

'Twenty-one if she's a day,' said Thomson, grinning. 'But she looks much younger, which is why she got the part.'

'Do you think we could get back to the nitty-gritty?' said Nick sarcastically. 'So, Compton went off to find Ben Latimer. Did they meet, or had Latimer already left by then?'

'We're not sure, sir. Nobody saw them

together after the rehearsal and, as far as we know, Lisa Catling was the last person to speak to Compton.'

Perhaps after my meeting this evening I'll be able to clarify that, thought Nick. Tony had already told him about Ben going off after he had failed to be persuaded to take a part in the show. Had he said where he was going, and had any of the three actually witnessed him leaving the building?

'We have to find Ben Latimer. Has anybody had any joy in tracing his movements after he left the hall?'

There was a conspicuous silence and Nick held up his hand.

'Right, our top priority is tracking down Latimer. His absence may have an entirely innocent interpretation, but we need to find him and talk with him. In the meantime, let's concentrate on Compton. What sort of picture of him have you built up after your interviews with the people who knew him?'

'He seems to have been a very popular guy. Nobody had a bad word to say about him.'

'Yes, he was well liked.'

'He enjoyed his work and got on well with his fellow workmates.'

'Very keen on this acting lark. Talked about it a lot.'

There were more comments along this line, and Nick listened shrewdly and then leant forward and addressed them.

'So, where does this leave us?'

'It's beginning to look as if he wasn't killed for who he was—' began someone tentatively.

'Yes?'

'—but because of something he witnessed. He got in someone's way and had to be wasted.'

'Quite. I want another fingertip search of the area where he was found, and we must widen the net of the house-to-house to include all the households in that part of town, not just those in the immediate vicinity.'

'What are we looking for?'

'Anything out of the ordinary that someone may have noticed. Strange vehicles parked where they had no business to be, any whispers of a heist being planned. God, man, use your initiative!'

'He could have been mistaken for someone else. These teenagers all dress alike. It's like a uniform – jeans, fleeces, trainers...'

'Point taken,' said Nick drily, looking at the speaker, who was dressed in the same gear he had just been describing and was not long out of his teens himself. 'Now, off you go and bring me back some results.'

They trooped off while Nick gathered together his papers and went to report to Tom Powell.

* * *

197

Nick called in briefly at his flat to have a shower and a change of clothing before going on to Reid Frobisher's place. He found the light flashing on his answerphone. The caller had been Dave Bloomfield, the private investigator he had put on to tracing Maureen. He rang him back immediately.

'I've had no luck in picking up the trail of your ex-wife since she left Geddington. Do you want me to continue?'

'I want to know what has happened to her.'

'Surely with the information I've supplied so far your magistrate is not going to refuse to grant your decree absolute? It's a ludicrous hold-up after all these years.'

'You're probably right, but I need to know about this son she had. You do see?'

'It will cost you.'

'I know, but keep digging away. They must be *somewhere*.'

'Do you know of any relatives in any other part of the country she could have gone to?'

'There was an aunt and some cousins in Scotland,' said Nick, dredging his memory. 'Dunfermline, I think, but as far as I know she never had much contact with them.'

'It's a long shot but worth a try. I'll be sending in my monthly account.'

'It will be honoured, don't worry. It's nice to know I'm keeping someone off the bread-line.'

After he had rung off, Nick made himself

a mug of tea and a cheese-and-pickle sandwich and downed them hastily before stripping off and getting under the shower. As he sluiced hot water over his head and shoulders he wondered what the outcome of the evening would be. Would it throw up information to help his enquiry? And how was Reid going to react when he told her that Ben Latimer was number one suspect?

He towelled himself dry, dressed, and tucked his pager and mobile phone into his pocket before going off to pick up Rachel.

'What am I going to do? Two months from the opening night and I'm without my Baby John!' Tony Pomfret stalked dramatically back and forth across the sitting-room floor.

'You really are a total shit, Tony,' said Reid angrily. 'That poor boy has been *murdered* and all you can think about is your bloody show!'

'You're right. I don't mean to sound callous, and you don't have to remind me of his brutal death – Christ! I had to identify him! But there are a lot of things at issue here. Cancelling the show won't bring him back, and think of how it's going to affect the rest of the cast.'

'I can't imagine any of them will want to continue under the circumstances.'

'Perhaps not, but perhaps it would be for the best.'

'The show must go on, you mean?'

'No, I mean it might be more therapeutic for everyone involved, especially the youngsters. They're going to be knocked up over this, but if we try and salvage the show it will keep them occupied and stop them brooding.'

'Do you imagine the police will allow it?'

'I don't see what it's got to do with the fucking police!'

'Try telling that to Nick.'

'Where is he, anyway? I thought he'd be slavering over the chance to grill us.'

'I think they're coming now. I heard a car draw up a minute ago.' Gordon Barnes spoke from his seat near the bay window, where he had been trying to ignore the fractious exchange between Tony and Reid.

'About time. Doesn't he realise that time is just as precious to us lesser mortals as it is to him?'

'For God's sake behave yourself, Tony. Nick is conducting a murder enquiry, he doesn't need you on an ego trip obstructing the case.'

'Me? Egotistical? I've—'

'Oh, shut up, Tony!' said Gordon Barnes. 'Hadn't you better answer the door?'

Tony looked as surprised by this remark from his business partner as if the worm had reared up and bitten the bird. Reid left them to it and went out to welcome the newcomers. She took their coats and ushered them into the room and then pounced.

'Nick, have you seen Ben? He's not answering the phone.'

'I asked you not to try and contact him.'

'I thought you meant until you'd had a chance to tell him about Kevin Compton. You *have* told him, haven't you?'

'Chance would be a fine thing. Ben Latimer has done a runner.'

'What! What do you mean?'

'He's disappeared. Vanished off the face of the earth.'

'But he can't have! Perhaps he went off for the day for a ... a nature hike.'

'With all his belongings? The room at Ranworth House where he was staying is empty. He's upped and left, Reid, and there is a general police alert out for him.'

'But why should he go without telling me? Why are you so anxious to find him?'

'Don't be obtuse, Reid,' said Tony, putting his arm round her. 'Our boys in blue think he did it, isn't that right, Nick?'

'There may be a quite innocent reason for his disappearance, but unless we can find him and he can talk himself out of it, he has to figure high on our list of suspects.'

'I don't believe this!' Reid shook off Tony's arm and turned to Rachel. *'You've* met Ben. You know he couldn't possibly have done it. Tell him!'

'Reid, I—' began Rachel unhappily, and Nick interrupted.

'Getting all emotional is not going to help matters, Reid. Let's get a few facts sorted out. You said Kevin and Ben had known each other before they met down here. How did it come about?'

'They were in the same home together when they were children. It was just coincidence they bumped into each other here in Casterford and recognised each other. What possible reason could Ben have for wishing harm to Kevin?'

'That remains to be seen, but what reason did Ben give you for coming here?'

'To find *me*. You *know* that.'

'That is what he told you. It could have been a trick.'

'I don't understand?'

'What proof have you got that the person who turned up here *is* Ben Latimer? He arrives on your doorstep, tells you he's your long lost son, and you welcome him with open arms. Did you check his identity?'

'Of course not. I *knew* it was him the minute I set eyes on him. We recognised each other – a mother *knows* these things!'

'You wanted to believe it. Con artists can be very persuasive.'

'I'm sure Ben was genuine,' put in Rachel, who had been listening to the exchange in growing dismay. 'I spoke with him and got to know him and I'm a good judge of character.'

'Beleaguered on all sides,' said Tony. 'I'm not sure you're doing this right, Nick. Shouldn't we be down at the station being grilled in a cell with our solicitors present and the whole caboodle on tape?'

'That can be arranged if that's how you want to play it,' said Nick wearily.

'Only joking, old chap.'

'You're not suspects, for God's sake. I'm just trying to piece together a picture of what happened last night when the rehearsal ended and I thought we could do it in a civilised manner.'

'What exactly do you want to know?'

'For starters, *your* movements.'

'I don't really know why I'm involved,' said Gordon plaintively. 'I left halfway through the evening before most of the men arrived.'

'Right, let's deal with you first. What time did you leave the centre?'

'About eight thirty?' Gordon looked to the others for confirmation. 'Tony had run through the scene I'm involved in with just the girls and as I had another meeting I left before the full-cast rehearsal started.'

'You went at eight thirty? Did you see anyone else in the vicinity of the building as you left?'

'Yes, I met all the men arriving. They were swarming into the place, I nearly got knocked over.'

'You came by car?'

'Yes, I'd left it in the car park. There were a lot more vehicles parked there but, by the time I'd opened the door, got inside and started the engine, all the newcomers had gone inside.'

'And presumably you're not familiar enough with the cast to know if there were any strange faces amongst them?'

'No.'

Nick turned his attention to Tony.

'Let's have your version.'

'What Gordon said about his movements is correct. He went off halfway through the evening and after a coffee break we resumed with a full chorus plus the principals. At the finish I went over to the side of the hall, where Reid and Rachel were sitting with Ben. We chatted for a short while and I tried to persuade Ben to take part in the show. He refused but agreed to help backstage. I then said we were going on to the Cock and Pie and did he want to join us, but he said he was meeting up with Kevin. Isn't that right?' he demanded of Reid and Rachel.

'He got up to go and while he was putting on his jacket I asked him about coming round for a meal later in the week,' said Reid. 'He wouldn't give me an answer there and then, said he would ring me.'

'He seemed to have suddenly had enough

of the rehearsal and us,' said Rachel, thinking back. 'He couldn't wait to get away.'

'But you don't know where he went after he left you in the hall?'

'Presumably he joined Kevin.'

'Kevin was last seen by Lisa Catling, and he told her he was going to find Ben Latimer. We have no witnesses to them actually meeting up. Nobody saw either of them after that.'

'You surely don't really think Ben attacked Kevin?' asked Reid.

'I've got to consider it a strong possibility, especially if the person you thought was Ben wasn't.'

'I'm sure Ben is my son and it can be easily proved. If he wasn't Ben, how would he have known his supposed name and how would he have found out about my attempt to find him? He must have been registered on the Adoption Contact Register, so he *must* be bona fide!'

'Explain how it works,' said Nick, and Reid told him.

'Well, it should be easy enough to check.'

'Isn't it confidential?' asked Rachel. 'Surely they can't give out sensitive information like that to all and sundry?'

'I'm not all and sundry, I'm the *police*. We'll get a magistrate's warrant if necessary.'

'Have you considered that Ben – whoever he is – might actually have witnessed Kevin's

205

murder and been so scared and upset that he scarpered?' asked Tony.

'Yes, Tony, we've got there too.'

'If that happened he may have gone back to his foster parents,' said Reid. 'He was close to them,' she added wistfully. 'Very fond of them and talked about them quite a lot.'

'Do you know their name and address?'

'No.'

'Well, we should be able to find that out also if he is the real McCoy.'

'So what happens now?' asked Tony.

'The press are on to it, so my superintendent is holding a press conference tomorrow morning and issuing a statement appealing for Ben Latimer, or anyone knowing his whereabouts, to come forward. I don't suppose you have a photo of him, Reid?'

'No, we never got as far as that,' she said sadly.

'We were rung up several times by the gentlemen of the fourth estate,' said Tony, indicating himself and Gordon, 'but I told them we had nothing to say.'

'Good for you, Tony,' said Nick, hardly able to believe his ears.

'They were hanging around outside the shop too when I left,' said Gordon, 'but I used the back entrance and gave them the slip.'

'Well, if nobody has anything to add to

206

what you've told me, I'll be off.'

'Aren't you going to stay and have a drink first?' asked Reid. 'You said this was *unofficial* business, so surely you can drink?'

'Love to, Reid, but I've got work to do. My evening is only just beginning.'

'I'll come with you, Nick,' said Rachel, hurriedly getting up, 'if you can drop me off on your way back.'

'Are you getting paid as an official grass, Rachel,' asked Tony, 'or are you the spy in the enemy camp?'

Nine

The press conference went ahead the next morning at twelve o'clock. Before it took place Nick had managed to contact the General Register Office in Birkdale about Ben Latimer. At first they had refused to divulge any information, but when assured that it was vital to a high-ranking police enquiry and would be pursued through the courts if necessary, they cooperated. The facts they supplied confirmed what Reid had told him. Ben Latimer had applied to go on the Adoption Contact Register, where a link-up had been made with his real mother, Reid Frobisher.

He had also found out the names and address of the foster parents Ben had been living with in York during recent years. Some liaison work with the York police had resulted in a visit to these people, a Clive and Laura Pendleton, who knew that their foster son was trying to make contact with his real mother, but hadn't realised that he had actually achieved this. They thought he was touring Cornwall, visiting nature reserves. They had produced a recent photograph of him, which was faxed through to the Wessex constabulary. Armed with this, Nick had made a quick visit to Reid Frobisher, who had agreed that the photo was that of the young man who had turned up proclaiming he was her son.

The results so far gathered from the ongoing house-to-house enquiry added nothing to the information Nick had already gathered the previous evening. No one had seen either Kevin Compton or Ben together or apart after they had left the rehearsal hall. Equally there had been no success in tracing Ben. No one had seen anyone answering his description leaving by train or bus. There was the possibility that he could have hitched a lift out of town and, when his photo appeared on television and in the papers, Nick hoped it might jog someone's memory.

The press conference generated the usual amount of phone calls from the public, and the staff manning the phones were kept busy. All calls had to be checked out, but a certain percentage of them were sure to be time-wasters or hoaxes, and most of the rest were unlikely to provide any new information or leads. Certainly nothing of any significance had emerged when Nick went to report to Tom Powell.

The superintendent was pleased at his handling of the press conference. He had got his message across and managed to side-track most of the awkward questions fired at him. A pity there had been no grieving parents to add an emotional appeal for help in tracing Kevin's attackers, but at least Joe Public knew that the police had someone in the frame and were pursuing a positive line of enquiry.

He was sitting at his desk with a satisfied smile on his face when Nick entered his office. Whilst Nick disliked intensely conducting or appearing in any press briefing himself, and was pleased that the superintendent usually took it upon himself to supervise such occasions, he was also aware that Powell was not averse to angling the story so that he appeared in a better light.

'No sightings of Ben Latimer?' asked Powell when Nick had brought him up to date with the investigation.

'No, but it is early days. The release of his photo may produce results.'

'Are you convinced he's our man?'

'No, sir, not at all – but I am sure he is in some way connected with the attack.'

'Don't talk in riddles, Holroyd. Are you implying this was a gangland thing and Latimer was one of many involved?'

'No, I think there are three possibilities. Either he did it, or he witnessed it and ran away in panic, or he too was a victim and we haven't yet found his body.'

Powell drummed his fingers on his desk and frowned.

'The whole area has been thoroughly searched, hasn't it?'

'Yes, but if he doesn't turn up alive in the next twenty-four hours I think it must be done again with more manpower involved.'

'Think of the cost. The house-to-house is costing a fortune in terms of overtime and extra men drafted in.'

'This *is* a murder enquiry.'

'Quite. But you haven't an atom of proof that Ben Latimer's disappearance is anything to do with Compton's death. His murder could be completely unrelated to Latimer.'

'We're looking at all possibilities, including the drugs scene, but I think we also have to consider that his murder may be connected with something that happened in his past, and I am trying to discover how the two of them knew each other and exactly when.'

'And?'

'At some point in their childhood they were in the same home together. That is all we know so far.'

'Social services should be able to come up with something from their records. Do we know where this home is?'

'Somewhere in Yorkshire.'

Nick paused and wondered how far to take the superintendent into his confidence as to the way his thoughts were running. He decided to stick his neck out.

'Mervyn Dooley was operating in Yorkshire.'

'What exactly are you getting at, Inspector?'

'Mervyn Dooley has been in the slammer twice for crimes committed in the Yorkshire area. Some people think there should have been a third conviction.'

'Ah, I'm with you now. The home that was closed down in the early '90s through some malpractice. It turned out later that there was a strong possibility that many of the children had been sexually abused, but by then no one could be found who would testify.'

'We know that Dooley had been employed there. Suppose it was the same home where Latimer and Compton stayed and they had suffered at his hands. They had hopefully put it behind them, then suddenly they are confronted by a face from the past. How would they react? Or, more to the point, how would Dooley react?'

'He would know they could finger him; their evidence could send him down for a long time.'

'So he decides to remove them from the scene. He seizes an opportunity and strikes down Compton. But what has he done with Ben Latimer?'

'And where is Mervyn Dooley? A good hypothesis, but that is all it is. Dooley will be miles from here by now, probably fled to the Continent if he has any sense.'

'I don't think so. We know he was hiding out at Grange Farm near Melbury Bubb; we've matched up his fingerprints. He took a bike from there when he scarpered and that bike has turned up only about half a mile from the community centre in Pankhurst Road.'

'This has been verified?'

'Yes. It was found lying in a ditch in a little copse at the end of Fermain Road. A sharp-eyed uniformed constable saw it and recognised it from the description circulating. It is an old-fashioned machine with a lot of new paintwork. Roy Sharpely, the owner, has identified it and, in any case, there are fingerprints plastered all over it. Dooley doesn't seem concerned about covering his tracks.'

'So, instead of looking for one man, we're looking for two,' said Tom Powell grimly, screwing the cap on his pen and rising to his feet.

'As far as the police are concerned the show can go on. They have no objections to us continuing, not that I think it's their deci-

213

sion to make.' Tony Pomfret addressed the small group of people gathered in Martin Boyd's study to discuss the future of *West Side Story*. Crammed into the small room were Reid, Gordon Barnes, Emma Spendlove, Hugh Smethers – the chairman of the operatic society – and Martin himself.

'So, what do you all think?' continued Tony, who had already made up his mind but wished to appear democratic.

'The heart will have gone out of it,' said Hugh Smethers, 'and I think my members would probably say it would be in very bad taste to continue.'

'Bad taste?' exclaimed Emma passionately. 'A young man has been brutally murdered, for God's sake! Surely that goes beyond the bounds of good or bad taste!'

'You think the show should be cancelled, do you, Emma?'

'No. I think the circumstances are so horrific that we need to get them all working together again as a sort of catharsis.'

'I'm inclined to agree,' said Martin, polishing his glasses vigorously. 'But is it safe? I mean, there's a homicidal maniac out there who could strike again. I have to think of the safety of my pupils and my duty to their parents.'

'I'm sure the police would not agree to us carrying on if they thought there was any danger. I believe they already have someone in the frame and it's just a case of marshalling the evidence.'

'How do you know that, Tony?' asked Hugh. 'You sound as if you have an inside line into the police investigation.'

'I have,' said Tony, tapping his nose. 'Detective Inspector Holroyd, in charge of the case, is a personal friend of ours.'

'Nick would never discuss the case with you,' Reid was stung to reply, thinking that Tony was referring to Ben as the suspect. 'This is all surmise on your part.'

'We have to consider what Kevin would have wanted,' said Tony, ignoring her. 'I'm sure he would want the show to go on.'

'How can you possibly know that?'

'If we do decide to go ahead,' said Hugh, trying to diffuse the situation, 'who could we use in the part of Baby John? It's late in the day to try and recast somebody else.'

'I think Garry Green could do it,' said Tony, who had already given some thought to the matter. 'He is bigger and won't look so good, but I think he's capable of taking over the part and making a success of it.'

'You seem determined to go ahead,' said Gordon, speaking out for the first time. 'I think it shows disrespect for the dead, but if it is for the common good...'

'Shall we take a vote on it?'

'I came here this evening thinking there was no way we could carry on; that no one would *want* to,' said Hugh. 'But I've come round to your way of thinking. Perhaps it *would* be for the best if we continued. To get everyone pulling together, determined to make a go of it, might help us all to come to terms with it, and stop the youngsters brooding.'

'So, we're agreed the show goes ahead?'

'I think you're railroading this through, Tony, but I think you've got us all behind you.' Reid looked round at them with a question mark in her raised brows but no one disagreed.

'Just one thing,' queried Martin. 'Where are we going to rehearse? They won't let us use the community centre.'

'That's where you're wrong. We can go back in there at the end of next week.'

'That's surprising. I would have thought the whole place would be sealed off for weeks. You see it on telly in those detective series: scene of crime, the area taped off and guarded by hoards of policemen.'

'I think they're working along the lines that we're going to do their work for them. Instead of setting up a big reconstruction like they do on Crimewatch, we'll do it for them and they're hoping it will jog somebody's memory.'

'What about the funeral? Kevin's funeral? We can't go ahead until that's over.'

'The body certainly won't be released until

216

after the inquest, probably not even then. Perhaps we can arrange some kind of memorial service instead. We'll have to think about it, but I think we should resume rehearsals as soon as possible. Martin, do you think we could use the school hall until we can get back into the community centre?'

'I expect it can be arranged. I'll have a word with the headmaster.'

The meeting broke up shortly after this and Emma Spendlove and Hugh Smethers went off together, leaving the others behind.

'Thanks for the use of your office,' said Tony to Martin. 'I'll leave you to rally the troops as regards the sixth-formers involved.'

'I hope we're doing the right thing. What do you think, Reid?'

'At least it will have brought home to them the reality of violence. That *Romeo and Juliet* is not just about courtly duels on stage, but real death and all the trauma and horror and emotion that goes with it.'

'A hard lesson to learn at their age.'

'But it will make for a more realistic performance,' said Tony, and hurriedly changed the subject when he saw the expression on Reid's face. ' Gordon's been doing some more research into the Thomas Hardy letters.'

'I thought they had been stolen,' said

Martin. 'You did tell me that, didn't you, Reid?'

'They've disappeared,' said Tony, 'but we know the content, so we can go on with our search.'

'I thought this was supposed to be kept under wraps?' Gordon looked across at Martin in embarrassment.

'Martin knows all about it.'

'I'm interested from a scholar's point of view. Have you had any luck in finding out where the addressee of the letters lived? I understand you think the AC stands for Arthur Curtis, a relative of the old boy who had them in his possession.'

'Yes, and I think I'm getting somewhere at last,' said Gordon, looking quite animated. 'I've been looking into land registry and farming records and if AC *is* Arthur Curtis, I think he was a farmer.'

'You didn't tell me that,' said Tony. 'You've been holding out on me.'

'I meant to, but this other business put it out of my head.'

'Do you know *where* he farmed?'

'Yes, I've discovered that too. It was at a Holmewood Farm out at Barmelton.'

'I don't believe this!'

Reid stared in amazement at Gordon, who looked puzzled at her exclamation.

'That's the farm where my aunt and I nearly got savaged by this crazy old man and his vicious dog – I told you about it, Tony.'

'Good God! Are you sure?'

'You don't imagine something like that. The place was an absolute ruin but he was guarding it as if it were Fort Knox.'

'Didn't you say he collected antiques?'

'According to local rumour the place is stuffed with valuables but it's hard to believe. It's literally falling down – rot and damp everywhere and he looked like a tramp.'

'What's his name?'

Reid searched her memory. 'Gorham. Matthew Gorham. Edith looked it up before we went.'

'What made you go there?' asked Gordon.

'Edith used to spend her holidays there as a child. Her relatives owned it and she wanted to look over the place again.'

'What was the name?'

'Edith Culham.'

'No, I mean the relatives she stayed with. Were they called Culham too?'

Reid thought about this, looking perplexed. 'Do you know, I have no idea.'

'But they were *your* relatives too, Reid,' said Tony. 'Surely you *must* know!'

'It was a cousin of my grandmother and her husband.'

'Maybe their name *was* Curtis. We must find out.'

'How?'

219

'Well, your aunt would know, surely? Give her a ring.'

'I suppose she would.'

'Then what are you waiting for? Give her a call.'

'What, now?'

'There's no time like the present. Is she likely to be in at this hour of the evening?'

'At her age she doesn't exactly lead a hectic social life.'

'You can use this phone.' Martin indicated the phone on his desk.

'No thanks, I'd like a little privacy. I'll use the phone in reception.'

To the three men left behind she seemed to be gone a long while. It was a good ten minutes before she returned, and she looked very upset.

'Edith has had a stroke! She's back home and she says she's alright – that it was only a mild one, and she is almost completely recovered, and she didn't let me know because she didn't want to worry me. But you'd have thought my mother would have told me. I can't understand my mother, but it's typical of her. She's always been jealous of the good relationship I've got with Edith – who is *her* aunt.'

Reid sighed and sat down. The men looked at her expectantly.

'Did you manage to find out?' Tony gave her a sympathetic smile and tried to keep the eagerness out of his voice.

'Oh yes, sorry. You were right. Their name *was* Curtis.'

'Bingo! We've struck pay dirt. If that manuscript *was* sent to Arthur Curtis for safekeeping, what's the betting it's still there somewhere in the house?'

'That's just wishful thinking. You're twisting the facts to fit your theory.'

'You did say this Matthew Gorham was into antiques,' put in Gordon, pinching the bridge of his nose and squinting through his glasses.

'He is reputed to have a fortune stashed away, but presumably it is stuff *he* has collected and not what was left behind by the previous owners.'

'It is as good a place to start looking as anywhere.'

'Excuse my hollow laugh,' said Reid dismissively. 'You don't know what you are talking about. How would you go about it? Knock on the door and say, "Oh, excuse me, Mr Gorham, but we believe you could have a valuable Thomas Hardy manuscript hidden in the house, may we come and look for it?" To start with you wouldn't get as far as the door. The place is impregnable, and even if you managed to get into the grounds you'd be shot or savaged by the dog before you could open your mouth.'

'Didn't you report his behaviour to the

police and weren't they going to look into it?'

'Yes. I'll have to ask Nick whether any action was taken. He seemed to think his shotgun licence would be revoked, always supposing he had one in the first place.'

'It sounds as if the old boy is a danger to himself and everyone else. Can't the social services move in and put him in a home?' asked Martin.

'Yes – and leave the place to be cleared out and sold,' added Tony.

'No, of course not. You can't just shut people away when they become old and decrepit. *They* have got to agree. I don't suppose he's seen a doctor for years and no one from social services would get near him. Anyway, suppose he *was* rehoused – I can't see how that would give you the authority to root through his belongings.'

'It is so tantalising to think that the manuscript could have been lying there all these years, forgotten and mouldering, and nobody knowing anything about it.'

'Mouldering is the right word. Under those conditions it would be completely ruined by now. Forget it!'

'What I think we ought to be considering is the theft of the letters,' said Gordon tentatively. 'Surely it means someone else is on the track? We know it wasn't one of us, so who could it be?'

★ ★ ★

Ben Latimer's face stared out from the papers and television screens and the calls started to come in. All the sightings and hearsay had to be checked out but at the end of the day the police were left with negative findings. No one had set eyes on him after he had left the community centre on the evening of Kevin Compton's murder. He had walked away from the rehearsal and virtually disappeared.

'I don't like it,' said Nick to Tim Court as the two of them sifted through reports. 'We know that he hadn't got wheels, so he must have either hitched a lift or caught a bus or a train, but no one remembers seeing him.'

'*Could* he drive?' asked Court, tipping his chair back so that it balanced precariously on two legs.

'That is something that will have to be checked. The foster parents are coming down from Yorkshire today and I've got a meeting with them this afternoon. That's something they'll be able to tell me.'

'I thought fostering stopped when the kid reached the age of sixteen. Why is Latimer still living with foster parents?'

'Search me. Perhaps they've offered him a permanent home. We'll have to check. Anyway, to get back to the wheels business, there are no reports of any vehicles going missing that night, so it doesn't look as if he made a getaway in a stolen car.'

'A bicycle? He's young and fit, he could cover quite a distance on a cycle.'

'Like Mervyn Dooley? And where the hell is he?'

'If he did knock them both off he won't still be around, that's for sure.'

'But nobody's seen him either. For obvious reasons we didn't plaster his photo all over the media, but it was shown to everyone we've interviewed – the bus drivers, taxi drivers, railway staff, transport caffs etc. – and we've drawn a blank.'

'You're putting your money on Dooley as being our man?'

'The way I see it is, if Ben Latimer didn't kill Compton, then Dooley did – and probably Ben as well.'

'So, where is Ben's body?'

'That's the million-dollar question. Let's think it through. Dooley recognises Compton and realises that he could finger him, so he follows him and lays in wait. When Compton leaves the hall, Dooley attacks him with the piece of girder he has already acquired for the purpose and drags the body behind the packing cases. He is about to make off when to his horror he sees another face from the past. What does he do? Does he attack him also there and then?'

'He's already chucked the girder, so he doesn't have a weapon and there are now other people about so he can't act immediately. Instead, he lures him into a dark corner and snatches him.'

'You mean he's being kept prisoner somewhere? No, I don't buy that. Dooley's on the run, he hasn't got a hidey-hole and he's a miserable specimen physically. He'd never overpower young Ben unless he's got a gun, and I'm pretty sure he's not into shooters.'

'Alright, then suppose he follows Ben, waiting for an opportunity to top him. If he was walking from the community centre back to Caister Road, Ben would probably have taken a short cut along the towpath. Dooley seizes his chance, grabs a rock or a branch, cracks him over the head and pushes him in the river.'

'That makes horrible sense, but surely by now his body would have turned up? We can't drag that whole stretch of river but if his body went in along there I should have expected it to have been carried downstream and caught somewhere along the bank. The water's high at the moment with all the rain we've had, and flowing fast.'

'I'll get part of the team to go over that area again, especially the water's edge. Can we authorise a dog handler?'

'I think we can in the circumstances. In the meantime, there is something else I want to check.'

Nick collected his car and drove over to

Casterford General Hospital. His objective was the mortuary, where he hoped to catch Dick Wickham before he went to lunch. The pathologist was just getting into his car when Nick drove into the car park, so he pulled up alongside him, winding down his window.

'Doc, I was hoping to have words with you. I didn't realise you bunked off so early for your lunch hour.'

'I have a full schedule this afternoon, starting at two o'clock with autopsies on the two victims of that pile-up on the A35. I need some sustenance first, so I'm going to the Angel Hotel. Would you care to join me?'

'Love to, but I can't spare the time.' Or the money either for their fancy prices, thought Nick. 'This is just a quickie. I'm sure you can fill me in off the top of your head. Our Kevin Compton – were there any signs of buggery?'

'You think he was into that scene? No, there was no evidence of it.'

'No, you've got me wrong. We think it is possible that he was sexually abused as a child.'

'You're talking how many years ago? No way I could tell after all that time.'

'I wondered if perhaps there might be some physical signs of old abuse.'

'Not unless he was severely injured at the time.'

'Ah, well, I was just hoping to confirm something. Thanks, Doc.'

'Does this tie in with the pervert who's gone missing?' asked Wickham shrewdly.

'No, what gave you that idea? We're exploring several avenues of enquiry.'

'Don't give me that line. You can keep that for your *holding-the-Press-at-bay* routine. It's insulting. You come and pick my brains and I give freely of my time, and then you stonewall me when I show an interest in your case.'

'I wish I had got something definite to tell you, but we're groping in the dark at the moment. Ben Latimer has gone missing, but whether he's our killer or another victim is anyone's guess at the moment.'

'At least my customers don't up and disappear! I'll see you at the inquest.'

Dick Wickham wound up his window and drove off. Nick looked at his watch, torn between the need to get back to the station and his desire to see Rachel. He decided that, as he was already at the hospital, he might as well try and spend a few minutes with her.

Rachel was at her office desk, almost obscured by the large pile of reports in front of her. She didn't see him hovering outside and he watched her for a few seconds through the glass panel in the door. She was frowning in concentration and scribbling on a notepad. A pot of chrysanthemums stood on the end of her desk and as she pushed a file aside it knocked against the plant and sent a shower of yellow petals across the surface. She brushed them aside with one hand and beat a tattoo on the paper she was perusing with the other.

Nick felt a rush of emotion. This was a crazy life they were living. They should be together, man and wife, not existing on snatched meetings and frustrating visits to each other's homes. When he'd got this murder case wrapped up he was going to make damn sure he got his decree absolute, and they'd get married and to hell with everything else. He tapped on the door and pushed it open. Rachel's face lit up when she saw him, then she looked worried.

'Nick! Is anything wrong?'

'What's wrong in wanting to see my fiancée? I had to see Wickham, the pathologist, and I couldn't resist calling on you to see if I can take you out to lunch.'

'I can't come, Nick, I really can't. I'm up to my eyes and I intend working right through my lunch hour. I'm sorry.'

'So am I, but I shouldn't be here either. I've got Ben Latimer's foster parents coming in for a meeting this after noon and a thousand things to do beforehand.'

'Are they staying down here?'

'Just overnight. They're putting up at the

Dove Hotel. They want to meet up with Reid.'

'She'll be anxious to see them too. Does she know they're here?'

'Not yet. They'll have to get together this evening. I think it would be better if she doesn't have Tony with her.'

'I couldn't agree more.'

'On the other hand, she could probably do with some moral support.'

'Meaning?'

'Could you go with her to the Dove this evening, if that meets with the approval of the Pendletons?'

'And what would my part be?'

'A friend of Reid who has also met Ben down here.'

'Are you sure you don't want me there as a spy?'

'I shouldn't think anything will come up that will help me in my enquiry, but keep your eyes and ears open.'

'You've got a cheek! There am I thinking you've called in to see *me* and actually all you want is some undercover work carried out!'

'I swear that's not why I came. I'm just thinking on my feet, that's all. I hadn't planned this.'

'Don't you think it's time I got paid for being a snout or whatever you call them? Or at least a retainer?'

Tony Pomfret sat nursing his pint in the local at Barmelton. It was half-day closing at the bookshop, but business was slack at the moment and he had taken the whole day off. Gordon thought he was at home working on the new Christmas catalogue but he had had other ideas. The fact that there could be an unknown Thomas Hardy novel lying hidden and waiting to be found exercised him greatly; and from what they had discovered so far the trail, if it could be said to be a trail, led here to Barmelton.

Gordon was interested and fascinated by the project but for him it was more an academic exercise. Tony wanted to actually find the damn manuscript and capitalise on it. Hell, the money would be useful, and why shouldn't he take advantage of it? He could make much better use of the sum it might realise than the Church. It would only go to swell the church coffers and be used for such mundane things as new hymn books or building repairs. Unthinkable. And now there was a new element in the equation. Someone had stolen the letters and was also in the know. Who could it be? One of Peter Stevenson's congregation? Someone to whom perhaps Rachel Morland had mentioned it, or even Reid? It was quite possible she had let it slip out casually in the course of a conversation with one of her friends.

Whoever the unknown quantity was they could have made the same progress in tracing the manuscript as him, and could even now be plotting how to get it into their possession. He had decided it was time to take things into his own hands and had driven out to Barmelton to suss out the lie of the land.

There had been heavy rain overnight again and water had lain in the gutters and puddled the fields. He couldn't remember ever visiting the village before but there was nothing remarkable about it to make it stand out in the memory. A nucleus of old houses huddled round the church and pub with a small council estate and two private housing estates fringing the perimeter of the village. He hadn't been able to find Holmewood Farm at first. He had driven down muddy lanes past waterlogged verges and under dripping trees, swearing as he bumped in and out of potholes. So well hidden was the farmhouse behind its jungle of overgrown hedge that he had passed it a couple of times before he'd become aware of its existence.

He had parked the car in a field gateway further down the lane and walked back, dismayed, when he had got near and glimpsed it through the foliage. Christ! Reid had been right – derelict wasn't the word for it. It was positively dilapidated to the point where you couldn't imagine anyone could actually be living in it. If there were antiques and valuable possessions in there, they'd be ruined and a complete write-off. And he had groaned at the thought of the state any book would be in.

He had heard a dog barking in the distance and had wondered how he could effect an entrance. Thoughts of baited meat and pretending to be some sort of official had floated through his mind with other equally bizarre schemes. Then it had started to rain again and he had sprinted back to his car and driven to the pub. Now, half an hour later, he was no nearer working out how he was going to get inside Holmewood Farm. He decided to enlist the help of the landlord.

He walked over to the bar and ordered a steak sandwich and another half pint and tried to engage the landlord in conversation. It was uphill work, the landlord being taciturn in the extreme. He was a tall, gangling man in his late forties with very little hair and a bony face that was all planes and angles. He was not Tony's idea of *mine host*, but as he discovered a little later, it was the wife who normally ran things front of house and she was on a visit to her mother. He tried to turn the talk to Holmewood Farm.

'I'm thinking of buying a property in this area and I've been having a look round. That place – what's its name – Holmewood Farm

– looks interesting.'

The landlord paused in his task of wiping the bar top, a spark of animation showed in his eyes and he became quite vocal.

'Presumably you want some place to live in, not a dump like that.'

'It does look rather run-down.'

'Run-down? I'd have put it rather stronger than that. It ought to be condemned.'

'But there is someone living there at present?'

'Oh, yes. Matthew Gorham his name is, and he's off his rocker.'

'Really?'

'Well, anyone who lives under those conditions has to be a few sandwiches short of a picnic, doesn't he? I hope you didn't try to approach him.'

'No. I heard a dog barking and I thought I'd better find out a little more about the situation before I intruded.'

'A good decision, my friend. That dog is as savage as its owner. If you're really looking for somewhere in the area you can do better than that. That place has long got past the stage of renovation.'

'There's a decent bit of land with it.'

'You're thinking you could pull the house down and build on the plot? I suppose you might get building permission for something like that. Most of the farmland was sold off years ago. I reckon there's just about an acre left now round the house, but you'll never get the owner out. He's been living there as long as I can remember.'

'Presumably he's getting on. Does he ever come in here?'

'You're joking? Matthew Gorham's a recluse. He don't come here and we don't go near him, not if we value our skins. God knows what will happen to the place when he pops his clogs. I've never heard tell of any relatives.'

Tony's sandwich appeared from the kitchen and the landlord grunted and placed it in front of him before removing himself to the other end of the bar, his oratorical powers evidently exhausted.

Ten

Clive and Laura Pendleton were in their fifties. Their own family was grown and scattered and they had been fostering for many years. Clive Pendleton was a lecturer in history at York University and Laura was involved in many voluntary organisations. They were quietly spoken but articulate and Nick was impressed by them. They were both obviously highly intelligent and had an air of integrity about them that was sadly missing in most of the people Nick came up against in the course of his work.

He met them in reception and took them up to his office, where he sent for coffee and tried to put them at their ease.

'Inspector, you don't really suspect Ben of being involved in this young man's murder, do you?' Laura Pendleton asked, a nice mixture of outrage and bewilderment in her voice.

Nick explained the basic facts of the case and their dismay and confusion deepened.

'Ben would never attack anyone, especially an old friend,' said Clive Pendleton firmly. 'He has a very gentle nature, doesn't stick up for himself enough, I've always thought.'

'You see my dilemma.' Nick leaned forward and spoke sympathetically. 'I hope you are right and Ben can be eliminated from my enquiry, but things are not looking good. It is three days since the appeal for him to come forward went out, and he hasn't materialised. If he is innocent I should have expected him to have made contact. On the other hand his disappearance could have a more sinister meaning.'

'You think he could also be dead?' asked Clive Pendleton gravely and his wife gave a little cry of distress.

'It is a possibility I have to consider.'

The coffee arrived at that moment and Nick thanked the WPC who had brought it and handed it round.

'Chocolate biscuits! You *are* honoured! It's more than I ever get.'

Laura Pendleton smiled weakly but refused the plate of biscuits and her husband took one and bit into it absentmindedly.

'Did Ben ever mention Kevin Compton to you?'

'That's the young man who was killed? No. We'd never heard of him before this happened.'

'They were in the same home when they were younger.'

'St Kilda's – that's where Ben was. In Ripon.'

'Did he talk about it?'

'No. I think it was a part of his life he wanted to forget, so we never pressed him. It had a bad name and was closed down by the authorities many years ago.'

Nick changed the subject, not wishing to bring up the possibility of child abuse at that point.

'Ben has been living with you how long? Six years? Surely you are not still acting as his foster parents?'

'We are quite happy to go on giving him a home.'

'But you don't get any financial help?'

'Not since he reached eighteen and finished school, but we manage. Ben is one of the family and the local authorities are quite happy with the situation. He has a permanent base while he takes up further education.'

'Have you had any contact with him since he left York?'

'A postcard from Dorset about a fortnight ago. We thought he was just passing through on his way to Cornwall. Ben is not one of the world's best communicators.'

'Has he got a girlfriend?'

'No. Certainly not as far as we know.'

Nick decided to ruffle the waters.

'Is he gay?'

He expected either a furious denial or embarrassment. Instead the Pendletons considered the question thoughtfully.

'Again, not as far as we know,' said Clive Pendleton carefully. 'We have considered the possibility, what with Ben not showing much interest in the opposite sex, but I don't think so.'

'Would it shock you?'

'I certainly hope we are more enlightened than that. I did try to discuss it with him once but he was far more embarrassed than myself. However, I think he got the message that he could confide in us without fear or recrimination.'

'I think Ben is just a late developer,' said Laura Pendleton, putting down her coffee cup. 'He's far more interested in his birds and animals and wildlife.'

'Did you know he was trying to contact his birth mother?'

'Yes, we thought it was a natural thing to do. His adoption had fallen apart and he was passed from pillar to post until he came to us, so we could understand his wanting to find his real roots. We hadn't realised, though, that he had actually made contact. He kept us in the dark over that.'

Let Reid tell them how that contact actually came about, thought Nick. The more he learned of Ben Latimer the more secretive a person he seemed to be.

'Reid Frobisher, his real mother, teaches at Casterford High School,' he told them. 'She is anxious to meet you.'

'We certainly want to meet her.'

'How long are you staying down here?'

'We have to get back tomorrow. I'm needed at the university and we have two toddlers we are fostering at the moment.'

'My sister is looking after them overnight but I must take over again tomorrow,' said Laura Pendleton. 'Can we meet Miss Frobisher today? Perhaps after school?'

'If you would like I'll get her to ring you at your hotel and perhaps it would be convenient if she came to see you at the hotel this evening?'

The Pendletons agreed that this would suit them and thanked Nick for his offer.

'I think Reid Frobisher would like to bring

someone with her.'

'I'm sorry, we never asked, is she married? Did Ben's existence cause any problems?'

'I believe she was married and divorced a long while ago. She has a friend who has also met Ben and is concerned about him. The friend's name is Rachel Morland and she is a ... a church woman.'

'You know her, Inspector?'

'She is my fiancée,' said Nick simply.

The car spluttered and stalled and Mervyn Dooley jabbed wildly at the starter, already regretting the impulse that had led to him hijacking the vehicle. It was an old banger – a Ford Capri on its last legs – and it had been left on a derelict building site with the key still in the ignition.

This is the story of my life, he thought, pulling the starter savagely, one failure after another. I decide to lift a car and I can't even pick one that will go! The engine wheezed and subsided and he forced himself to leave the ignition alone. He'd probably flooded it by now. He must sit still and wait a while before trying again. He drummed his fingers on the steering wheel and stared out of the window. He reckoned he had travelled a couple of miles before it had given up on him and he wasn't sure where he was. Somewhere on the outskirts of Casterford, that was for sure, in a residential area. He hoped he was on the southern side of the town. He needed to pick up the A354.

He knew it was vital that he got away, put as much distance as possible between himself and Casterford, and he had hit on the idea of getting himself to Weymouth and going across on the ferry to the Isle of Wight. Surely once there he could find somewhere to lie low until he had sorted out what he was going to do? The face staring out at him from the hoarding had almost paralysed him with fear. He was a marked man and he wouldn't be welcome in the network. Events were escalating out of control and he didn't know what to do.

A couple of pedestrians were approaching along the pavement and he cringed back and pretended to be studying his notebook. They passed by with just an idle glance at the car. He gasped in relief and looked at himself in the mirror. The beard was coming along but, hell, how it itched. He scratched beneath his jaw and pulled his cap lower across his forehead. He *did* look different, surely no one would recognise him now?

He decided if and when he got the car to start again he would drive out into the countryside and find a place to hide overnight. He'd get off the road somewhere, hide behind a hedge or get in amongst the trees and try and get some sleep. Then he would make an early start. Get on the road again and make for Weymouth before there was much traffic about.

But first he would have to get some petrol. The petrol gauge was on empty and he had a horrible feeling that might be the reason why the car had given up the ghost. He must also get some food. One of the big, anonymous service stations would probably be the best bet. They dealt with so many customers in the course of the day they were unlikely to remember individual faces and they also served a good selection of fast food. The only problem was, they usually had CCTV cameras in action.

'What did you think of them?'

Reid Frobisher had persuaded Rachel to meet up for coffee in the town centre. As it was Saturday morning the café was crowded but they had managed to get a table in a corner where they had a little privacy.

'The Pendletons? I liked them. They seemed very genuine, good people.'

'They would appear good to you, she's another church woman, isn't she?'

'You didn't like them?'

'What was there to dislike about them? Good law-abiding citizens, pillars of society, if we're going to talk in clichés. Do-gooders of the first order.'

'Reid, what *is* the matter?'

'They made me feel so inadequate, so

lightweight—' Reid grimaced and made patterns in the sugar bowl with her spoon.

'They made me realise what a lousy mother I would have been. I guess Ben was lucky to end up with them. If they had been the ones to adopt him as a tiny baby, I bet he wouldn't have bothered tracing *me*.'

'I do believe you're jealous.'

'Well, of course I am. They've had him for six years and I've only just met up with him and he's been snatched away!'

'They were very upset too. They couldn't take on board the possibility that he might be implicated in Kevin's death.'

'Of course he isn't. Surely you don't think that?'

'I only met him that one time,' said Rachel slowly, trying to be tactful, 'and I thought him a very pleasant young man, but that doesn't mean that he wasn't trying to hood-wink us. I don't know the real Ben Latimer. He could be a very different person from the first impression I got.'

'What a nasty, suspicious mind! You're getting as bad as Nick, always believing the worst of people.'

'You know that's not true. I always try and think the best of everyone, though I have sometimes got my fingers burnt in the process.'

'Sorry, Rachel. I guess I'm on edge. Every-thing seems to be rushing out of control and

I feel so *helpless*. I found my son and lost him and there's a murderer at large and Tony—'

'What about Tony?'

'He can't seem to understand how I feel. *He* thinks Ben is guilty and he just seems to be relieved that he didn't impinge any further on our lives. He's managed to push it all into the background. All he's concerned about is his show and those blasted letters. Has Nick said whether they've got any further in tracing the thief?'

'No. He's heading the murder investigation now. I think Peter's burglary has been put on the back burner.'

'He's obsessed with trying to trace that missing manuscript.'

'Reid, are you ... are you sure that Tony didn't help himself to those letters? He is one of the only people who knew about them and he is aware of their true value.'

Reid looked outraged but Rachel thought she was bluffing and that the same thought had probably occurred to her. She might be smitten by Tony but she wasn't blind to his faults.

'I won't deign to answer such a ridiculous question,' said Reid, glaring at her friend. 'All I can say is, if you'd heard the way he's been going on about the theft you'd realise that he's as sick as a parrot over the whole business.'

243

'Well, the letters are gone and I reckon the manuscript disappeared years ago – if it ever existed – so I think we should draw a line beneath this and forget the entire episode. Do you want some more coffee?'

Reid pushed her cup over and Rachel filled it and offered her the milk jug. The chatter around them rose in volume and people pushed past laden with shopping. We ought to drink up and go, thought Rachel, there are people waiting for a table.

'Didn't Tony come into town with you today?' she asked. 'I thought you usually did the shopping together on a Saturday.'

'No, he's busy trying to sort out rehearsals. You know the show is still on?'

'Yes.'

'You are still going to help me as prompt, aren't you?'

'Well, I'm not sure—'

'You can't let me down! Won't Nick insist?'

'What do you mean?'

'You're his stool pigeon, aren't you? His little inside line to what goes on.'

'I don't believe this! *You* twisted my arm to help out at rehearsals.'

'But I bet Nick thought it was a good idea. Did you report back to him? Have you given him your version of meeting with the Pendletons yet?'

As this was too near the truth for comfort Rachel found herself retaliating.

'I can see you're determined to pick a quarrel.'

'No, I'm not, but you can't deny you give him the lowdown on what you've seen and heard.'

'I thought I was there yesterday evening to support *you*!'

'Oh, God, yes, I'm glad you were there. I should probably have made a complete fool of myself if I'd been on my own. Sorry, I'm being a real bitch.'

'You're overwrought, we both are. The sooner this murder mystery gets solved the better.'

'Does Nick discuss it with you? Confide in you?'

'Only the things he wants me to know.'

Rachel glanced round the room and wondered just what Nick was doing at that moment. She only knew that he was busy following up lines of enquiry and she would be lucky to set eyes on him over the weekend. Her attention was drawn to a woman who had just entered the café and was bearing down on them, ignoring the other customers who were waiting to be shown to a table. She was about the same age as Rachel, smartly dressed and with a petulant expression on her expertly made-up face.

'Do you know that woman?' she asked Reid.

'Uh-huh, it's Fiona Boyd, Martin's wife.

Damn, she's coming over to us!'

'Good morning, Reid, you don't mind if I join you, do you?'

'We're just going, actually.'

'Oh, I am sure you can find time to keep me company for another coffee.' Fiona Boyd looked pointedly at Rachel and reluctantly Reid introduced them.

Fiona Boyd appropriated a spare chair from a nearby table and sank gracefully on to it. She slipped off her coat to reveal an elegantly cut suit that screamed *designer* and that Rachel knew she would never, ever, be able to afford.

'You're lucky you have your weekends to yourself,' said Fiona to Reid. 'Poor Martin has had to go back into school this morning.'

As she was sure that Martin deliberately worked overtime to avoid keeping his wife company, Reid ignored this and asked instead how the building work was coming along.

'It is chaos at the moment. The kitchen is finished but the conservatory is taking ages. You can't get workmen to do a decent day's work these days. They come and go as they please and the place is like a building site.'

'This wet autumn can't have helped,' put in Rachel, trying to ease the conversation.

'My dear, yes, the garden is like a quagmire where they've carted materials backwards and forwards.'

And that will require the attentions of a landscape gardener to sort out later if I know my Fiona, thought Reid.

'Of course, the other problem,' continued Fiona, 'is that you can't *get* the right materials here in this backwater. I want these Italian tiles for the floor but do you think I can find a supplier in Dorset? I'm going to have to go up to London myself to look for them.'

'Have you got a family?' asked Rachel.

'Yes, two girls. They are away at boarding school. We simply must get everything finished before they come home for the Christmas holidays.'

Rachel began to see why Reid was so antagonistic towards her colleague's wife. Reid had very strong views on teachers who taught in the state system but didn't deem it good enough for their own children and educated them privately, and she sympathised with her.

'You must miss them.'

'Oh, I do, but I'm relieved they're out of the way with this dreadful murder case going on. Thank God it wasn't one of Martin's sixth-formers who was killed. To my way of thinking they shouldn't have been involved with this musical in the first place. Martin's got enough on his plate without taking on any more extra-curricular activities like that. They should be concentrating on their studies and not cavorting on stage. I'm surprised Martin encouraged it.'

'I really must go,' said Rachel, getting to her feet and ignoring the pleading look Reid threw at her. 'I have things to do in town. It's been nice meeting you, Fiona, I hope your building work gets finished soon. I'll give you a ring, Reid.'

She made her escape and remembered when she was outside on the pavement that she hadn't paid for her coffee. Perhaps Fiona Boyd would pick up the tab, she mused as she wended her way through the congested crowds towards the market, but somehow she didn't think so.

The fog that had been threatening all morning clamped down at midday and Rachel had a difficult drive home. Familiar landmarks were distorted and once she had left the town behind the road became a narrow channel tunnelling through blankness. It is like the parting of the Red Sea, she thought, squinting through the windscreen. I'm crossing the floor of the sea and the grey and white shapes looming from the side of the road are the petrified waves. She was relieved when she reached the village and the sanctuary of her cottage. She parked under the carport and walked round to the front porch, suddenly loath to go inside.

What was Nick doing now? Would he have remembered? Remembered that today was to have been their wedding day? She fumbled in her handbag for the key and shuddered as an icy drip ran down her face and found its way inside her collar. Perhaps it was as well that it had been postponed, this certainly wasn't wedding weather and Nick had other things to occupy him now. He hadn't mentioned recently how the search for his ex-wife was progressing; he was so engrossed in this murder case that he had probably pushed it to the back of his mind.

Would he have had to postpone the wedding anyway, she mused, even without this hitch, because of his involvement in this case? She let herself into the cottage and took off her coat. Would it always be like this, with his work coming first? But no, that was unfair. She had known what she was taking on when she had agreed to share her life with him. He was a good policeman and she admired his commitment to his job, and he, in turn, respected her involvement with the church.

The answerphone was flashing when she walked into the sitting room and there was a message from Nick.

'I haven't forgotten what today is. We'll celebrate it soon, I promise you. I can't get away until this evening but I'll definitely come round then although it may be quite late before I make it. Love you.'

He *had* remembered – how could she have doubted him. She went through into the kitchen and heated up some soup, determined to spend the afternoon writing her sermon for the next week. Peter was letting her preach at the family service the following Sunday and she wanted to make a success of it. It was to be no solemn address from the pulpit but a talk that would involve visual aids to grab the attention of the children.

She worked through the afternoon and made herself a scratch meal from the ingredients in the fridge, then prepared to go out again. She was reading the evening office in her local church, so she grabbed a torch from the hall table and let herself out of the cottage. The fog now seemed more patchy. As she squelched through damp leaves she moved through pockets of fog that sucked her into the dank banks of mist swirling round her like an impenetrable miasma; then she would suddenly find herself out in the clear again, the hedgerows and trees springing into prominence and lighted windows illuminating the dusk.

When she had completed her devotions she locked the church behind her and hurried down the path. At the gate she hesitated. Nick wouldn't be round yet, should she go over to Barminster and see Peter and Jenny? An owl hooting from a nearby tree decided her; the sooner she was back inside her warm cottage the better, and Nick might get over sooner than expected.

She swung the heavy gate back and it creaked like something out of a gothic horror film before clanking shut behind her. She started up the road towards the village green. A form suddenly loomed up in front of her. Startled, she sidestepped to avoid it but it reached out a hand and clutched at her arm. Thoroughly scared by now she reeled back against the churchyard wall and the figure took substance, startling her even more.

'Ben? Ben Latimer? Is it really you?'

'I'm sorry I scared you.' His face so close to hers looked set and remote. 'I must speak with you.'

Bruce Downing took the letter out and re-read it. The envelope was addressed to him in crude capitals and it had been sent by first-class mail. He unfolded the single sheet of paper and ran his eyes over the contents although he already knew them by heart:

Protect our children! There is another pervert living in our midst. Matthew Gorham is a canker in our society. He thinks he is safe hidden away in his

251

farmhouse but he must go. Root him out! He lives at Holmewood Farm in Barmelton.

At the bottom of the page was a rough map showing the location of Holmewood Farm in relationship to the village.

Who had sent it to him this time? As leader of the vigilantes he had received several anonymous pieces of information about known sex offenders living in the area, but not since he and his fellow ringleaders had been hauled up before the magistrates. His easily-roused temper flared afresh at the memory of how they had been treated like common criminals by the police. He and his friends were doing society a kindness by exposing these evil monsters, and their reward was to be bound over with criminal charges to answer. And what were the police doing now that they were muzzled? Sweet fucking nothing! They knew who was on the sex register, and instead of driving them out they kept stum, actually providing protection for the scum. It made his blood boil!

It wasn't going to be easy to follow up the letter's bidding. He was a marked man. The police would be on to him in a trice if he was caught leading another protest, and they'd really throw the book at him. He must get the others together and see what they thought. They had vowed that they wouldn't rest until all the known perverts were driven out of the area, and now here was another one that they hadn't been aware of before.

Bruce Downing racked his brains. The name Matthew Gorham rang a bell. He'd heard it before but he couldn't remember in what connection. Perhaps one of his mates could fill him in. He put the letter in his pocket, switched off the television and went into the hall. He scowled at his reflection in the hall mirror, shrugged into his anorak and called out to his wife, who was in the kitchen.

'I'm off out.'

'Where are you going?' His wife put her head round the kitchen door, an anxious expression on her careworn face.

'Out! I don't have to get my wife's permission to go out for a drink with my mates.'

'Oh, Bruce, do be careful. You know what that magistrate said.'

'Boring old fart! No one's going to stop me cracking a bottle with my mates.'

'Don't you go plotting no more trouble. I don't trust them so-called friends of yours.'

'Shut up, woman! You don't know nothing about it, you're talking a lot of drivel!'

He banged out of the house and walked towards the crossroads, the glimmering of an idea beginning to form in his head.

'Do you realise that the police force of the

entire country is looking for you?'

Rachel stared at Ben Latimer, hardly able to believe her eyes. He didn't look like a fugitive who'd been living rough, and she felt in no way threatened. Here she was, in a remote country lane, no one else within call, face to face with a man who was a possible murderer, but she didn't feel afraid.

'But I don't understand why. What am I supposed to have done?' He looked genuinely puzzled and brushed away some droplets of moisture that were clinging to his eyebrows.

'Where have you *been*?' Rachel shivered as another column of fog swirled round them, damp and choking. 'We can't talk here, we'd better go back inside the church.'

She led the way back up the churchyard path and Ben followed her carrying a rucksack and grip, which she hadn't noticed at first. She unlocked the door and snapped on some lights.

'We'll go in the Lady Chapel, it's warmer there.'

The Lady Chapel was a Victorian addition bristling with much Gothic decoration. Ben dumped his gear on the floor and sat on a bench pew opposite her. The muted light threw grotesque shadows across the walls and carvings and the chrysanthemums bunched on the little altar smelt old and rank. Rachel repeated her question.

'Where have you been?'

'Lundy.'

'Lundy?' She decided to pass on that one for the moment and moved on. 'Do you know about Kevin Compton?'

'I found out yesterday. It's terrible! It must have happened just after I left that evening!'

'Ben, what happened that evening?'

'How do you mean?'

'You were watching the rehearsal with Reid and myself, and afterwards, when we were discussing it, you refused to take part in the show but agreed to help backstage. Then you rushed off and we thought you had gone to join Kevin.'

'Well, no.' Ben looked embarrassed. 'I guess I felt that you were all pressing me to get involved and I wasn't sure what my long-term plans were, how long I was going to stay in Dorset, so I decided to take off for a few days. I'd always intended going on to Cornwall, so I went back to the house and collected my stuff and walked to the A35 to hitch a lift. I meant to ring Reid and Kevin and let them know where I was but I got picked up by this couple of guys who were on their way to Barnstaple. It turned out that they were going across to Lundy; they were both keen birdwatchers and we got talking and I decided to go with them. We stayed in a remote cottage and there was no phone or television. I never even saw a newspaper. It was very primitive but great, we saw all sorts of seabirds. Anyway, I felt rather guilty as I hadn't let anyone know where I was, so I decided to come back here and give Cornwall a miss until next year.'

He shrugged and shook his head in bewilderment. 'When I got back to the mainland I was walking past this newsagent's and I saw *my* photo staring at me from a hoarding. I couldn't believe it! I bought a paper and read that Kevin had been murdered and that the police wanted to contact *me*! It didn't make sense. Why was Kevin killed?'

'I think the police are hoping *you* can tell them that.'

'I don't understand...'

Rachel leaned forwards and spoke carefully.

'Ben, Kevin was killed that evening soon after he left the rehearsal. He was hit over the head and his body hidden nearby. The police thought you were probably the last person to see him alive, but when they tried to find you, you had disappeared. They jumped to the obvious conclusion.'

'They think I killed him? Christ!' Ben glanced warily round the chapel as if he feared divine retribution for the expletive.

'They think that either you had something to do with it or you were harmed too. As

256

they haven't found your body and they discovered that you had taken all your belongings, I'm afraid they favour the first option.'

'But this is awful!' Ben jumped to his feet and mooched up and down the flagstones. 'I didn't do it, Rachel, I swear to you! Why should I want to harm Kevin?'

'I believe you, but you must admit it looks bad. You were an old friend of his, can you think of any reason why someone would want to kill him?'

'I don't really know much about him – I mean about his life here. We were in a children's home together when we were kids and I hadn't seen him since then until I bumped into him the day I arrived in Casterford. I can't believe he had any enemies!'

'That's what everybody says.'

'What am I going to do?'

'You must go to the police. If you're innocent you've got nothing to fear.'

'What about Reid?'

'*She* thinks you're innocent but she is very concerned about you.'

'I feel guilty because I went off without telling her. I was going to go straight to her place today but then I wondered how she would receive me, whether she might regret ever meeting up with me, so I decided to talk to you first and see how things were.'

'I'm flattered.'

'Well, you're connected with all this...' His gesture took in their surroundings and the entire Christian doctrine. 'I knew I could trust you to put me right. Will I be arrested?'

'Not if you can prove that what you have just told me is true, but you must go and be interviewed.'

'I think they probably know I'm back in Casterford. I got a lift with a lorry driver. He was very chatty to begin with, then he began giving me odd looks. When we got to a service station on the outskirts of the town he filled up and went into the kiosk to pay. I could see him talking to the cashier and pointing back at me and then the cashier made a phone call. I knew that they had recognised me from the papers and I didn't wait to see what would happen next. I got my stuff and slipped out of the cab and walked the rest of the way here.'

'You *walked*? All that way? You must be exhausted.'

'I'm used to long hikes, but I *am* starving.'

'Look, my cottage is over on the other side of the village. We'll go there and I'll contact Nick. He's my fiancé and is the detective inspector in charge of the murder enquiry. I'm expecting him this evening and he may be there already. If he isn't, I'll phone him and tell him you've turned up, and while we're waiting for him to arrive I'll find you something to eat.'

Rachel once more let herself out of the church and locked up accompanied by a silent, pensive Ben. Whilst they had been inside, the fog had almost dispersed. Visibility was reasonable in all directions and the single street lamp positioned opposite the church gate illuminated them as they turned and started to walk up the lane towards the Green.

The car engine sounded unnaturally loud as it approached. The headlights temporarily blinded them and they hesitated at the side of the road as the car accelerated towards them. Pinioned in the glare they only just managed to jump back on to the verge as the car swerved at the last moment and swept past them.

'Maniac!' said Ben. 'He *must* have seen us.'

They squelched off the wet grass back on to the road and Rachel held up her hand.

'He's turning round.'

They could hear the car reversing and manoeuvring in the distance and then it was coming back towards them.

'Must be lost. He's probably going to ask us for directions.'

But the car didn't slow down as it got nearer. Instead it bore down on them at an alarming speed.

'Look out, Rachel!'

She felt a hand on her arm pushing her

towards the verge but even as she stumbled back she felt an almighty blow on her hip and then she was sailing through the air towards blackness.

Eleven

There was a light burning on her eyelids, drawing her back. Back from the nightmare depths she was swimming in. She had to make an effort, to claw her way back to the glow hovering just out of reach. She tried to move but a terrible pain shot through her and she groaned and froze. Somewhere, a long way away, someone was calling her name, urgently, repeatedly. ' Rachel, Rachel, Rachel...' She made a supreme effort and forced open her eyes. The light was blinding, searing, car headlights bearing down on her remorselessly. She gasped in terror and sank back into oblivion.

The next time she surfaced she was dimly aware of a soothing sensation in her hands. Someone was stroking them, massaging them gently. The voice was calling again. This time the light was not so terrifying when she blinked her eyes and a face swam in and out of focus. A familiar face, blue eyes brimming with anxiety and a wedge of fair hair falling over his forehead.

'Rachel. It's alright, Rachel. You're going to be alright.'

'Where—?'

'You're in hospital. You were hit by a car. He didn't see you in the fog and didn't stop.'

'No... No.' She must make him understand what had happened but the pain shot through her body again and she sank back into unconsciousness.

Some time later she opened her eyes to find herself staring at a muted blue light in a dim ceiling way above her head. Trying not to move, she slid her eyes down and caught the edge of a curtain in her vision. It was pale pink with a pattern of green foliage. She had no curtains like that— She twisted on the pillow and this time the movement was not so painful, just a throb somewhere behind her temples.

'Mrs Morland, you're back with us. How do you feel?'

A woman in nurse's uniform, with a sympathetic face, was bending over her.

A nurse. Hospital. She was in hospital. Memory started to return.

'Nick?'

'Your husband will be back soon. He's been here with you all night but he had to go out for a short while.'

'I'm here.'

Nick's face loomed beside the nurse and then the nurse had gone and Nick was there beside her, asking the same question, 'How do you feel?'

'I— I don't know... My head is throbbing but I daren't move. My hip— Have I broken my pelvis?'

'No. You've badly bruised your hip and all down that side but there are no broken bones, The car must have caught you a glancing blow on your hip and threw you on to the verge, where you must have landed on your head. Fortunately the ground was very soft. You were knocked out but according to the scan your skull isn't damaged. You must rest and relax. There's nothing to worry about and the doctor says you will soon be as right as rain.'

'I remember the car's lights bearing down on us—' Memory suddenly kicked in. 'Ben! What's happened to Ben?'

'Ssh, don't upset yourself.'

'He's dead, isn't he?'

'No. He took the brunt of the impact and he's unconscious, but I promise you he isn't dead.'

'How bad is he?'

'He's in a coma but they hope he will recover.'

'He saved me, pushed me out of the way when we saw the car returning—Why did it run us down?'

'It was an accident, Rachel, try not to dwell on it.'

'No, no ... you don't understand – it was deliberate.'

'What are you trying to say?' He was still solicitous, anxiety and love plainly written on his face, but the policeman was taking over. She could hear it in his voice even in her weakened, muddled state.

'He deliberately ran us down. Don't look at me like that, Nick, it's true, I'm not wandering! He made one attempt and when that failed he turned round and drove back at us again – it was awful...'

'But the fog?'

'It had cleared. He could see us, he knew what he was doing.'

'Not upsetting your wife, are you, Mr Morland?' The nurse was beside the bed again, admonishing Nick. 'She needs rest and quiet, not to be reminded of the unfortunate accident.'

They moved away and Rachel was dimly aware of Nick's voice telling the nurse that he was her fiancé, not her husband, and that he was a detective inspector and this was very important. Their voices became muted and she drifted off into an uneasy sleep punctuated by ghastly dreams in which she relived the horror of being mown down by the unknown car.

* * *

Nick Holroyd stared through the window of the intensive care unit at the still, corpse-like figure lying on the bed, attached to numerous drips and machines. So, this was Ben Latimer. He looked more dead than alive, what were his chances of pulling through? The detective was waiting to speak to the doctor in charge and, meanwhile, questions buzzed round and round his head unanswered. Where had Ben Latimer been since the night of Kevin Compton's murder? Why had he suddenly reappeared? How had he come to be with Rachel? And why had they been deliberately mown down and left for dead?

'Detective Inspector Holroyd? I'm Doctor Mukerji.' Nick turned round to the speaker and found himself confronted by an Indian of about his own age, who looked haggard under the fluorescent light.

'You wanted to speak to me?'

'Your patient – how is he?' Nick indicated Latimer. 'Is he going to live?'

'He has serious head and abdominal injuries. We have removed a cerebral haematoma – blood clot – from his brain but he has massive bruising of the brain tissue. If we can stabilise him and there are no further complications he should make it. He's young and healthy.'

'And the abdominal injuries?'

'Several ribs were broken and one has

punctured a lung.'

'How long is he likely to be unconscious?'

'We'll keep him under for at least a week.'

'Keep him under? I don't understand.'

'As I said, he has extensive bruising of the brain and must be completely immobilised to enable healing and subsidence of the swelling. Which means that he is drugged and the ventilator takes over his breathing.'

'So, even if he recovers, we won't be able to speak with him yet?'

'Inspector, I am only concerned with the welfare and recovery of my patient and *not* whether he can help you with your enquiries!'

'Quite, I appreciate that. But you think he should make a full recovery?'

'We can only hope. Head injuries are always tricky. He could develop another clot and there is always the risk of infection and pneumonia because of the lung injury.'

'Are there any other injuries?'

'A dislocated shoulder and extensive bruising but they are minor problems.'

'I think a deliberate attempt was made on his life. He could still be in danger if his attacker realises that he is still alive. Security needs to be stepped up. I want a police officer on duty round the clock.'

Dr Mukerji shrugged and knuckled his eyes. 'You're in the ICU. Patients are under surveillance at all times and there is always a nurse in attendance.'

'I still want an officer in.'

'That's up to you. As long as he doesn't get between my staff and their duties.'

'Can he have visitors?'

'Yes, that is quite in order – as long as you can vouch for their credibility,' added the doctor, a flash of humour lighting his dark face. At that moment his bleeper went off. 'I have to go.'

'Thank you, doctor, I'm sure he's in good hands.'

Dr Mukerji departed and Nick looked back at his patient. A nurse was now bent over the bed adjusting a piece of machinery. What secrets were locked away in that frozen brain? he wondered. Perhaps they had been confided to Rachel. Perhaps she now held the key to the whole mystery? He hurried back to her beside.

Rachel was now fully conscious and her face lit up when Nick appeared.

'How do you feel now?'

'Much better. My head is not throbbing as badly but I'm still very stiff and sore.'

'Do you feel able to talk about it, or would you rather not dwell on it for the time being?'

She knew how much it had cost him to say this and she clutched his hand and shook her head.

'I'm quite okay to talk, but how is Ben?'

Nick told her what the doctor had said and she closed her eyes briefly and murmured, 'Pray God he makes a full recovery.'

'Are you sure you were deliberately run down?'

'Yes.'

Once more she told him what had happened in the road outside the churchyard.

'Did you recognise what make of car it was or catch sight of the driver?'

'No, I'm sorry, this sounds feeble, but I was dazzled by the headlights. There was no way I could have seen who was behind the wheel and I don't even know what colour it was...'

'Okay, don't distress yourself. Was it a large vehicle?'

Rachel searched her brains. 'Well ... it wasn't a Mini or a Metro, something bigger than that— I'm not being of any help at all, am I? I've been going over it and trying to understand why it happened. No one would want to harm me, it was Ben they were targeting – why?'

'That's what I hoped you might be able to tell me. How did you meet up with him? Where had he been?'

She explained what had taken place the previous evening and Nick listened intently.

'So you see, Ben had nothing to do with Kevin's murder. He was just as puzzled as us as to why he had been killed,' she said, when she had told him all that she could remember of events.

'Mmm.'

'I'm sure he was telling the truth, Nick, and surely his story can be verified?'

'Yes, we'll get to work on that straight away, and we're already checking out the claim of a long-distance lorry driver that he picked up someone answering to Ben's description.'

'That will be the driver who gave him a lift back here.'

'Probably. And Ben definitely said that he had had no contact with Compton since they left the home as children, and met up with him unexpectedly here in Casterford?'

'Yes. This goes back to something that happened to them in that home, doesn't it?'

'I think it does.'

'You're talking child abuse?'

'There is a distinct possibility that something along those lines took place in that home. It was closed down very suddenly and later, when details of abuse started to come to light, it was too late to get evidence and mount a prosecution.'

'So how does that link with what's happened now?'

'I'm thinking aloud here, but what I think may have happened is this: Ben and Kevin meet up after a long interval. They may have discussed what had happened to them in their youth, they may have suppressed it and tried to pretend it hadn't happened. Anyway, they are together again and suddenly they're confronted by a face from the past—'

'The person who abused them?'

'Yes.'

'But wouldn't they have contacted the police? Reported him?'

'The recognition may not have been mutual. In any case, they didn't get the chance. This person may have thought that he'd been recognised and that their evidence could send him down for a long spell, so he decides to eliminate them. He kills Kevin but Ben disappears before he can be tackled.'

'But when Ben turns up again this person is on to him immediately and tries to kill him?'

'Yes.'

'You know who this person is, don't you?'

'I have a pretty good idea.'

'It's this sex offender the police are looking for? Merv the Perv they call him, don't they?'

'Yes,' said Nick grimly. 'He went underground when the name-and-shame mob attacked the house he was living in but we know he's still in the district. Don't worry, we'll get him. Every policeman in the West Country is looking for him and we know

now that he has acquired a car.'

When he returned to the station, Nick's attention was drawn to the report of a stolen car that had come in a couple of days before.

'It was an old banger and nobody's much concerned with its recovery, but I thought it might be significant in the light of what's happened,' said Tim Court, grimacing as he slurped at a cup of cold, congealing coffee.

'You mean it could have been nicked to carry out the hit and run? Have we got a description?'

'Ford Capri. "A" reg. Blue. According to the owner – a student – in a battered state.'

'The impact will have done some damage to the front, but even if we find it, it is going to be difficult to tell old from new. We'll put out a general alert for it – it'll probably turn up abandoned somewhere. If he's got any sense he won't hang on to it.'

'Mervyn Dooley?'

'I know we shouldn't jump to conclusions but my bet is on him.'

'I can't understand why he's still hanging round the area,' said Court, pivoting his chair from side to side.

'I don't know,' said his superior. 'Look at it from his point of view. He reckons he has been recognised by Compton and Latimer, so he has to stop them fingering him. He does for Compton but Ben disappears. No one knows what has happened to him, so

Dooley waits around hoping he'll turn up and can be dealt with. When he does, Dooley immediately grabs the opportunity, nicks a car, and mows him down.'

'Injuring Rachel at the same time.'

'Yeah, he must be getting desperate.'

'How is she?'

'She's going to be alright, only superficial injuries.'

'Good. Well, we know she wasn't the target.'

'No, but he may be afraid she saw him and can identify him and the car.'

'Hell, she could still be at risk.'

'Yes. I want an immediate press release sent out.' Nick scribbled away furiously at his desk. 'This should do.' He read out what he had written:

A man and woman were struck by a hit and run driver yesterday evening in Melbury Magna. The accident happened in the fog. The man, believed to be in his late teens, sustained serious head injuries and is not expected to live. The woman received minor injuries and is recovering in hospital. She can remember no details of the accident and the police are appealing for witnesses.

'I'll see it goes straight out.'

'Get the team together. I want a briefing here in an hour's time.'

'*Is* Latimer going to make it, do you think?'

'They're doing their best for him. The next couple of days are going to be crucial but they hope he'll pull through. If we stress the seriousness of his condition in the press release it may encourage witnesses to come forward – it's a very emotive issue. The foster parents are coming back this afternoon. It's hit them hard.'

'You know what I'm thinking?'

'I'm sure you're going to tell me.'

'It's a pity the lynch mob didn't catch up with Dooley when they chased him out of Hawk Street.'

Reid Frobisher stared down at the comatose figure on the bed and a tear slipped down her face as she whispered, 'Ben. Ben, you mustn't die. *Please* come back to us.'

There was no response, only the measured clicking and soughing from the innumerable machines he seemed to be attached to. There were drips feeding into his body and drains leading out, including an horrendously large pipe protruding from his chest that she had been told was a chest drain. There was even a clip attached to one of his fingers. She reached over and picked up the other hand and caressed it gently.

'You *can't* leave me now, Ben. Not now I've just found you again.'

A nurse materialised at her side. 'Don't distress yourself, my dear, he's in with a chance.'

'He looks so – remote, so far away...'

'Are you a relative?'

'I'm his mother.'

'His mother?' The nurse looked surprised. 'So you are *Mrs* Latimer?'

'No ... no. It's too complicated to explain but I'm his birth mother.'

'I see,' said the nurse, who clearly didn't. 'Why don't you go along to the canteen and get yourself a nice cup of tea. His condition's not going to change for the time being. Have a break.'

'Perhaps I will,' said Reid, but after she left the intensive care unit she didn't go to the canteen. Instead, she made her way through the maze of corridors to the ward where Rachel was.

Rachel was dressed and sitting in a chair beside the bed, turning the pages of a magazine. She took one look at her friend's pinched, haunted face and apprehension flared through her.

'Ben? He hasn't—?'

'No, his condition is unaltered.'

'I'm sure he'll make a full recovery, Reid. He's in good hands – they're doing their best for him.'

'I know, but he's so pale and still... Suppose they say he's brain dead and want to switch off the ventilator?'

'I'm sure there's no question of that.'

Reid perched on the end of the bed and shook her head.

'I wish I had your faith. They say troubles never come singly, don't they?'

'Why? What else has happened?'

'My aunt has died – Aunt Edith. My mother rang this morning to tell me. She had another stroke, a fatal one.'

'Oh, Reid, I'm so sorry.'

'She seemed so fit and well when she was down here visiting recently, and now she's gone. I must go to the funeral but I don't want to leave Ben.'

'You can't keep vigil day and night. I know you want to be at his side, but at present he's not aware of whether you're here or not.'

'Yes, I suppose you're right. His foster parents are coming back today. I don't know how long they plan to stay around but they'll be here for a time.'

'What about Tony?'

'He's very concerned but he's tied up at the shop at the moment. Gordon is up in the Lake District attending an important book sale so Tony is on his own. Help! You must think me a selfish pig. I haven't even asked you how you are.'

'I'm feeling much better, as you can see. I

274

feel a fraud, taking up a valuable hospital bed when I'm sure I'm well enough to be discharged.'

'They know best. Have they said when you can go home?'

'No. They're concerned that I live on my own and there's no one to keep an eye on me.'

'Can't Nick move in? I'm sure he'd welcome the excuse.'

'He seems to think I should stay here a little longer. I think he's afraid of delayed concussion, and anyway, he's so tied up with his case he's not going to be around much. I just want to get back to work and put this behind me.'

'You're not thinking of going back to work yet?' Reid was scandalised.

'No, I wouldn't be of much use to them at the moment. I think I'm in need of some therapy myself.'

'Physician, heal thyself. I bet your staff would like to get to work on you.'

'They're not going to get the chance. I'm only bruised and that will heal in its own good time. If they insist on keeping me in I don't see why I shouldn't go and sit with Ben.'

'Oh, Rachel, would you? And will you pray for him? He needs all the help he can get, even if—'

'Even if you think it's all mumbo-jumbo?'

suggested Rachel helpfully.

'No, I didn't mean that. It's just that I've never really given religion much thought and it seems a cheek to suddenly turn to it when you're in trouble.'

'That's what God is for. Ben will be in many people's thoughts, certainly all Peter Stevenson's congregations will be praying for him.'

'That's a comfort and I know it means something.'

'Have you got time off school?'

'Not really. Martin is covering for me at the moment but I have to go back tomorrow; though how I shall cope with trying to stuff unwanted facts into unreceptive brains when Ben is lying there fighting for his life, I don't know.'

'It will help to keep your mind occupied. When Ben will really want you is when he comes round and is recuperating and wanting a lot of TLC.'

The glow in the sky could be seen for miles around. At first sight it was similar to the red nimbus that hovered over a city at night. But this was no conurbation, illuminated by thousands of street and domestic lights; only an isolated farmhouse sprung to prominence by the flames shafting through the ancient rafters.

By the time the police and fire brigade

arrived, more or less together, Holmewood was well alight and beyond saving. The police had been alerted to trouble by a call from an indignant householder in the nearby village reporting that an unruly mob had converged on the village a short while ago and was heading eastwards towards open countryside. As the flames spread, the crowd scattered but not before the police realised that they were dealing with another vigilante group who had latched on to Holmewood Farm as the supposed hide-away of another person outed from the Sex Offenders Register. Discarded signboards and banners proclaimed the same crude messages and the remnants of the group rounded up by the constabulary insisted they were protecting society by chasing out the evil perverts.

Superintendent Powell turned up as the fire brigade finally got the fire under control and the flames subsided, leaving smoking timbers and charred, twisted wreckage. He stood watching the activity, his hands rammed deep in his pockets, frowning as the sergeant in charge briefed him.

'Is this Bruce Downing's doing? Is he behind it?'

'Not in person. Neither he nor his close cronies appear to have been acting as incitors or, indeed, being in the crowd at all.'

'I bet he masterminded it, organised it. I

277

want him and his known associates arrested on suspicion. He won't be able to talk himself out of this one. But why, in God's name, did they target a deserted farm?'

'There's a tenant, sir. A Matthew Gorham lived here.'

'Somebody actually *lived* here – in this dump?'

'Yes, he was a recluse. No one seems to know much about him.'

'So, where is he? Did the mob harm him?'

'There's no sign of him, sir. If he had any sense he took to his heels and is out there somewhere.' The sergeant gestured towards the fields behind them.

'Well, get a party out there looking for him.' Tom Powell nudged a blackened timber with his foot, then grimaced and coughed as the smell of acrid smoke caught him in the chest.

'Where is the fire officer? I want to know exactly how this fire started. Was it deliberate or accidental?'

'There's no need to search for the owner. I think we have found him.'

The chief fire officer materialised out of the smoking ruins looking grim. The two men acknowledged each other and the fireman continued, 'We've found a body. It's burnt beyond recognition but it appears to be that of a man.'

'Let me see.'

'You can't go in there yet, it isn't safe.'

'If you've got a dead body in there this involves us very much. We need to get the team in – the pathologist, forensics, photographer—'

'I know the score, Superintendent, but no one is going in there until I give the say-so, not even our own investigators.' Tom Powell resigned himself to a delay.

'Any idea where the fire started?'

'The seat of the conflagration seems to be in the area where the body is, in the centre of the house. One would have expected it to be in one of the outhouses or the roof if one of that howling mob had tried to torch it from outside.'

There was an interruption in the form of a young constable, who came round the corner rubbing his soot-stained face.

'Sir, there should be a dog.'

'A dog?'

'Yes, sir. According to the locals, Matthew Gorham had a dog. A ferocious brute that he kept as a guard dog.'

'Didn't do him much good tonight, did it? Have you got two corpses in there – a human and a canine?' He turned back to the fireman.

'Could well have,' said the other man heavily, 'it's not a pretty sight in there.'

The call from Weymouth Division came in

just after Nick Holroyd arrived in his office early the next morning. He listened intently, asked a few questions, then went in search of his sergeant. Tim Court was sitting in front of his VDU, one hand tapping idly away at the keyboard, the other clutching a large bacon butty from which he took a bite from time to time, oblivious of the crumbs scattering over the desk.

'The Ford Capri has been found.'

'Locally?'

'No, it's turned up in Weymouth. Was involved in an accident yesterday evening.'

'So, they've got Dooley?'

'No such luck. According to the driver of the other vehicle involved, the Capri came round a corner on the wrong side of the road and was in a direct collision course with him. At the very last moment the driver of the Capri wrenched at the wheel and the car spun out of control, shot across the road and embedded itself in a brick wall. The driver jumped out unharmed and scarpered away from the scene of the accident.'

'He seems to bear a charmed life.'

'Yes. The front of the car sustained considerable damage, so you know what that means?'

'Any damage caused by an earlier incident is going to be impossible to detect?'

'Yes. The good news is, there were prints all over the inside and out and, unbelievably, they've done a match already and they're Dooley's.'

'So, we've got our proof.'

'You're jumping the gun. All we've got proof of is that Dooley stole the Capri and wrote it off. We haven't got any evidence that it was the car used to run down Ben Latimer and Rachel.'

'It must be, it's too much of a coincidence not to be. Whereabouts in Weymouth did it happen?'

'In a side road off the street leading to the port area.'

'He was m 'ing for the docks, trying to get across to the sle of Wight! What do you bet I'm right?'

Court got up in excitement and the re-mains of his breakfast fell on to the floor.

'I think you may be right. If he *is* there we've got him. It should be easy to run him to ground on an island.'

'The Isle of Wight is a big island,' said Court doubtfully. 'If he holes up there—'

'He's got to eat, find somewhere to sleep. With everyone looking for him and the ferry terminal under surveillance to make sure he doesn't slip back again we *must* be able to pick him up.'

'Any signs of Ben Latimer regaining con-sciousness?'

'No, it doesn't sound too good. I've just spoken to Smithers, who's on duty there, and he says that they tried to take him off the ventilator last night but he couldn't breathe normally so he's back on again and they're concerned about a chest infection.'

'What about Rachel?'

'She's made a brilliant recovery. There'll be no excuse for keeping her in hospital much longer.'

'Well, with Dooley out of the way, she's no longer in any danger, is she? We'll soon have this tied up.'

'I'm not so sure.' Nick drummed his fingers on the desk, looking thoughtful. 'Even if we catch up with him I'm not sure we can make out a case that the CPS will accept. Rachel can't identify him as the person who ran her down. If Ben croaks, he can't either, always supposing that he saw any more than Rachel. There's going to be no forensic evidence to tie him in with Kevin Compton's murder. It's all supposition on our part.'

'Let's catch the little bleeder first. Once he's inside, I'm sure we can wring a confession out of him.'

'I didn't hear that, sergeant.'

The investigation into the fire and death of Matthew Gorham at Holmewood Farm took on a new twist when the autopsy results were known.

'Gorham did not die as a result of the fire,' said Tom Powell at the briefing that had been hurriedly convened.

'There was no detectable carbon monoxide in his blood, which there would have been if he had breathed in smoke. In other words, he was dead before the fire started and, although the body was badly burnt, Wickham had enough to work on to establish that he had had a severe blow to the head, which undoubtedly killed him. It has also been established that the fire started in the section of the house in which the body was found – there is evidence that petrol was used as an ignitor. So, what does that tell us? Can I have some feedback.'

'One of the mob broke into the house, came face to face with Gorham. There was a fight, Gorham was killed and the fire was started to cover up his killing.'

'By his assailant, who just happened to have a can of petrol with him?'

'They've torched other places. They could have meant to drive him out and then set light to the place.'

'Are we sure the body *was* that of Matthew Gorham?' asked someone else.

'Good point, that. Dental records would be of no use, as I don't suppose he ever visited a dentist, but we got lucky. Gorham had a metal plate in his leg as a result of an accident several years ago and that survived the fire.'

'What about the yobs we arrested?'

283

'They insist that no one went inside the place. Their intention was to scare the shit out of him and make him run. They were noisy and in a nasty mood but not organised. Once the fire started that place was a fireball within minutes and it was the crowd who took to its heels.'

'*Someone* must have planned the little exercise. Who gave them Gorham's name? We know he was a bloody-minded old sod but he wasn't a pervert.'

'Word of mouth and anonymous phone calls, according to them. And, for your information, Bruce Downing spent yesterday evening in the Red Lion watching a football match on Sky TV, although I've no doubt he was behind it. What we need to do is find out who gave him the tip-off.'

'Gorham was supposed to have a lot of valuable antiques stashed away. Maybe inciting the mob to attack the place was a means of getting inside and ransacking it.'

'Then it went horribly wrong, didn't it? Whatever he had of value in there is now reduced to ashes. But I think you're right – that may have been the motive.'

'The insurance assessors are going to have a hell of a task sorting that little lot out.'

'I don't think Gorham had any truck with insurance companies. He had set himself up as a one-man security service, patrolling the place with his dog, and the locals all knew it was dangerous to meddle with him. I don't reckon we'll ever know what he had in there and whether he *was* sitting on a fortune.'

'What happened to the dog?'

'No identifiable remains have been found but they are still sifting through the debris.'

'Whoever attacked him would have had to deal with the dog first – it's a real maneater. He had a shotgun too.'

'No. We confiscated his shotgun and revoked his licence recently after his threatening behaviour to passers-by. For all his antisocial behaviour, Gorham was basically a vulnerable old man and somebody took advantage of this and clubbed him to death. We are treating his death as murder. We are going to find out who killed him and why, and the place to start is to find out who started the rumours that he was a sex pervert. I want to know just how that message was spread and how the mob was mobilised. Lean on Bruce Downing and his cronies. I'm damn sure he was behind it and I want to know who motivated *him*.'

As the meeting was splitting up news came through that Gorham's dog had been found dead on the outskirts of a neighbouring farm. It looked as if it had been poisoned and had dragged itself away from the turmoil to die. A postmortem would be carried out to ascertain exactly what it had died from but Tom Powell was in no doubt that it had been got out of the way to enable someone easy access to the building.

Nick Holroyd had been giving evidence in court in a case of larceny he had been involved in. He arrived back at the station as his fellow officers were piling out of the CID general office.

'What's going on?' he asked the duty sergeant as he passed the front desk.

'Christ, Nick! I sometimes wonder whether you work here at all. Why weren't you in on it? There's been another murder – out at Holmewood Farm at Barmelton.'

'Bloody hell, the old geezer's finally done for someone!'

'No, mate, *he's* the one who's bought it.'

Twelve

Rachel had been discharged from hospital on the strict proviso that she did not return to work for at least a week. However, she was back at Casterford General the next day visiting Ben Latimer. Nick found her there when he called in to see how the patient was progressing. She was bent over the bed talking urgently to the still figure and her eyes were closed.

'Is he coming round?' asked Nick eagerly. Rachel shook her head.

'It looked as if you were having a conversation.'

'No, I was praying. His condition has deteriorated overnight. He's developed pneumonia.'

'Is he going to die?'

'They're optimistic he'll pull through.' Rachel indicated the nurse who was marking up charts at the far end of the room. 'Staff nurse says there's always a risk of infection with lung injuries, but they're pumping massive doses of antibiotics into him.'

Nick put his arm round her shoulders and gave her a gentle squeeze.

'I didn't expect to see you here, this is a bonus. I thought you would be fed up with the hospital scene.'

'They can't get rid of me but at least they're not feeding and watering me now.' She smiled at him. ' Reid has had to go up north for her aunt's funeral and the Pendletons won't be in until this afternoon, so I've come to keep vigil. I take it you are here officially?'

'Yes, I was just hoping he might have regained consciousness and would be able to give us his version of what happened.'

Rachel looked at the comatose figure on the bed and sighed.

'That's not going to be yet. By the way, I was listening to the local radio before I came and on the news bulletin they were reporting a fatal fire at Holmewood Farm at Barmelton. That's the place Reid went to with her aunt.'

'Yes, it's a nasty business.' He told her briefly what had happened and explained the police theory as to why it had taken place.

'You mean the name-and-shame mob were deliberately incited to target Holmewood Farm to cover up something else?'

'Yes. The old chap was reputed to be sitting on a little goldmine of antiques. We think someone was after those and used the riot as a diversion. Unfortunately, this person must have come face to face with Gorham and in his panic killed him and set fire to the place to cover it up. What's the matter? You're looking very pensive.'

'There's something you should know. Reid mentioned it to me a few days ago. I didn't think much about it at the time, though I passed on the information to Peter, but now – it could be important – what a horrible thought...'

'Rachel, *what* are you talking about?'

'The missing Thomas Hardy manuscript. Tony and Gordon Barnes have been doing some research and somehow they found out that the person the letters were addressed to was an ancestor of the old boy who owned them – and he used to live at Holmewood Farm. They have this theory that the manuscript could still be there – hidden somewhere in the building.'

'You seriously think that Tony or Barnes could be behind the attack?'

'No, of course not. Don't be ridiculous!'

'So, who else knows about this?'

'Peter could have mentioned it to any number of people, I really don't know. And of course, there is always the person who stole the letters in the first place. You never cleared that up, did you?'

At that moment Nick's mobile phone

rang. The staff nurse glared at him and started to speak but he muttered an apology and hurried outside. When he returned to Rachel a short while later she could see that he had received some momentous news.

'That was my counterpart in Weymouth. A body has been found in the harbour. It is almost certainly that of Mervyn Dooley.'

'Not another murder!'

'No, it was found wedged between a groyne and a fishing vessel not far from where the ferry docks. They think he was trying to sneak on board the ferry and slipped and fell into the water.'

'Poor man. I know he murdered Kevin Compton and tried to kill Ben and me but you can't help feeling sorry for him. He was like a cornered rat.'

'We still have no proof that he was our man.'

'So, what will happen now?'

'Under the circumstances I'm sure my superintendent will want to draw a line under the whole affair. With a scapegoat who can't be brought to trial we don't have to prove our case.'

'But you're not happy about it?'

'I like to have all the ends neatly tied up, but perhaps it is for the best. It will save Ben having to give evidence – if he recovers – and dredging up the past, which can be a nasty process in cases of childhood abuse. I suppose you can say that Dooley has paid the price with his life; he would still be alive if he hadn't tried to flee justice.'

As Nick predicted, Tom Powell was adamant that the case of Kevin Compton's murder had been solved and the enquiry brought to a satisfactory conclusion.

'We would have had a hell of a job getting a conviction or even mounting a viable prosecution, so his death is very opportune. Justice has been done,' declaimed Powell, looking at Nick over his glasses. 'And now this one's been cleared up I want you back on the other case: the name-and-shame mob violence out at Holmewood Farm. Matthew Gorham's death was no accident, so you have another murder enquiry on your hands. The antiques he stored on the premises were probably the motive for the attack. That angle needs looking into.'

This was the point at which Nick should have divulged the information that Rachel had passed on to him about the Thomas Hardy manuscript, but he decided to keep it to himself for the time being and carry out some enquiries before it became public knowledge. Instead, he asked, 'Do we know who tipped off the vigilantes?'

'Bruce Downing has admitted that he received an anonymous letter – which he has conveniently burnt – naming Gorham as a known paedophile. "Because I'm on bail and can't do nothing, I didn't do nothing" – quote, unquote – but he passed the message on to others in his mob; probably arranged the attack from his armchair.' Powell snorted in disgust. 'It's all yours, Nick, and I want it cleared up quickly. This sort of outrage rebounds badly on us. We need to be seen to be doing something. The press are already hinting that the situation is out of control and we're under mob rule – as if the Mafia had moved business to Dorset!'

Nick had hardly got back to his office before another call came through on his mobile. It was Tony Pomfret sounding very agitated.

'How did you get this number?' demanded Nick but Tony ignored the question.

'I've just seen the local rag – the front page is all about this fire at Holmewood Farm. Is the place really destroyed?'

'To all intents and purposes, yes.'

'Oh, this is terrible – was nothing saved?'

'A few charred timbers and burnt-out debris. What had you in mind?'

'The Hardy manuscript. We think it may have been hidden somewhere in the building.'

'Well, it will be dust and ashes now.'

'It would have been priceless! This is a tragedy!'

'It was a tragedy for Matthew Gorham too.'

'Oh, God, yes! The old savage got caught in the fire also.'

'The "old savage" was murdered and the fire started to cover up his death by someone who was looking for something.'

There was a stunned silence at the other end and then Tony's voice sounding very subdued asked, 'What are you saying?'

'Just where were you last night, Tony?'

'Oh Christ! You're so banal! I don't believe this!' And Tony cut the connection.

'I really don't see why you can't come and stay at our place,' said Reid, as she drove herself and her mother back to Casterford. 'It's ridiculous you going to a hotel.'

'I'm not staying with you and your paramour.'

'Christ, mother! Whatever sort of literature do you read!'

Reid struck the steering wheel in frustration and the car swerved slightly, causing the driver behind to hoot angrily.

'Do watch what you're doing, you'll cause an accident!' Helen Frobisher clutched the dashboard in front of her and Reid, spying a lay-by up ahead, signalled, pulled the car over and drew to a standstill.

'Mother, let's get this quite clear. Tony and I are partners, equal partners. I am not his mistress, or his floozie, or his bit on the side—'

'There is no need to be vulgar, Reid.'

'—and I have no intention of signing a marriage contract just to please you. We live together and we are committed to each other and that is the way it is done these days.'

'There is no security, he could walk out and leave you.'

'Which I'm sure would suit you fine.'

'I only want your happiness.' Helen Frobisher veered off on to a tack she had used many times before.

'I am perfectly fine, an independent woman who can look after herself. If it doesn't work out, we'll part company with no recriminations on either side.'

'It's not natural, marriage is for life.'

'A life sentence, you mean. Your marriage wasn't exactly made in heaven, was it? My most vivid memory of my childhood is of hearing you two arguing, day in, day out, until he upped and left.'

'Your father was—'

'Oh, don't start on dad again,' interrupted Reid. 'I've heard it all before, so many times. What I want to know is, if you are so opposed to my lifestyle, why are you coming to Casterford?'

'I want to see this boy.'

'Your *grandson*, mother, whether you like it or not, and the only one you're likely to have!'

'Don't shout, Reid, I'm not deaf.'

'You made me give him up. I've never forgiven you for that.'

'It was for the best, you must see that. You've got a university degree and a good job.'

'I'm only an ordinary teacher in an average comprehensive, not an Oxford don or a university professor.'

'You've got a career and he had the start in life that you couldn't give him.'

'That's where you're wrong. He had a hellish childhood and now ... now that I've found him again it's probably too late...'

Tears glittered in Reid's eyes and she fumbled for a tissue. Helen Frobisher opened her handbag and produced a spotless lace-edged handkerchief, which she passed to her daughter. Reid blew her nose violently, thinking how typical it was that her mother still used real handkerchiefs whereas a box of tissues sufficed for most people.

'Is he going to die?'

'I don't know. It's in the hands of God, mother; the deity you go to church to pray to each Sunday.'

'There's no need to be blasphemous.'

'I'm sorry, if prayers will save him, please pray hard. My friend Rachel is also pulling out all the stops.'

'Rachel?'

'You've met her, mother. Rachel Morland

– she's a committed church woman and utterly convincing. It's real to her – all this religious thing – she doesn't just pay it lip service.'

'Are you suggesting—?'

'Give it a break, I'm too upset to start arguing the finer points of religion.'

'It was you who brought it up. But I can see you're overwrought and it's understandable, what with Edith's death and now this. Are we going straight to the hospital?'

'No. I'll drop you off at the hotel first and you can book in and tidy up and I'll pick you up a little later. I've got to do some shopping.'

'Will Tony be with you?'

'No, mother, he's no more anxious to see you than you are to see him.'

'I only asked.'

'Sorry, I didn't mean to snap. We'd better get going, it's not far now.'

Reid started up the car and pulled out into the traffic, which was building up into the rush hour. Three-quarters of an hour later she drew up outside the hotel her mother had chosen. She deposited her mother at the reception desk, carried in her case and got back in the car. As she drove off she pondered her relationship with her mother. She loved her – didn't she? But they only had to be together a very short while to get at cross purposes with each other. Tony's attitude didn't help, of course, and what about Ben? What would he think of the grandmother he'd never met when, and if, he recovered?

Nick Holroyd stood in the still-smouldering ruins of Holmewood Farm and felt a horrid sense of déjà vu. Just so had he stood in the fire-blackened house in Hawk Street where Mervyn Dooley had lived, not so long ago. There was black slime underfoot and the same stink, acrid and choking, that caught in his throat – and beneath it a whiff of something else; something that reminded him horribly of roasting meat. He told himself not to be so morbid and fanciful and went to talk to the two firemen who were still on duty, keeping a watchful eye on the smoking ruins.

'Has anything at all survived? He was supposed to have had a large collection of antiques.'

The firemen led him round to what had been the east wing of the building. There, beside the buckled wall that had formed an alcove near the chimney breast, were some twisted shapes that turned out, on closer inspection, to be the remains of pictures. The glass had shattered and melted, the frames were black and distorted, and whatever paintings they had held were charred beyond recognition.

'They could be Old Masters, we'll never

know,' said one of the firemen. 'The only other things that weren't completely consumed were over in the old stables across the yard. That was the last place the fire reached, and we managed to douse it before it was completely razed. There's the remains of some old carriages – a dog cart, a landau or some such vehicle, and some carriage lamps and old harness. Do you want to see it?'

Nick declined. He had learnt enough to know that the rumours about Matthew Gorham's antiques had been correct. But whether they were the reason for the attack or whether someone had been after a specific valuable manuscript was another matter. He would set up a house-to-house in the village in the hope that someone might have seen someone suspicious hanging around the farm. In the meanwhile, the pub would be the best place to start, and with any luck he'd get a meal as well as information.

'We're not open yet, luv, another ten minutes to go.' The landlady of the Fox was polishing the bar counter when he pushed open the door and walked in. She was everyone's idea of the archetypal barmaid from the dyed-blonde hair to the blowsy figure squeezed into a clinging black top that left nothing to the imagination.

'Police.' Nick showed her his warrant card and she eyed him speculatively.

'You've come about that business at Holmewood Farm. Shocking it is. He were a right old sod but nobody deserves to be burnt alive in their own home.'

'Have you noticed any strangers hanging around in recent weeks?'

'Do me a favour, officer, we're on the tourist trail. We get visitors coming in all the time. Even the family room out there,' she nodded to the large conservatory tacked on to the back of the building, 'has wall to wall children at the weekends. Not that you'd be interested in them.'

'Did you see the mob moving in? Did they come this way?'

'Heard them. It sounded like an advancing army. We didn't know whether to call in extra staff or board the place up, but in the end they gave us a miss, took the other road through the village.'

'So you had no contact with any of them?'

'Tell you what, I reckon there were some locals there.' She leaned across the counter, displaying a vast area of cleavage, and winked a mascara-laden eye. 'Later on that evening we had a full house and there was an awful pong of smoke hanging around the place. You know how it clings and makes hair and clothing reek.'

'Anyone in particular you could name?'

'Oh, I couldn't be naming names. I don't think they were involved – just went along afterwards to have a shufti.'

Realising he was going to get nowhere with his questioning, he asked if they did lunches.

'It's our chef's day off but I can do you a nice ploughman's.'

He agreed to a stilton and pickles ploughman's and asked for a half of cider. With a very pointed look at the clock she pulled it for him and he took it over to a table near the window and awaited the arrival of his food. Almost immediately the landlady reappeared from the kitchen area.

'It won't be long but I've just remembered something Dennis said. There was someone in here asking about Holmewood Farm last week. Wanted to buy it, believe it or not.'

'Who is Dennis?'

'My husband. It would be just over a week ago, the day I go and see my mother. He takes over front of house then.'

'Then I'll speak to Dennis.'

'Right, I'll call him. He's down the bottom of the garden.'

A short while later she came back accompanied by her husband, who was in shirt sleeves and was drying his hands on a towel. He looked many years older than his wife but probably wasn't, reckoned Nick. She was fighting the ageing process with every artifice she could lay her hands on, whilst he had settled into comfortable middle age.

'This is Dennis. Tell him about that man

300

you told me about. The one you thought was a poof.'

'Alright, Myra, you go and get the Inspector's food.'

She exited reluctantly and Nick prompted the man, who seemed in no hurry to start talking.

'Someone was interested in Holmewood Farm?'

'That's right. He said he wanted to buy a property in the area and was particularly interested in that place. Sounded as if he had had a nose around, because he mentioned the dog. I soon put him right, told him the place should have been condemned years ago and that nobody would get old Gorham out.'

'Can you describe him?'

'Very flamboyant type with a plummy voice. Lots of dark-red hair, swept back as if he'd just come from the hairdresser's. And he was wearing *red velvet trousers*.' The landlord sounded outraged. 'Can't imagine anyone like that wanting to settle in the heart of the countryside. I'll tell you something else. He were driving a big old Volvo estate – not the sort of car you'd expect someone like him to drive at all, if you see what I mean.'

At this point the landlady brought his order over to the table. She fussed about with cutlery and serviettes and asked the question her husband had omitted to ask.

'Do you think this man had something to do with the attack on Holmewood Farm?'

'I doubt it, but he will be checked out,' replied Nick smoothly, attacking his cheese and granary bread.

'Is there anything else you want?' she asked, hovering hopefully.

'No, this is fine, thank you. Whilst I'm eating, perhaps you could write out a list of the names and addresses of all the villagers who frequent this pub.'

As he drove back to Casterford later he mulled over what the landlord had told him. There was no doubting the identification of the mysterious man; it was as good a description of Tony Pomfret as anyone could give. Things were beginning to look very bad for Reid's partner, but surely the man wouldn't have been so careless about covering his tracks if he had intended raiding Holmewood Farm in search of this mythical manuscript? But then, it hadn't been meant to end like that, had it? The death of Gorham and the fire had happened as a result of the planned incident going hideously wrong.

Pomfret had a lot of explaining to do and Nick couldn't wait to start questioning him, not least because he was looking forward to witnessing Pomfret's reaction on being told that he had been labelled 'one of those'.

★　★　★

Peter Stevenson held a midweek communion service at St James's at ten thirty every Wednesday morning. Normally Rachel was unable to attend because of her work commitments but, as she was still on sick leave, she took part in the service that week. She was surprised at how well attended it was. It was true that most of the congregation were women, members of the Mother's Union and other church groups – tell me something new, she thought – but there were also several retired couples and at least two visitors. Peter had recently come back from a synod meeting in London and, after the service was over and they were in the vestry, he brought her up to date with the proceedings.

'I didn't expect to see you out there in the congregation,' he said, stripping off his cassock to reveal a decidedly grubby sweatshirt bearing the legend, 'Save the Whales and Vote for Jesus'. 'Shouldn't you still be resting?'

'I'm fine, I feel a right old fraud.'

'Well, I'm glad to see you in more ways than one. I had a rather disturbing phone call yesterday evening that I think Nick ought to hear about. See what you think.'

Peter perched on the edge of the table that was used for signing the marriage register and Rachel moved a pile of hymn books off a chair and sat down.

'I met up with an old friend at the synod. Name of David Ransom. He's vicar at St Bede's in Scarborough. We were at ecclesiastical college together, although he is several years older than me. He trained as a mature ordinand after a brief career in engineering. Anyway, we got talking about the churches and parishes we were looking after now, and discussing the various problems they throw up, and I happened to mention the troubles we were having locally with the group of vigilantes.'

Peter paused and plucked at his earring, and Rachel wondered what was coming next.

'David said that he had read something about it in the papers,' he continued, 'and agreed that it was a delicate situation and needed careful handling. Nothing more was said about it and the talk moved on to other topics. We all went our separate ways at the end of the convocation and I didn't expect to hear from David again until the usual Christmas card arrived, but he phoned me last night.'

Peter got up and mooched round the vestry, running his hands over the bunched-up choir vestments hanging along one wall.

'About eight years ago he was vicar in Welby in Yorkshire and one of his parishioners was a man who was involved with the church youth club. This man also helped out at the local Children's Home – a place called St Kilda's.'

Rachel looked up, startled.

'But that's the name of the home that Ben and Kevin Compton lived in, and that was in Yorkshire. It must be the same place. So what about this man?'

She was all attention, knowing and dreading what she was about to be told.

'He was a devout churchgoer but he seemed to David to be very troubled, on the verge of a breakdown. Eventually he confided in David and confessed. He'd become involved in this paedophile ring in the home. The children, all boys, were being abused by some of the very people supposed to be caring for them. David was horrified, but the man told him the home was closing down, and David assumed the culprits were being dealt with and that this man's involvement had been overlooked. He was full of remorse and convinced David that he would never offend in that way again. He also swore that he had never touched any of the children in the church youth club, and David believed him – otherwise he would have reported him to the police. As it was, he felt genuinely sorry for the man, who insisted that he was a reformed character, and who said he was leaving the area and starting a new life elsewhere. He said he intended moving to the West Country, where he had enjoyed holidays as a child. So, having given a solemn promise that nothing like that would ever happen again, he left the district. But David has always had it on his conscience – wondered if he had done the right thing by turning a blind eye. After our talk at the synod meeting he decided he ought to speak out.'

'Did he tell you the name of the man?'

'Yes, but I'm afraid I've forgotten it,' confessed Peter.

'Was it Mervyn Dooley?'

'No, but he would probably have changed his name, wouldn't he?'

'He was certainly connected with St Kilda's. The police have established that. It must be the same person, it's too much of a coincidence to be otherwise. Mervyn Dooley already had a couple of convictions for child molestation.'

'David certainly never knew that or he would never have kept silent. Are the police any nearer to catching this man?'

'Peter, don't you ever read the papers or listen to the news?'

Rachel told him what had been reported in the media about Mervyn Dooley's untimely end.

'Nick will certainly be interested in hearing about this, it may tidy up some loose ends for him. Can you come and explain it all to him as you've just told me?'

'Sure. I never thought I was going to be part of a police investigation when I took on this parish. By the way, did he have any luck with tracing those stolen letters?'

'There's been a development there too,' she said, deciding that she would leave it to Nick to explain as much or as little as he wanted about the disaster at Holmewood Farm.

'Bring him in. We'll do this by the book.'

Nick was briefing Tim Court about his visit to the Fox and the information he had gleaned relating to Tony Pomfret.

'You're arresting him? You reckon we've got enough on him for an arrest?'

'No, he'll be helping us with our enquiries, but you can put the fear of God into him. He should be in his bookshop at this time of day, but send someone else for him – Fenton? He seems to be kicking his heels out there – I want *you* to conduct the interview.'

'You aren't doing it yourself?'

'There's nothing I'd like better,' said Nick feelingly, 'but on reflection it wouldn't be appropriate.'

'He's a friend of yours?'

'He's no friend of mine but, as he's the partner of Rachel's friend Reid Frobisher, we've met socially, God help me.'

'He seems to be popping up all over the place. He was connected with Compton through *West Side Story*, Ben Latimer is Reid Frobisher's son, and now you reckon he's involved with Matthew Gorham's death.'

'Yes, he'll have a job of it talking himself out of this one, but he's a smooth-tongued bastard, so don't let him tie you in knots.'

It was a couple of hours later that the matter of Tony Pomfret was again brought to Nick's attention. He had been liaising with the fire officer and checking the reports coming in from the team carrying out the house-to-house enquiries at Barmelton, and had just returned to his office when Court collared him.

'He's determined to speak with you. Refuses to say anything else without you being there,' said Court in exasperation.

'Have you got anywhere at all?'

'He insists that he had nothing to do with what happened at Holmewood Farm; says he was at home with his partner all evening.'

'Well, that can be easily checked. Has he asked for a solicitor?'

'Says he's got nothing to hide and he's not having one of life's parasites getting rich on his behalf,' quoted Court deadpan.

'I must remember that one. Right, I'll just check this alibi and I'll be with you shortly.'

A phone call to Casterford High School caught Reid Frobisher just as she left her last class of the morning.

'It's Nick Holroyd here, Reid. Can you

remember what you were doing last Thursday evening?'

'Last Thursday? I was up at the hospital with Ben. Why?'

'You're sure about that?'

'Of course I am, I've spent most of my time up there recently. What is this?'

'Was Tony with you?'

'No, he was at rehearsal.'

'All evening?'

'I presume so. I was at the hospital until about eight thirty and when I got home he was still out. Nick, are you checking *alibis*?'

'Yes.'

There was a pause at the other end of the line and then Reid's voice sounding very subdued asked, 'Tony's or mine?'

'Tony's.'

'Did he say he was with me?'

'Yes.'

'Oh, God! What's he supposed to have done? Is he in some trouble?'

'I can't talk now, Reid. I'll be in touch.'

'Where is he?'

'He's here at the station.'

'You've *arrested* him?'

'He's not under arrest yet. He's trying to explain what his connection is with the business at Holmewood Farm.'

Nick grimaced as he put the phone down on Reid's expostulations and went to tackle her lover. When he entered the interview room, Tony lurched to his feet and flung out his arms in a theatrical gesture.

'Thank God you're here, old chap. There's been a ghastly mistake! Please sort it out with your minions.'

'There's no mistake, you're here on my orders,' said Nick, whilst Court recorded his presence and the time on the tape recorder.

'Turn that bloody thing off! Go on,' said Pomfret, glaring at the machine. 'You said this was unofficial, so turn it off.'

Nick nodded and Court flicked the switch.

'And send them away. There's no need for all this show, you're trying to intimidate me. Why can't we just have a man to man, I'm quite happy with that.'

'I'm afraid it's not a case of what you're happy with. You've got some serious explaining to do.'

Nick dismissed the young constable sitting by the door and turned back to Pomfret.

'My sergeant stays. I'm sure he's told you why you're here.'

'He's accused me of killing the old geezer at Holmewood Farm and setting light to the place. Oh, and instigating the riot in the first place,' added Pomfret sarcastically.

'Did you accuse him, Sergeant?'

'I suggested that circumstantial evidence pointed to him being in bad trouble.'

'This is preposterous!'

'Look at it from my point of view,' said

Nick, leaning across the table. 'I find out that you have been making enquiries about Holmewood Farm, pumping the locals about the owner and how to access the place. Then, less than a week later, the place goes up in flames and Matthew Gorham is found dead, killed probably in panic by someone who was searching for something. Now, you've made no secret of the fact that you're desperate to get your hands on this so-called valuable manuscript, which may or may not exist, and which you thought you had traced to Holmewood Farm – so, in my position, what would you think?'

'I can prove I wasn't there that evening.'

'Can you?'

'Yes. Ask Reid. She'll tell you that I spent the whole evening with her at home.'

'Now, isn't that strange? I've just spoken with Reid and she assures me that she was at the hospital and you were at a rehearsal.'

Tony checked and started to bluster.

'Well, I must have made a mistake on the date. I'm a busy man, I can't be expected to remember every little detail of my life.'

'So, you're now saying that you were at a rehearsal? That should be easy to check.'

'Not a full rehearsal. I'm still busy with *West Side Story* and I have these coaching sessions.'

'Coaching?' queried Nick, thinking that he sounded like Lady Bracknell.

'If you must know, I spent the evening with our female lead. The young woman who plays Maria. We were going over her interpretation of the part. And you needn't look like that, I didn't get my leg over!'

Not for want of trying, I bet, thought Nick. 'What time was this?'

'I went to her flat about seven thirty.'

'And how long did this session last?'

'About a couple of hours.'

'That only takes us up to nine thirty. The mob violence and fire happened later than that.'

'I went to the nearby pub for a drink afterwards. What is it's name? The Owl and Firkin I think.'

'Did you see anyone there who would remember you?'

'I didn't meet any friends, if that's what you mean. The place was crowded but someone must have noticed me.'

'Yes, you stand out in a crowd, don't you? The landlord at Barmelton Fox thought you were a poofter.'

Tony's eyes glittered angrily.

'That's not politically correct, *Inspector*.'

'No, it isn't, is it?' said Nick cheerfully. 'What a good thing this is not being recorded.' He leaned back and put his hands behind his head. 'Well, you'd better be on your way.'

'You mean I can go?' Tony was startled.

'Why Tony, you sound as if you want to sample Her Majesty's hospitality.'

'You believe me? I'm not still under suspicion?'

'You still figure largely on our list of suspects, but that will be all for now. We shall want to speak with you again, so don't fly the country, will you?'

After he had gone, Court rubbed his chin thoughtfully and tackled his boss.

'You're not letting him off the hook, are you?'

'No, but we've got no proof, and, to quote an old cliché, if we give him enough rope he may hang himself.'

Thirteen

No sooner had Nick Holroyd got rid of Tony Pomfret than the desk sergeant rang through to say that he had two people in reception asking to see him. To his astonishment it was Rachel and the Reverend Stevenson.

'Peter has something to tell you,' said Rachel. 'He's acquired some information which I think you may find very important, so we've come to give it to you. Is that alright?'

'Any excuse to see you brightens my day, and if it has any bearing on my case that is a bonus. Come up to my office.'

He took them up and arranged for coffee to be brought. Peter looked about him with interest and said sheepishly, 'I've never been further than the enquiry desk before. I don't know what my parishioners will think if any of them have seen me disappearing into the bowels of the police station accompanied by a police officer.'

'I don't know whose reputation will suffer most,' said Nick with a grin, 'yours, or mine for entertaining a man of the cloth in my office – not to mention my fiancée.'

'It's business, not pleasure, Nick,' said Rachel, wondering when she was ever going to see him off duty and just where their relationship was going; a thought that had been exercising her greatly in the last few days, since she had time on her hands to worry about the future. Nothing had been said recently about the search for his ex-wife and her son, and Rachel was determined not to bring it up unless he mentioned it himself. He was engrossed in his current case and looked harassed and tired. Would it always be like this, she mused, as he poured out the coffee and handed it round, and could she cope with it long term? Or was she being negative because she was also very much involved in this investigation and was still feeling under par? She sipped her coffee and listened whilst Peter Stevenson relayed to Nick the facts he had told her earlier. Nick heard him out without interruption and, when he had finished, assured him that he had done the right thing in bringing it to his attention.

'Rachel says this man – Mervyn Dooley – is now dead,' said Stevenson, 'so how will this information help?'

'It fills in another part of the jigsaw. We have a case where we are 99 per cent sure of what happened but we have no proof. What you've told me bolsters up our findings.'

Nick took down the name and address and details of the vicar from Scarborough and shook hands with Stevenson when he got up to go. Rachel also scrambled to her feet, and her fiancé hesitated and glanced at his watch.

'It's alright, Nick, Peter is taking me back home. We have some church business to discuss.'

'Fine, well, I'll give you a ring later,' he said, unable to keep the relief out of his voice and she went off feeling even more alienated and vexed.

When they had gone, Nick went in search of his sergeant.

'How do you fancy a trip to Scarborough?'

Tim Court put down the Mars bar he was chewing and raised an eyebrow.

'It's the wrong time of year for the seaside, but anything is better than this dump. What gives?'

Nick told him and Court whistled.

'So we can actually put Dooley at St Kilda's at the time Compton and Latimer were there. What do you want me to do?'

'We could bring this Reverend Ransom down here to identify Dooley's body, but I think that is jumping the gun. Go and see him and show him a mug shot of Dooley. See if he can give a positive identification from that and we'll take it from there.'

'You could always fax it through to the Yorkshire force.'

'No, I want you there to shake all the information you can from him – and you can also take photos of Compton and Latimer and see if they mean anything to him.'

'If he had spoken out at the time, Compton would still be alive.'

'I know, but be tactful. We need him on our side and according to the Reverend Stevenson he has a bad conscience about the whole thing.'

'Well, that won't improve when he learns what his turning a blind eye has led to. These do-gooders...' Court sighed and heaved himself to his feet. 'When do you want me to go?'

'Might as well get it done with. I'll clear it for tomorrow. In the meantime, chase up this woman Tony Pomfret says he was with on the night of the fire and see if you can find anyone who saw him later that evening.'

When Reid Frobisher and her mother arrived at the hospital, Dr Mukerji was talking to the nurse on duty in intensive care. When he saw them, he broke off his conversation and came towards them and Reid felt her heart plummeting.

'Is he—?'

'Don't look so worried, he's progressing well. The antibiotics have taken effect and the chest infection is under control. If he maintains this improvement, we'll try the ventilator in manual mode again.'

As Reid looked puzzled, the consultant continued, 'The machine is breathing for him now, but I hope he'll soon be able to function without it. When he starts respiring normally, the ventilator will shut off but will kick in again when he lapses. Then we'll encourage him to come round and he can be moved to a room on his own.'

Dr Mukerji went back to his conversation with the nurse and Reid led her mother to Ben's bedside. Was it relief at what she had just been told colouring her perspective, or did he look more *alive*? Was there a slight warmth in his still, pale face? Did his skin look more *real* and not so much like carved marble, or was she imagining it and

317

clutching at the proverbial straws?

'You can't tell who he looks like,' said Mrs Frobisher, a strange catch in her voice, as she looked at the figure on the bed. What hair hadn't been shaved off was covered by the bandages that swathed Ben's head and he could have been a sarcophagus on a tomb.

'He has my colouring. It's no good denying he's my son.'

'I never thought things would turn out like this.' Helen Frobisher dabbed at her eyes. 'If he recovers will he be *alright*?'

'What do you mean, *alright*?'

'I mean, will his *brain* be damaged?'

'That would be a skeleton in the cupboard, wouldn't it? An illegitimate grandson who is deranged!'

'Reid, don't be so bitter and don't pick on everything I say and twist it.'

'I'm sorry, mother, I reckon I'm a little unbalanced myself at the moment.'

'It's understandable.' Her mother put a hand on her arm and Reid felt strangely comforted. 'We must be positive. That doctor sounded hopeful, didn't he?'

'Yes, he did. He seemed to think he is on the mend.'

They stayed by Ben's bedside for an hour and then Reid drove her mother back to the hotel, first calling in at Casterford High to pick up some papers. She left her mother

318

sitting in the car and hurried into the building. When she returned a few minutes later her mother was peering through the windscreen and looking agitated. Oh, Christ, what was bugging her now? thought Reid as she walked back to the car. Had she seen a pupil smoking or behaving in a manner she considered unsuitable?

'Reid, that man over there...'

'What man?'

She followed her mother's gaze, which was locked on a figure letting himself into his car over on the other side of the staff car park.

'That's Martin Boyd, my immediate boss. He's head of the English department.'

'But he's the man who visited Edith the week before she died,' hissed Mrs Frobisher.

'What are you talking about?'

'I went round to visit Edith the weekend before she had her fatal stroke. She seemed very well, no hint that she was going to be snatched from us so soon. That man was just leaving her cottage as I arrived. We nearly collided on the garden path. Edith told me later that he was an historian and genealogist, and was doing research into some Dorset villages and their inhabitants. Apparently he had traced Edith as being related to one of the families he was investigating, and was hoping she could give him some more information about them.'

'You must be mistaken.'

319

'No, I'm not. I'm sure that is the same man.'

At that moment Boyd started up his car and drove past them.

'Yes, that is definitely him.'

'But ... what family was he interested in?'

'Something to do with those cousins she used to stay with as a child.'

'The ones at Holmewood Farm? In Barmelton?'

'Yes, I think that was the name Edith mentioned,' said her mother in surprise. 'So you *do* know about it?'

'Not in the way you mean,' she replied grimly.

She was silent on the journey back to the hotel, pretending to concentrate on her driving, but her thoughts were racing. She believed her mother, who had excellent eyesight and a good memory, and horrible suspicions were beginning to form in her mind. What *was* going on? Tony had spent the morning at the police station and, although he had insisted to her over the phone that it had all been a big mistake and the force had got its knickers in a twist over nothing, she knew he was badly shaken, and now it looked as if he had involved Martin in his scheming. She wished Rachel had never told her about the Thomas Hardy letters; wished she had never shown them to Tony, and wished most of all that the idea of searching for the missing manuscript had never been mooted. Sick with suspicion and dread she left her mother at the hotel and drove home to confront Tony.

As she had known he would be, Tony was already at home. It was early closing day at the bookshop and his car was in the driveway. She squeezed in behind it, grabbed her handbag and briefcase off the back seat and marched into the house. He was sprawled in an armchair in the sitting room, idly flicking through television channels, and he jumped to his feet when she burst through the door.

'Dear heart, am I pleased to see you! What a day I've had. Do you know that bloody Nick Holroyd had me in a cell giving me the third degree? Can you believe it?'

'Yes, I can,' she said in a quiet, cold voice, and he looked at her, mystified.

'Just what have you been up to? Did you kill that poor old man and start that fire?'

'I don't believe I'm hearing this! If my other half doesn't believe me, what hope have I got?'

'*Did* you, Tony?'

'Of course I fucking didn't! And you've changed your tune – "poor old man"! You didn't call him that when he chased *you* off the premises. I reckon he deserved all he got! No, I shouldn't have said that, but how can you believe that I could do something like that?'

'How do I know what to believe? You were poking around the place just before it happened and now I've learnt that you got Martin doing your dirty work for you, too.'

'What the hell are you talking about?'

'Persuading him to go and pump Aunt Edith with some cock and bull story about family history research because you knew if you went she'd recognise you and—'

'Wait a minute, you've lost me. Martin Boyd we're talking about? You're saying I sent him up to see your Aunt Edith? You must be out of your mind! Why should I do that?'

'You're a man possessed about this Hardy manuscript. You'd do anything to get your hands on it—'

'Including murder and arson? Thanks for the vote of confidence! At least I now know what you really think of me! If that bloody manuscript ever existed and *was* at Holmewood Farm it's now destroyed. Burnt to ashes, incinerated, kaput! Neither you nor I, nor the Holy Church are going to get rich on it!'

'I'm sorry, Tony, I just thought it was some conspiracy between you. I mean, what *was* I to think?'

'Hang on, just what has Boyd been up to?'

Reid told him what her mother had told her and Tony exploded again.

'Have you told the police?'

'The police?'

'Holy Jesus, Reid! I'm practically under arrest for this crime and now it looks as if your precious colleague is in the frame!'

'Martin? Surely not...'

'Well, it all seems very fishy, don't you agree? The police need to know about this.'

'Let me speak to him first.'

'I'll speak to him now. What's his telephone number?'

Reid told him and Tony punched out the numbers and glared into space as the phone rang the other end. It was answered eventually by Fiona Boyd. After a short exchange Tony put the phone down in disgust.

'He's out. That was his wife.'

'I'll speak to him in the morning before classes start. Don't do anything until I have, *please*, Tony.'

'I believe you'd rather have me under suspicion than him. He'd better have a very good explanation, and Nick should be told anyway.'

Reid caught up with Martin Boyd the next morning as he pushed his way through the doors leading to the sixth-form rooms.

'Martin, I must speak with you.'

'What, now?'

'Yes, it's important.'

Martin consulted his watch.

'You'd better come through to the office. Is

something wrong?'

'You could say.'

'Not Ben?'

'No, he's improving all the while. This is something personal.'

'Well, I hope it won't take long. The hoards will be descending in a little while.'

Reid followed him up the stairs into the little cubbyhole that served as an office and he dumped his gear on the desk and turned to face her. She thought he looked dreadful, pale and drawn.

'Are you alright?'

'Bad night. Now, what is all this about? Is the workload getting too much for you?'

'This is not about me, it's about you, your actions...'

He frowned. 'What *do* you mean?'

She was suddenly bereft of words. How did you accuse your colleague and boss, your *friend*, for heaven's sake, of murder and arson? It was unthinkable. But so was the alternative. She believed Tony, didn't she? So that left Martin, and she *must* tackle him about it.

'Just what did you think you were doing chasing after my Aunt Edith in Pickering?'

He looked stunned. 'You've got it all wrong—'

'No, I haven't. Don't bother to deny it, my mother recognised you. She's staying down here.'

'Alright, I *did* go and see her. I was up in that area for the weekend and I suddenly thought it might be a good idea to go and talk to her, see if she could come up with any more information that would help us in our search.'

'Without telling me? Or Tony? And how did you get her address anyway?'

'Tony and Gordon have been hard at work with their research. I thought this was a chance for me to do my share...' he said lamely.

'Which you never mentioned.'

'I knew she'd died soon after my visit and I didn't want to upset you.'

'Are you sure you didn't upset Edith? That you didn't bring on the stroke that killed her?'

'You're surely not accusing me of being responsible for her death?'

'Not *her* death, Martin, but what about Matthew Gorham? Did you kill him and start the fire at Holmewood Farm?'

'You can't believe that! This is ridiculous!'

'Did you know that Tony was down at the police station most of yesterday afternoon being questioned? That they've all but accused him of it? Now I discover that whatever's gone on, you're up to your neck in it.'

'I see. To save Tony you'd drop me in it.'

'I'm not going to stand by and see Tony charged when you appear to have just as much to answer for. *Did* you go to Holme-wood Farm?'

'Yes, but only to have a general look around. I didn't set foot in the place. I drew the same conclusion as Tony, it was a no no.'

'You must tell all this to the police.'

'But—'

'If you don't, I shall.'

'Alright, I admit it does look bad and I have some explaining to do.'

'Do it now, give them a ring.'

'Have a heart, Reid, let me put it right with Fiona first. Can you imagine what she'd say if the police turned up on our doorstep and she didn't know what it was all about?'

Reid could imagine all too well. She hesitated.

'Well—'

'I'll tell her this evening, explain just what happened, so she's prepared; then I'll make a statement to the police in the morning.'

'Okay, if you promise to do it tomorrow, but it's a horrible thing to have hanging over us. Somebody killed Matthew Gorham and burned down his home, so if it wasn't you or Tony the police need to eliminate you from their enquiries and get on with finding the real culprit.'

Tim Court did not go to Scarborough as planned that morning. Instead, he was involved in following up a breakthrough that

326

came from an unexpected quarter. A motorist, stopped for a minor traffic offence, was found to have the back of his van loaded with stolen goods. He was arrested and a search warrant issued for his premises led to the discovery of a large cache of hot items in his lock-up garage.

'Sheer chance, and all due to the sharp eyes of a constable on the beat,' said Nick Holroyd, reporting to Tom Powell later that day. 'The cigarettes and booze definitely came from the Patel's shop, which was raided on the occasion when the mob went after Dooley. There are numerous electrical goods: televisions, videos, microwaves, computer equipment etc., some of which have already been identified by householders who were done over at the same time.'

'This Dave Hilton who you've picked up for the job – we know him, don't we?'

'Yes, he's got form and we've been pretty certain he was still up to his old tricks but couldn't pin anything on him.'

'So, what came first, the chicken or the egg? Did he take advantage of the name-and-shame activities to move in, or did he instigate the riots and use them as cover?'

'The latter. He's come clean about it.'

'So, how did he get hold of the names on the Sex Offenders Register?'

'He has a niece who works for the probation service.'

'Not much longer she won't,' said Powell grimly.

'No, quite. He planned it all like a military operation. Got in with the right-wing element in the neighbourhood watch, stirred things up and goaded them into taking action, and then wrote letters to the ringleader – our Bruce Downing – giving names and addresses. It worked like a dream. Whilst the mob were rampaging down one part of the street, Hilton and his pals were working a heist at the other end under cover of the general mayhem going on.'

'What about Holmewood Farm? Were they after the antiques supposedly stored there?'

'He won't put up his hand to that one. He's admitted to all the others but insists that was nothing to do with him.'

'Do you believe him?'

'The obvious reason for not owning up to that is the fact that someone died and he doesn't want to face a murder rap; but, much as I hate to admit it, I don't think he was responsible for it. Someone else was making use of his little scheme for their own ends.'

'You're still rooting for the theory of this apocryphal Hardy manuscript being behind it?'

'I think it is a strong possibility. It can't be dismissed out of hand.'

'So what are you doing about it?'

'I'm following up one or two lines of enquiry,' parried Holroyd.

'Well, let's hope you get some results. It would have been good to wrap this whole thing up. And don't forget, even if this damn manuscript *did* exist, it certainly won't have survived that fire.'

'I'm not so sure. We're just taking it for granted that everything was destroyed but perhaps the culprit *did* find it and got away with it after starting the fire to try and cover up his murder of Gorham.'

'Well, he won't benefit from it. If it turns up in literary circles he'll know we can trace it back to him.'

'Not necessarily. It doesn't have to come on the open market. We know only too well that there are plenty of unscrupulous collectors about who are quite prepared to pay vast sums to add to their collections without being too fussy about provenance.'

'That's true, but all this supposition about something that probably does not exist is not our main concern. Our primary business is to catch the villain who incited a riot and murdered an old man in the process.'

Tony had persuaded Reid to attend a rehearsal that evening. They were still being held at the school and, as she knew that Ben's foster parents were visiting him, she agreed. Tony had left early as he had a meeting with the stage crew first but it was after eight o'clock before she pulled into the staff car park, having dined with her mother at the hotel. The food had been good but she was glad of an excuse that saved her from having to spend the rest of the evening with her mother.

Her mobile phone rang as she was getting out of the car. It was Fiona Boyd.

'Reid, do you know where Martin is?'

'No, I'm afraid not.'

'There's not a school meeting he's forgotten to tell me about?'

'No.'

A twinge of unease fluttered through her. Surely Martin hadn't done a runner?

'It really is too bad of him,' Fiona's voice squawked in her ear. 'He knew we were having a dinner party tonight with some important people. I've been up to my eyes all day arranging it and now the host has gone missing!'

Fiona felt relief at these words. Fiona Boyd's infamous dinner parties were well known amongst the staff. The people invited were those she considered important in aiding her climb up the social ladder. Wealth and status were the passport and they would have little in common with poor Martin. He was probably skulking somewhere, putting off the evil moment when he was forced to join them; possibly still trying to think of a way of confessing to her his part in the Holmewood Farm affair.

'I wondered if he might still be at school,' continued Fiona's disembodied voice. 'If he's engrossed in something he's quite likely forgotten the time.'

'I'm just going into school myself; do you want me to see if he is there?'

'Oh, yes please, Reid, and if he is send him home *at once*!' Yes, madam, said Reid to herself with a grimace as the call was abruptly ended.

The rehearsal was being held in the sports hall, which formed part of the new complex over on the far side of the senior playground. To reach it one didn't have to go into the main school building, but as she'd promised to chase up Martin she went into the reception area and made her way towards the sixth-form unit. She didn't think he would be there. The school was in darkness and the cleaners had long since been and gone.

She didn't need to put on any lights, she could see her way clearly from the moonlight filtering in through the windows. As she walked along the corridors the smell, peculiar to all schools, assailed her nostrils, more potent in the still, quiet atmosphere. A mixture of sweat, chalk, trainers and the still-vaguely-discernible sour milk. That was a smell familiar from her own schooldays but she surely must be imagining it here, school milk had finished years ago.

She let herself into the sixth-form rooms knowing she was on a wild goose chase. Martin wasn't here, he was probably already home being scolded by Fiona. The pipes clicked and groaned as the heating system shut down and in the distance she could hear a train speeding along the track that formed one of the boundaries of the school grounds. She went from classroom to classroom, across the area given over to individual study cubicles and pushed open the door of Martin's office. It was empty but she noticed that his usually cluttered desk had been cleared. The surface was bare apart from a single large envelope which lay in the centre, pristine and white.

She idly picked it up and turned it over. It was addressed to the police. So he had kept his word but had chosen to explain his actions in a letter rather than face to face with the constabulary. Typical Martin, she thought, but she was sure he wouldn't get away with it and was convinced that the next day he would be hauled down to the station as Tony had been.

She replaced the envelope on the desk, wondering when he intended posting it or handing it in, and went back into the corridor. As she walked past the door leading into the sixth-form library she remembered that there was a reference book she had been meaning to consult. She pushed open the door and went inside. The moonlight, flooding in through the tall windows that ran the length of one wall, was almost as bright as daylight and she didn't bother to switch on the overhead lights. Instead, she went over to one of the computer consoles, clicked on the desk lamp and booted up the machine; flicking through the visual catalogue until she found a reference to the book she wanted. She made a note of where it was supposed to be shelved and went to the relevant bookstack.

The library consisted of a ground floor and a mezzanine floor, which was in reality a narrow gallery that ran round the upper reaches of the room and was accessed by a wrought-iron spiral staircase. As she walked past this staircase a shaft of moonlight reflected off something hanging in the stairwell. She looked up puzzled at the small disc glinting and oscillating in the gloom. It was a watch face and as she peered closer she saw it was a wristwatch and this was attached to an arm. She felt apprehension sweeping through her and reached up towards the dark mass. Her hand brushed against a shoe. A shoe containing a foot. She fought the hysteria that was threatening to overcome her and plunged across the library floor blindly seeking the light switches. She snapped them down and looked back.

'Oh, my God! Sweet Jesus!' She leant back against the wall and stared in horror at the body hanging in the stairwell, gently swinging in the current of air flowing in from the corridor. It was Martin Boyd and he was obviously very dead.

Fourteen

Her first feeling was of guilt. This was her fault. She'd driven him to this by her accusations, she had hounded him to death. Following on this came the thought: how on earth was she going to tell Fiona? Fiona who sat at home with her guests waiting for Martin to put in an appearance. Trying to stem the sickness rising in her gorge she stumbled like a drunkard to a chair in the nearest alcove and sank on to it, clutching the arms for support. As she fought for control common sense took over. She didn't have to tell Fiona, that was a job for the police. She must get help. Martin was beyond human assistance but there were things to be done.

Tony was on the school premises, should she go and get him? Or could she get in touch with Nick Holroyd? In the end she fumbled for the mobile in her handbag, dragged it out and dialled 999. Whilst she waited for someone to answer her SOS she went into the cloakroom, gulped down some water and splashed her face with it, then went and sat by the door leading from the sixth-form unit into the assembly hall.

It was there that Tony found her thirty minutes later, surrounded by police officers and looking very distraught. He had been alerted by the police cars and ambulance sweeping across the playground and had called a break in rehearsal and come in search of her.

'Reid, what's happened? Are you alright?'

'It's Martin. He's hung himself!'

'He's dead?'

'Yes. Oh, Tony, it's dreadful! I found him – in the library.'

'Christ! So it *was* him. I suppose he couldn't live with his conscience.'

'And who would you be, sir?' DI Stephen Morton, the officer in charge, tackled Tony.

'I'm Tony Pomfret, Miss Frobisher's partner. She's very upset, can I take her home?'

'All in good time. Miss Frobisher discovered the body, so she is a key witness.'

'I've told you what happened. There is really nothing more I can tell you.'

'Martin Boyd was a close colleague of yours. Have you any idea what can have driven him to take his own life?'

'We've got a pretty good idea, officer,' said Pomfret importantly. 'Didn't he leave a suicide note?'

'Oh, my God, I've just remembered—' Reid clutched DI Morton's arm. 'There is a letter addressed to the police on the desk in his office. I found it there when I was looking for him. I never dreamed it was a suicide note.'

'It's a confession,' said Pomfret. 'At least it will let me off the hook.'

'I'm afraid you're a step ahead of me,' said the policeman. 'To what do you think he is confessing?'

'I suggest you go and find the letter and read it, then you'll know what I'm talking about. In the meantime, can I take Miss Frobisher home?'

'Oh, no, sir. I think you have some explaining to do. Exactly how are *you* involved with Martin Boyd?'

'Look, get hold of Nick Holroyd. He's one of you and he knows what this is all about.'

'I still can't believe it.' Reid sat in Rachel's sitting room that evening and regarded her friend and Nick Holroyd with tragic eyes. 'It's so out of character; Martin being violent, I mean. I suppose he was defending himself and he accidently struck Matthew Gorham too hard.'

'It was no accident,' said Nick grimly. 'He'd planned it all down to the last detail. He poisoned the dog to get it out of the way and when Gorham happened on him whilst he was searching the place he deliberately killed him and then set light to the building to try and cover his crime – using a can of petrol he'd taken along with him for the purpose.'

'I suppose there is no doubt he *did* commit suicide?' asked Rachel, who, like Reid, found it difficult to think of Boyd as having been a violent man.

'No doubt at all, he left a full confession, admitting to the murder and arson and also explaining how he had instigated the mob violence in the first place by copying the previous attacks.'

'How did he poison the dog?' said Reid, latching on to the lesser crime, still unable to take on board the enormity of Boyd's actions.

'The autopsy on it revealed rat poison, of the sort too many people still have hanging around in their garden sheds.'

'I suppose he didn't find the manuscript?' queried Rachel, pushing the wine bottle over to Reid, who topped up her glass and took a generous gulp out of it.

'No, his confession says that he was in debt and pressed for money and he had thought finding and stealing the manuscript and

337

then selling it privately would be a way of getting him out of his monetary troubles. It seems when he realised what he had done he couldn't live with the knowledge and decided the only way out was to take his own life. He asked for forgiveness and understanding.'

'I blame Fiona for this,' said Reid. 'She drove him to it with her demands, always wanting money spent on improvement in the house, entertaining and private schooling. Money she knew full well he didn't have and couldn't possibly earn in the teaching profession.'

'How is she taking it?' asked Rachel.

'She's run home to Mummy and Daddy, and I hope for their sake they've got deeper pockets than poor Martin had.'

'Was it Martin who stole the letters?'

'Yes, I meant to tell you.' Nick helped himself to a handful of crisps from the tub Rachel had placed at his elbow and waved them in the air, scattering crumbs everywhere. 'He'd put them in the envelope with his confession. He stated that he got into the vicarage when all the occupants were out, took the letters and tried to make it look like an opportunist burglary.'

'What will happen to them now?' asked Reid.

'When we've finished with them they will be returned to the rightful owner – St

James's Church. And if Peter Stevenson has any sense he will see that they are passed on to some reputable dealer in London to be sold. There is no way that Tony is going to get his hands on them again.'

'No, I can understand that,' said Reid sadly. 'This has really knocked him for six. He's decided to cancel *West Side Story*. He's very upset about it but there really doesn't seem to be any other option. The show seemed to have a jinx on it.'

'Where is Tony tonight?'

'Telling his cast the sad news, or in other words, consoling his groupies,' said Reid savagely. 'He hasn't come out of all this very well, has he?'

'How is Ben?' asked Rachel, tactfully changing the subject.

'There's been a great improvement,' she said, brightening up. 'They are moving him to his own room tomorrow and he's not as deeply unconscious as he was. His eyelids are flickering and there has been some movement in his hands.'

'That's marvellous.' Rachel turned to Nick. 'I suppose now that Dooley is dead you don't have to keep him guarded now?'

'No. When he regains full consciousness we hope what he may be able to tell us will fit in with the other evidence we've accumulated. In the meantime, I'm sending my sergeant up to Scarborough to tie up some loose ends.'

'Scarborough?' queried Reid. 'Why Scarborough? That's not the part of Yorkshire that Ben is connected with.'

'Police business,' said Nick, tapping his nose. 'Now, are we going to broach this second bottle of wine?'

'I shouldn't really...' said Reid, eyeing the bottle eagerly. 'I've got to drive home.'

'My dear girl, you're way over the limit already. I'll get you a taxi later.'

Tim Court returned from Scarborough three days later. With little to report he stopped off first at his home, where he spent a couple of hours catching up with his family and downing the enormous fry-up his wife put in front of him, before calling in at the station.

'Complete waste of time,' he told Nick Holroyd, who was still dealing with the aftermath of Martin Boyd's death and only giving him perfunctory attention. 'But I enjoyed the drive. Bloody cold up there, though. I reckon the wind comes straight across from Siberia.'

'You did see this Ransom, the vicar?'

'Yes, and he knows nothing about Mervyn Dooley. Whoever was playing with little boys in his old parish, it wasn't our Merv.'

'His appearance could have changed a lot in the years since he left Yorkshire. Was he taking that into account when you showed him the photo?'

'Yes. He says there is no similarity at all between Dooley and the Maurice Benton he knew, and to prove it he produced a photo of Benton taken not long before he left Welby and I had to agree with him. Even allowing for ageing and a deliberate attempt to alter his appearance, there is no way they could be the same person.'

'Ah, well, it was a long shot. Hopefully Latimer will soon be recovered enough to finger Dooley. He's starting to pull out of his coma.'

'That's good.' Court started to rummage through the drawers of the filing cabinet. 'Where are the claim forms?'

'Claim forms?'

'I want to write up my expenses before I forget.' He took out his wallet and extracted a couple of receipts and a photo fell out.'

'Oh, that's the photo of Benton.' Court bent down and picked it up and handed it to his colleague. 'The good vicar thought we might as well have it.'

Nick glanced at it cursorily and then snatched it out of his sergeant's hand. 'Wait a minute...'

'What's up?'

'*This* is Maurice Benton?' He tapped the photo.

'Yes. Why? You don't know him?'

'Oh my God! I believe I do...!'

The photo showed a man with two young boys in running gear. He had his hand up as if protesting to the photographer and his head was turned slightly away presenting a three-quarter view of his face but to Nick's horrified gaze he was only too familiar. Even allowing for the passage of time there was no mistaking him; the same buttoned-up expression, the same fawn-coloured hair and sallow complexion.

'...Only I don't know him as Maurice Benton. *This* is Gordon Barnes!'

'Who the hell is he?'

'He is Tony Pomfret's partner in the antiquarian bookshop he runs. He knows about Ben Latimer and he actually had a part in *West Side Story*, so he would have met Compton.'

'You're not saying—?'

'Christ! I believe we've been making a terrible mistake!'

'You think we've got the wrong man in the frame?'

'We've been so bloody sure that Dooley was our man that we haven't bothered to look any further. We took it for granted that Dooley was guilty and we fitted the evidence to match that assumption – something a good police officer should never do.'

'But one photo – an old one at that – is not evidence that – Barnes? – is the culprit.

342

We've got nothing else on him.'

'Not yet, but just think, man: if that *is* Barnes in this photo – and I'm a hundred per cent certain it is – he's a self-confessed child molester. He leaves Yorkshire and settles in Dorset. We don't know that he is a reformed character but let's give him the benefit of the doubt. He thinks he has put his past behind him, then by a sheer fluke he meets up with two of his victims who he never expected to see again. So what does he do?'

'He decides to knock them off before they can finger him.'

'It makes horrible sense. It must have been a terrible shock to him to come face to face with Compton at a rehearsal.'

'So, why didn't Compton speak out straight away if he recognised Barnes as someone who had interfered with him as a child?'

'He didn't get the chance. Barnes must have acted immediately he saw him. We've always thought it wasn't a premeditated crime. He must have grabbed that girder and struck him down as he left the hall.'

'But he didn't attack Latimer.'

'He must have seen him there too, but before he could act Ben had disappeared. I tell you something else: I don't think Ben saw or recognised him. From what he told Rachel before they were mown down he knew nothing about Compton's death and the reasons behind it. But, of course, Barnes couldn't know this.'

'He must have been on tenterhooks wondering what had happened to Latimer and whether he was going to resurface, but how the fuck did he know when he *did* return?'

'Must have seen him by sheer chance.'

'We're making out a very good case against him,' said Court, flicking his pen from hand to hand, 'but it's all supposition again. Barnes *may* have been connected with St Kilda's but that doesn't mean that he was there when Compton and Latimer were in residence, or that he interfered with them. Come to that, we don't even know if they *were* abused, and won't know until Latimer recovers enough to tell us. Barnes may have genuinely reformed and know nothing of Compton and Latimer's past. We can't rule Dooley out of the picture; Barnes could be completely   innocent.'

'It's a hell of a coincidence though, isn't it? And I don't like coincidences. I reckon *this*—' Nick waved the photo to and fro, '—is a good enough reason for some serious questioning of Gordon Barnes and there's no time like the present. It's Saturday morning, he should be at the bookshop, so what are we waiting for?'

The shoppers were out in full force and it took them longer than expected to cover the distance between the station and the book-store. Court drove and Nick sat tapping his finger impatiently on the fascia board as they crawled through the milling crowds. They parked on double yellow lines outside the shop and Nick nodded at the old Volvo estate parked in the alleyway between the buildings.

'I think that's Pomfret's car but possibly Barnes uses it as well. We'll have a quick dekko, see if there's any sign of damage to the front, or a respray job.'

They were bent over the bonnet of the car when Tony Pomfret emerged from the shop.

'I thought I recognised you,' he said curtly to Nick. 'What's the matter now? You're determined to nick me for something but the road tax is up to date, as you can see, and it is MOT-ed and insured.'

'Just checking. What about Mr Barnes? Does he share this as a business car or has he one of his own?'

'Got an almost identical one. We both drive old bangers. We do a lot of mileage and cart hundreds of books about in the course of the year and, let me tell you, there is nothing as filthy as books – and I'm talking covers here, not contents. Come inside.'

Tony Pomfret led the way into the shop and flung back over his shoulder, 'Mind you, Gordon's car had a nasty knock a couple of weeks ago. He was up in the Lake

District on a book-buying trip and someone ran into the front of him when he was parked. Had to have it sorted out up there before he could drive back.'

He didn't see the look that passed between Nick and Court as they followed him into the interior.

'Now, I don't know what you want,' he continued, 'but I reckon you owe me an apology. Carting me down to the station and giving me the third degree when all the time it was Martin Boyd who was guilty, God rest his soul. If it wasn't for the fact that I know you and don't want to get you into trouble with your superiors, I reckon I would make an official complaint to the Chief Constable.'

'Actually it's not you we're interested in,' said Nick smoothly. 'It's Mr Barnes we've come to see.'

'Then you've struck unlucky, he's not here. He's taken Reid up to the hospital.'

'He's *what*?'

'Run her up to the hospital,' said Pomfret, looking surprised at Nick's tone. 'She was here earlier this morning when a call came through from the hospital to say that Ben was coming round. Of course, she wanted to go up there immediately, but she's lent her car to her mother – the old bat – so Gordon offered to give her a lift. And before you ask, I couldn't take her as I'm expecting an important client from London, who I always deal with personally.'

'How long ago was this?' snapped Nick, already halfway out of the shop.

'About an hour. Why? Is something wrong?'

But he was talking to an empty shop. Nick and his sergeant were outside, leaping into their car, and he watched in astonishment as the engine was gunned and they roared off down the road.

'Surely he can't do anything in broad daylight in a busy hospital ward?' protested Court as they screamed round a corner, narrowly missing a pedestrian, who leapt back on the pavement just in time.

'Latimer's in a room on his own. If Barnes is panicked, God knows what he'll attempt. Reid Frobisher could be in danger as well. Slap the light on and the siren.'

Whilst Court concentrated on his driving, Nick called up reinforcements. He and his colleague should get to the hospital first but he didn't know what sort of situation they would be facing. They parked outside the main doors in a bay reserved for ambulances and raced inside the building.

'I think he's in a private room attached to the ICU. You go along here and up in the lift to the second floor.'

They charged along the corridor, almost colliding with a bed plus patient being wheeled towards them. At the lift Nick jabbed the call button and they waited for what seemed long-drawn-out minutes for the lift to descend. When the doors slid open they were astonished to see Reid inside.

'Where is Barnes?' demanded Nick.

'He felt a little faint, so I'm fetching him a cup of tea from the café.'

'Is he with Ben?'

'Yes. What's the matter?'

Nick bundled her out of the lift. 'Stay here!'

'But—'

Before she could object further the two men were in the lift and she found herself staring at a blank steel wall.

Pray God we're in time! thought Nick as they hurtled out of the lift and along another corridor. What could Barnes possibly do here to silence his victim? Then he remembered all the machines Ben was attached to and how easy it would be to tamper with them. They crashed through the door into the intensive care unit and a startled nurse jumped to her feet from behind the nurse's station.

'Where is Ben Latimer?'

'What—?'

'Police. This is an emergency!'

She pointed to a door off to the right and the two men ran towards it and flung it open and paused on the threshold.

Gordon Barnes was there and he was reaching up to the bag containing the saline drip poised over the bed in which Ben lay. He was holding a small jar in one hand and when he saw them a look of desperation flickered across his face and he jerked the bag off the stand and tried to pour the contents of the jar into it. He was not quick enough. Court felled him with a rugby tackle and the jar flew out of his hand and smashed on the floor spilling white powder around.

'Gordon Barnes, I arrest you for the murder of Kevin Compton and the attempted murder of Ben Latimer,' began Nick. As he recited the rest of the caution there was the thud of feet behind them and police reinforcements arrived accompanied by shocked medical staff.

Fifteen

If it hadn't have been for a sheer fluke Mervyn Dooley would have gone down in the records as guilty, the case would have been closed and a murderer would be walking free.'

It was a week later and Nick was at Rachel's cottage bringing her up to date with his investigation.

'You got the right motive,' she pointed out. 'You thought all along that child abuse was at the root of it.'

'Just got the wrong man,' said Nick gloomily, pacing the floor, his hands in his pockets.

'For goodness sake sit down and tell me exactly what happened. I don't know why you're so miserable. With the two cases you were working on cleared up you should be in great spirits.'

Nick flung himself into a chair and gave her a sheepish grin.

'This is all sub judice, but I know it won't go any further and, as you've been so closely involved, I think I owe you an explanation. To start with, Gordon Barnes has admitted to everything.'

'He has?'

'Not at first he didn't. When I charged him in that hospital room he denied everything. Then a most extraordinary thing happened...' Nick paused and Rachel looked at him expectantly.

'If it had happened in a book or a play it would have been condemned as unbelievable and contrived—'

'What *did* happen?'

'We were all milling around in that small room and Ben was lying on the bed, apparently still comatose. I suppose the bed was jostled or the noise must have got through to him because he suddenly opened his eyes. It was weird; his gaze sort of flickered from one person to another and he was obviously out of it and not connecting, and then— He saw Barnes and this terrible expression passed over his face— We all witnessed it, it was sheer horror. He recognised Barnes and he was looking into hell. For a few seconds he appeared to be struggling mentally and we thought he was going to speak but he shunted off into unconsciousness again. But it was enough. He'd condemned Barnes and Barnes knew it. He was a broken man after that and couldn't confess quickly enough.'

351

'He was really going to try and kill Ben that day?'

'Oh yes, he had a lethal combination of drugs in a bottle he took with him. You name it, he had it: crushed up sleeping pills, paracetamol, aspirin... He was just about to feed it into the saline drip when we arrived.'

'Thank God you got there in time. I suppose he hadn't been able to make the attempt whilst Ben was actually in the ICU.'

'That's right. He was hoping against hope that Ben wouldn't come round; that he'd snuff it or be permanently brain-damaged, but as an insurance he had prepared his lethal little cocktail.

'He'd actually been up to the hospital earlier to suss out the lie of the land. A nurse has said she saw him looking through the window at Ben but as she didn't like the look of him – her own words – she told him only relatives were allowed in. Anyway, Barnes hung on, hoping that if Ben did recover he'd get the opportunity to finish him off before he could condemn him. Reid was in the bookshop with him when the call came through from the hospital saying that Ben was regaining consciousness. Barnes knew he had to act quickly. He offered to drive her up to the hospital, went in with her to see Ben and thought of an excuse to get her out of the way. The rest you know.'

'Ben is going to make a full recovery. The

medicos are confident there's no permanent brain damage. He has no memory of the actual hit-and-run but they think that is only temporary amnesia. Have you managed to interview him yet?'

'Yes, I've been to see him. The doctors insisted that I didn't pressurise or worry him but I managed a short chat. As you say, he couldn't remember anything of meeting you and being mown down by Barnes, but he did remember events at St Kilda's and Barnes's part in them. They are obviously very upsetting memories and I didn't press him, but one thing is clear – he didn't see Barnes at the rehearsal that night and had no idea this spectre from his past was here in Dorset.'

'So, he was no threat to Barnes? He didn't need to be eliminated?'

'No. Hopefully Ben will be able to tell us more as he recovers.'

'What I don't understand,' said Rachel, frowning as she remembered the evening of the accident, 'is how Gordon Barnes knew that Ben had returned.'

'That is another weird coincidence. He was on his way up to the Lake District and he stopped at a service station to fill up and he actually saw Ben getting out of the lorry he had hitched in.'

'That's unbelievable!'

'I know. He immediately changed his plans

and followed Ben back into Casterford.'

'Ben walked all the way out to where he met me outside the church, he told me so. And Gordon Barnes was following him? All that way?'

'Yes. Monitoring him and hoping he'd get the opportunity to act. He could do nothing whilst Ben was walking the streets in broad daylight with other people around but as it got darker and the fog came down and he reached open countryside he thought he'd get his chance. Then Ben met up with you and you went inside the church. By this time Barnes was getting desperate. He was afraid Ben was confiding in you and when you came out together he reckoned he had to get rid of both of you. He ran you down and thought he had killed you both but daren't stop and make sure as he heard another vehicle approaching.

'Instead, he drove hell for leather up to the Lake District. Booked into an hotel the next morning for his stay up there, telling the receptionist that he had spent the previous night in Penrith, taking the opportunity to explore that part of the area, and booked the car in for repairs at the local garage after spinning some yarn about having had a flock of sheep collide with him on a mountain road.'

'He thought of everything, didn't he? So, when I came round with only superficial injuries he must have been horrified. I must still have been in danger from him?'

'Now you know why I was so insistent that you remain in hospital as long as possible with a police guard. Once it was known that Ben had no idea why Compton had been killed and you thought you were just a victim of a hit-and-run incident, Barnes knew you were no danger to him.'

'I still can't believe it.' Rachel shuddered. 'He always seemed such a meek and mild man.'

'You could have been killed instantly when he ran you down and no one would ever have known the real reason behind it. It doesn't bear thinking about.'

'What doesn't? The fact that you'd lost me or that you'd come to the wrong conclusions about your case?'

'I'm not going to deign to answer that. Don't torment me.'

He pulled her into his arms and was kissing her very thoroughly when there was the sound of a car pulling up outside. He released her with a groan.

'Are you expecting anybody?'

Rachel glanced out of the window.

'Oh no, it's Tony. I wonder what he wants? I haven't seen anything of Reid these last few days.'

Tony Pomfret walked up the path and hammered on the door. Nick answered it and Tony pushed his way inside.

'It's Rachel I want to see, where is she?'

'And good morning to you too, Tony.'

'Sorry, Nick. I'm distraught!'

Rachel walked into the hall and Tony pounced on her.

'She's left me!'

'What are you talking about?'

'Reid. She's walked out on me. What am I going to do?'

'Look, I have to go.' Nick eyed the agitated man warily and edged towards the door. 'I've got a meeting at the station.'

'Coward!' hissed Rachel out of the side of her mouth and Tony looked surprised.

'I thought the pressure was off you now? Your case is solved and everything is going your way, whereas I...' Tony paused dramatically. '...My life is falling to pieces around me. I've lost my woman, my partner, and the show is kaput!'

'I'll give you a ring later,' said Nick to Rachel. 'Sorry, Tony, I can't stay and give you a sympathetic ear but Rachel is better at this sort of thing than I am.'

'Come and sit down, Tony,' said Rachel, grimacing after her fiancé's retreating back. 'Do you want a coffee?'

'I need something stronger, but I don't suppose hard liquor is available in this household.'

'I expect I can oblige, but do you really

356

want it this early in the day when you're driving?'

'No, you're right. A coffee would be great.'

He followed her into the kitchen, looking suddenly like a lost puppy.

'I want to marry her. Did you know that?'

'I thought marriage was not on Reid's agenda?'

'Well, she knew I wouldn't contemplate it, but I've changed my mind. I suddenly realised how much she meant to me and how transient life is – here today, gone tomorrow. When you have a chance of happiness you have to grab it and hold on to it. But Reid has changed her mind about us, or so she says. She said I was a self-centred bastard and she'd come to her senses! I know I've behaved badly but I really want Reid – I *need* her. She's the only person who can reform me!'

'Have you asked her to marry you?'

'Yes, and she refused.'

'Did you ask her before or after she said she was leaving you?'

'After. And don't look like that. I know it sounds as if it was a desperate ploy to make her change her mind but it wasn't like that at all. I was all set to propose and then she threw this at me. You must believe me.'

'I do, but does Reid? You must see how it might appear to her.'

'Yes. So you think I might still be in with a

357

chance if I can make her understand?'

'I don't know, Tony. This is between you and her.' Rachel handed him a mug of coffee. 'Did she say why she was ending the relationship?'

'Apart from slagging me off – yes.' Tony paused and rubbed a hand over his face. 'Look, hasn't she said *anything* to you?'

'No, I haven't seen her.'

'Well, she went on at great length about my shortcomings – which we'll take as read – and said there was nothing to keep her down here and she was going back up north. She said that, with Martin's death, teaching at the High School was now untenable – even though she might be offered head of sixth-form English – and she wanted to be nearer Ben when he goes back – and also her mother. I can't imagine why she should want to be at her mother's beck and call but I suppose the old girl is getting older and frailer.'

'Tony, what do you intend doing now?'

'A good question. The bookshop is finished. Being in partnership with a murderer, who also happened to be a paedophile, is not good for business. A lot of our trade comes through word of mouth and it's going to be bad-mouthing from now on. I suppose I'll try and sell my share and salvage what I can – though God knows what the legal position is with Gordon's stake.'

'So, there is nothing to keep you in Caster-ford?'

'No, I suppose not.' Tony gulped down the remains of his coffee and put the mug back on the table.

'Then you could move somewhere else and start again?'

'Are you telling me to follow her?' He looked suddenly more hopeful.

'Don't put words into my mouth. I'm not telling you to do anything. Reid has had some awful knocks and shocks just lately. She needs space. You mustn't crowd her, but if you're sure of your commitment you can tell her how you feel and let her know you'll still be around when she's had time to come to terms with her trauma. She won't give up on Ben, you know. He *is* her son and she'll want to build on that relationship.'

'Yes, I realise that now. I guess I was a little crass about Ben. Thank God the blighter is going to be okay. I'd like to get to know him better; as far as I'm concerned the advent of a fully-grown son is far better, at my age, than all the business of nappies, toddlers and temper tantrums.'

Tony seemed suddenly to realise that Rachel had become a little withdrawn and was staring into space with a rather strange look on her face.

'Anyway, when are you and Nick tying the knot?'

'God knows. They say marriages are made in heaven, but this one has very earthly parameters,' she replied, and firmly changed the subject.

Ben Latimer continued to make good progress and was soon able to function fully without artificial aids. He had made an official statement to the police, which, besides condemning Gordon Barnes, tied in Mervyn Dooley with events that had taken place at St Kilda's during the relevant years.

Reid Frobisher was adamant that she was leaving Dorset – and Tony – permanently. She had given in her notice to the Education Department and was working with an acting head of English seconded from another school until the end of term. She was refusing all importuning from Tony Pomfret to resume their liaison and had moved in temporarily with Rachel. She was determined to settle in Yorkshire and had already applied for a teaching job in that area. Her greatest desire was to keep in touch with Ben when he went back up north and they had agreed that they wanted and needed to get to know each other better and build on their relationship.

Tony was not giving up on Reid. He also intended moving north when he had sorted out his financial problems, but the notoriety that Gordon Barnes had brought to the bookshop meant an upsurge in business, albeit temporary, and he was not slow to take advantage of it.

Helen Frobisher had returned home far more shaken by events than she cared to admit and was equally determined to keep in touch with her newly-found grandson. She was delighted that Reid had split up with Tony and was already making plans to introduce her daughter to more suitable men when she started her new life nearby; a fact that would have caused Reid great amusement had she known of it.

Holmewood Farm had been levelled and great interest was being shown in the site by several building companies. It would never be known whether the ash still drifting over the countryside and settling in hedgerow and ditch contained the remains of the last novel penned by Thomas Hardy. The letters were now being examined by experts in London and Peter Stevenson was hopeful that their eventual sale would realise a welcome sum for the church. Martin Boyd's death was seen by many people as a tragic climax to a plan that had accelerated out of control and had been prompted by a desperate desire to haul himself out of the pit of debt that his wife had driven him into. Surprisingly, his suicide evoked more sympathy than that shown for the death of Matthew Gorham, and if Fiona Boyd hadn't defected to her parents' residence it was common opinion that she would have been hounded out of Casterford.

Six Sixth Form pupils regretted the cancellation of *West Side Story* but went to their A-level exams with a greater understanding of the passions and emotions encapsulated in *Romeo and Juliet*, and the local Operatic and Dramatic Society decided to stage *Oklahoma* as their next production.

All in all, reflected Rachel Morland, as she sat in the chancel of St James's after choir practice, most of those involved in the recent tragedies were rebuilding their lives and planning their new futures. Only she, always on the periphery of events, seemed to be living in limbo. She saw Nick several times each week and their meetings were happy and satisfactory, but that was all they were – meetings – which also meant partings. They came together for a few snatched hours and then went their separate ways. Sharing her cottage with Reid helped to take her mind off things, but it was Nick she wanted to share with, not Reid.

She sighed and looked down the aisle. The nave was in darkness, only the chancel lights were on, and shadows arched over the chancel steps from the black mass of the main church beyond. The sanctuary light gleamed like a red-jewelled pendant above her and the candlesticks and cross on the altar glimmered dully in the diffused light. She felt restless and unfulfilled, and the usual solace of prayers seemed to be denied her that evening. She collected up the hymn books and music sheets and stowed them in the vestry cupboard, then she switched off the remaining lights and let herself out of the church.

As she crunched down the gravel path she was horribly aware of the last occasion when Ben had been with her and the car had roared out of the night and charged towards them. There was no frost tonight. It was cold and clear with a touch of frost in the air but there was a car approaching just like that other time. It was moving fast, only slowing slightly as it negotiated the bend in the road, and then she was caught in the glare from the headlights.

She reeled back into the hedge, dazzled and fighting sheer terror. The car screeched to a halt and someone jumped out.

'Rachel – are you alright?'

Nick's voice cut through her panic and she rushed into his arms, half sobbing, half laughing.

'Oh, Nick, you gave me such a scare! I heard a car and for an awful few seconds I thought I was going to be run down again!'

'Christ, I never thought! Forgive me. I wanted to meet you out of choir practice

363

and I thought I was too late and I'd missed you.'

'I stayed behind to clear up. Is anything wrong?'

'No, just the opposite. I've had some news...'

She looked at him quickly. There was an air of tension about him and suppressed excitement. His hair was ruffled as if he'd been running his fingers through it and his eyes glinted under the street light.

'Is it—' she began but he interrupted her.

'Let's get in the car, it's freezing out here.'

He held open the passenger door, she scrambled inside and he joined her. He grasped her hands in his and spoke in a rather strange voice. 'How would you like to get married in church?'

She stared at him, trying to read his expression, and then understanding dawned.

'She's dead, isn't she? Maureen's dead?'

'Yes. I've just heard from Dave Bloomfield. He traced her to Scotland and ran up against a blank wall at first. Then he was reading through some old copies in the Dunfermline newspaper archives and discovered that she had been in a rail crash near Dundee four years ago. She was one of the fatal casualties.'

'And the boy?'

'He was killed too.'

'Oh, Nick, I'm sorry. He was so young to die.'

'Yes, and I'll never know now whether he *was* my son.'

'No, that's something you will have to learn to live with.'

'I never knew him. It is time to bury the past and make a new start. I'm a widower now, not a divorcee, so I repeat my question: how would you like to get married – in church?'

'I should like that very much.' She smiled at him. 'I wonder what Peter Stevenson will say?'

'Let's go and ask him, shall we?'

And he started up the engine, reversed the car and drove back towards the rectory.